D0466075

THE
OTHER WOMAN

PATRICIA KAY

BERKLEY BOOKS, NEW YORK

THE OTHER WOMAN

A Berkley Book / published by arrangement with
the author

ISBN: 0-7394-1874-2

BERKLEY®
Berkley Books are published by The Berkley Publishing Group,
a division of Penguin Putnam Inc.,
375 Hudson Street, New York, New York 10014.
BERKLEY and the "B" design
are trademarks belonging to Penguin Putnam Inc.

PRINTED IN THE UNITED STATES OF AMERICA

For Mary Jane Booker—bridesmaid, old friend, and number-one fan—with much love. Those late nights in your mother's kitchen are among my fondest memories.

Acknowledgments

As always, there are so many people to thank: Alaina Richardson and Heather MacAllister, who read this book and gave me invaluable suggestions and comments; Muna Shehardi Sill (writing as Isabel Sharpe), who answered my questions about Yale and New Haven; Robert W. Shields, Jr., M.D., staff neurologist with the Department of Neurology at the Cleveland Clinic Foundation, who shared his medical expertise in the area of spinal injuries; Bunny Paine-Clemes, Ph.D., who taught me how to get started and how to finish once I did; Helen Breitwieser, my wonderful agent and friend; and Cindy Hwang, my terrific editor.

Prologue

New York City, New York
December 1997

Adam Forrester whistled as he took the stairs leading to Natalie's apartment two at a time. Although this wasn't the way he would have chosen to live, for some reason tonight he felt more optimistic than he'd felt in a long time. He couldn't wait to see Natalie. It had been at least six months since they'd had an entire weekend together, but with Julia gone to Mamaroneck, he was free. *They* were free.

Maybe they would go somewhere. He'd bet Natalie would like that. He smiled. It would be nice to take her somewhere.

Clutched in his hand was a bottle of her favorite port. Whenever he came to her place, he always brought her something—wine or flowers or books—because from the very first she had refused to take any money from him. She wouldn't even let him pay for half the food they ate.

"No," she'd said, "when you take me out somewhere, then you can pay. When we're at my apartment, I'm the hostess, and I'll pay."

"But—"

"I won't be a kept woman," she insisted. Her beautiful blue gray eyes held that determined glint that meant she would not change her mind, no matter how much he protested or what arguments he used.

Adam, shaking his head, finally gave in. Natalie might look delicate, but underneath that slender frame and deceptively gentle manner was a core of steel.

He was huffing a bit by the time he reached her third-floor landing. He grimaced as he rang her doorbell. Lately, he hadn't been going to the gym as often as he should. He'd better remedy that. Forty-four was no age to slack off on your exercise program.

He waited impatiently, but finally he heard the sound of her footsteps, followed by the distinctive grind of her deadbolt being released. In that last second before she opened the door, there was a familiar tightening in his gut. There had been times over the years when he'd wondered if he would still feel the same excitement and anticipation about being with her if they were married, if he saw her every day, if their relationship wasn't clandestine. The answer was always the same. It wouldn't matter what their situation was. From the day he'd first laid eyes on her, Natalie had been the only woman in the world for him, and she always would be. She was the reason he looked forward to each day. Without her, his life would be empty.

He smiled when the door opened.

"Hi." Her return smile seemed a bit tired. "You're early."

"Yes, the meeting didn't last as long as I thought it would." He shut the door, set the wine down, then took her into his arms and gave her a lingering kiss. Afterward, he held her close, reveling in her warmth and softness. "God, I've missed you."

"It's only been three days," she said with a soft laugh. But she didn't try to pull away. Instead, she lifted her face to his again. Just before their lips met, he saw a glimmer of something in her eyes that disturbed him, and he wondered if there was anything wrong. But he quickly forgot about it, because this time there was a kind of desperation in the way she clung to him and in the intensity of her kisses so that dinner and everything else was wiped from his mind. All he cared about was Natalie. Loving her. Wanting her. Needing her. Blood pounding in his veins, he swept her up and into his arms and carried her into the bedroom.

Most of the time, when they made love, Adam didn't like to rush. He loved touching Natalie, brushing his fingers over her breasts and belly and thighs and looking at her while he did. He loved seeing the way her eyes would drift shut and the way her body trembled as desire built. He loved hearing the little catches in her breath, the soft moans and whimpers. Her pleasure excited him and increased his own anticipation. He especially loved taking her close to the brink and then stopping—giving her a few seconds to fall back a little—then starting again so that her eventual pleasure—and his, too—would be more prolonged, more intense and satisfying.

But tonight there was none of that long, slow buildup of passion. Tonight she was ready for him almost immediately, and he was more than ready for her with one of the most painful erections he'd ever had.

"Adam, Adam!" she cried as he plunged into her, pushing deep and hard. Her fingernails dug into his back.

"I love you," he managed to gasp before he shuddered out of control.

When his body calmed, she wouldn't let him pull away. Instead, she held him tightly. So tightly Adam remembered his earlier misgiving. Something *was* wrong.

It was then he felt the wetness on her cheek. She was crying. Natalie rarely cried, at least not in front of him. She hadn't even cried that day so long ago when he'd told her he was going to marry Julia instead of her.

This time when he tried to pull free, she didn't stop

him. "What's wrong?" he said, sitting up. Was she sick? Had something happened?

She sat up, too, and swiped at the tears on her cheeks. "Let's get dressed first."

Adam stared at her. Fear caused his heart to pound. Still he managed to answer calmly, "All right."

She pulled the quilt off the bed and wrapped it around her—almost as if she was embarrassed to be naked in front of him—before walking to where their clothes lay jumbled together in a pile. Not looking at him, she began to get dressed.

Suddenly, with a sick feeling, Adam was afraid he knew exactly what it was she was going to say. Still, he told himself not to jump to conclusions. Maybe he was wrong.

But once they were dressed and seated next to each other on the sofa in her tiny living room, he knew he wasn't wrong. The expression on her face, half sadness, half resignation, told him everything. The day he had feared for years, a day he had hoped and prayed would never come, was finally there.

She closed her eyes for a second and took a deep breath. "Oh, God. This is so hard. I . . . Adam, I can't go on like this anymore."

"Natalie, don't—"

"No, wait. Please let me finish before you say anything. You know how much I love you. How much I will always love you. For a long time I've thought that would be enough and that the worst thing that could ever happen to me would be losing you again, but—" She swallowed. "But now I know that's not true. Loving you isn't enough." Her eyes pleaded with him to understand. "You see, lately, I've realized that I have become a person I don't like very much, and . . . I am so very sorry, but I just can't be that person anymore." For the second time that night, her eyes filled with tears.

Adam wanted to beg her. Get down on his knees and

plead with her not to do this. Not to leave him. How could he go on without her? Yet he knew to do so would be the ultimate act of selfishness on his part. Knowing Natalie as he did, he knew she had not come to this decision easily, and if he tried to change her mind, he would only make things harder for her. She had already given up too many years of her life for him; he had no right to ask for more.

So, even though inside he was bellowing his despair and frustration and rage at the fates that had first given but were now taking away, he used every ounce of control he possessed to will himself to accept her decision and say nothing in protest.

"Your place is with Julia," she continued brokenly. "I accept that." Brushing at her tears, she took a deep, shaky breath. "But my place is somewhere else." Her eyes met his. "I'm leaving New York, Adam. I gave Jack my notice on Wednesday. I'll be gone before Christmas. I'm sorry," she whispered. "I'm so sorry."

Adam felt frozen, as if his heart had been ripped out of his chest and plunged into a tub of ice. He wasn't sure he'd ever be warm again. "Where will you go?" he asked dully.

"To Emerson for the holidays." Emerson, a small town in northern Connecticut, was her hometown. "After that, I don't know. Maybe to L.A. Brooke has been after me to move out there."

"I see."

"Adam . . ." She touched his cheek.

Her touch was nearly his undoing. Suddenly he knew he had to get out of there. Now. Because if he stayed, he would do or say something he would be sorry for later. If he left now, at least he would still have his dignity.

"It's okay," he said stoically. "I understand. And I don't blame you for feeling this way. But I think the best thing I can do right now is leave."

"Oh, Adam, you don't have to go. You can still stay the weekend the way we planned."

He shook his head. "No. I can't." Blindly, he got up, found his coat, put it on. He didn't look at her. Couldn't.

"Adam, don't leave like this." She was openly crying now.

Somehow he managed to choke out, "I'll always love you." Then he opened the door and walked out.

Part One

One

New Haven, Connecticut
October 1978 to January 1979

It was one of those glorious, crisp autumn days—the kind Natalie Ferrenzo had always loved. The cloudless sky was an intense blue, and the sunlight the kind that hurt your eyes. In Natalie's opinion, this was the prettiest season in New England, which was now experiencing a dazzling display of fall color. The red maples with their brilliant scarlet leaves were especially beautiful this year, she thought as she cruised along on her ten-speed. She was on her way home, finished with classes for the day. A sophomore English major, Natalie attended Southern Connecticut State University and lived only a few blocks from the campus.

Almost home now, she rounded the corner and turned onto her street. Her garage apartment was located midway down the block and, as she got closer, she saw she had company. Red hair blazing just as bright as the maple leaves in the afternoon sun, Brooke Gallo sat on the bottom step of the outside stairway that led to Natalie's place. She stood and waved as Natalie pulled into the driveway.

"What are you doing here?" Natalie braked, then

walked her bike over and parked it under the stairway.

"Is that any way to greet your best and most admired friend?" Brooke countered with a cheeky grin.

Natalie rolled her eyes. "I thought you had class." She fastened the lock she hoped would deter anyone from stealing the bike.

Brooke pushed a stray strand of hair out of her eyes. "Professor Miller canceled. Something about his wife being sick. So I thought I'd come over and talk to you about tonight."

They climbed the stairs to the apartment. "What about tonight?" Natalie unlocked the door.

"We've been invited to a party."

Natalie made a face. She didn't much like parties.

Pretending not to see Natalie's expression, Brooke walked inside. "I think it'll be fun."

Natalie shrugged out of her backpack and dropped it on the coffee table. Brooke headed for the futon that doubled as Natalie's bed and plopped down on one end, folding her legs under her Indian fashion. Her knees poked out of the holes in her Levi's.

"Where is this party, anyway?" Natalie reached up under her sweater and unfastened her bra. "Oh, man, that feels better."

Natalie hated wearing bras, yet she didn't feel comfortable going without one the way Brooke did. Of course, Brooke had nice, small A-cup breasts, whereas Natalie's were like her mother's and required a C cup.

"The better to nurse babies with," Connie Ferrenzo always said whenever Natalie or her sisters—who were also C cups—complained. Connie always assumed her four daughters would marry and have lots of babies.

"Somewhere over by the Yale campus," Brooke said. "I have the address written down."

Natalie made a noncommittal sound and headed for the kitchen, calling over her shoulder, "Want a Coke?"

"I'd rather have a beer."

"Sorry. It's Coke or ice water."

"Oh, well. Coke, then, I guess."

While in the kitchen, Natalie decided she wasn't going to let Brooke pressure her into doing something she didn't want to do. Returning to the main living area with two cans of Coke, she handed one to Brooke, then curled up on the other end of the futon. Her jeans, reflecting her orderly personality, had no holes. In fact, they were clean and still showed signs of the crease she'd ironed into them. She pulled the tab of her drink and took a long, thirsty swallow.

"So?" Brooke said after drinking some of her Coke, too. "What do you say? Want to go?"

Natalie shook her head and picked at a loose thread in the futon's upholstery.

"Oh, come on, Nat."

"I'm sorry, Brooke. I just don't want to."

"Why not?"

"Because I hate that whole party scene. Watching a bunch of guys barf into the privet hedge is not my idea of a great Friday night. Besides, there's bound to be drugs."

"So? Just because they're there doesn't mean we have to mess with them."

Natalie sighed.

"C'mon," Brooke wheedled. "I don't want to go by myself. Anyway, it'll be good for you to get out and mix and meet some new people. You never go anywhere."

"That's not true."

Brooke's expressive face wore a pained expression. "Oh, yeah, sure, you work, go to class, go to the library, go to church, but you never go *out*! You're totally boring. You never have any fun!"

"Yes, I do. I read and I write and I go to movies—" And *why* was she explaining herself to Brooke, anyway?

"Oh, for Pete's sake, how can you call that fun? What

about guys? What about sex? Are you gonna remain a virgin your entire life?"

"I'd hardly say I'm a decrepit old woman at nineteen," Natalie answered, telling herself not to get mad. "You know how I feel about sex."

"Yeah, yeah, I know. Only when you fall in love. Only when it's the real thing, whatever *that* is."

"You can make fun of me, but I believe in true love."

Brooke made a face. "You and my mother." Brooke's mother had been married three times and was well on her way to number four.

"*My* parents are happily married."

"I never said they weren't. It's just . . . Oh, shoot, Nat, you're too young to live like a nun. Haven't you heard about the sexual revolution?"

Natalie shrugged. Right now, sex was the furthest thing from her mind. From what she could see, when a girl got heavily involved with a guy, the relationship seemed to take over her life. Natalie didn't want that. She didn't *need* that. She had a goal, and she'd made up her mind when she started college that nothing, *nothing* was going to deter her from reaching it.

Ever since she'd started working at the Emerson Library in her junior year of high school, she'd known what she wanted. Unlike her older siblings, she was going to college, where she would work very hard, earn top grades, get her degree in English, and then head for New York, where she intended to land a job with a publishing company. And then someday, after she learned the business, she might take a stab at writing a book herself.

That part of her dream was still her secret, though. But her goal would not be met if she spent her free time mooning over some guy. It was hard enough going to school and working, too. "I don't have time for guys."

Brooke gave her an exasperated look. "An occasional party doesn't mean you're committing your *life*!"

"I know that. But why waste time on something that's

not important to me? You know the terms of my scholarship. I have to do well, or I'll lose it." At Brooke's long-suffering look, she added, "Anyway, this is a Yale party, right?" The moment the words were out of her mouth, she could have kicked herself. Why couldn't she just say what she felt and leave it at that? Why did she always feel guilty when she couldn't please other people?

"Yeah. So?"

Natalie sighed. "Oh, come on. You know those guys look down their noses at us. I'm sure they think if we had any brains, we'd be going to Yale."

"You're paranoid. Besides, even if they *do* think that, who cares? We're not gonna marry 'em. We're just gonna eat their food and drink their beer and have some fun."

"*You're* just going to eat their food and drink their beer. *I'm* not going."

"But I don't have anyone else to go with," Brooke whined, pouting. "Just come with me for a little while, okay? If it's awful and you hate it, we'll leave. I promise."

"Brooke . . ."

"Please? Pretty please?" At this, Brooke slid off the futon onto her knees, her hands clasped together as if in prayer. She gave Natalie a pitiful look.

Despite herself, Natalie started to laugh. "Oh, honestly."

Brooke's face broke into a delighted grin. "Does that mean yes?"

Natalie sighed again. It was Friday, and even though she was working tomorrow, she had all Sunday to finish her English lit paper on Jane Austen. She guessed it wouldn't kill her to go to one party. Hoping she wouldn't be sorry, she finally said, "Oh, I guess so."

"Thank you, thank you." Brooke jumped up, very nearly spilling her Coke in her exuberance.

"But remember," Natalie added, "if I want to leave, we're going. No arguments. Understood?"

"Understood."

"You promise."

"Cross my heart."

"I'll hold you to it."

"Fine," Brooke said, waving her hand airily. "Now, what're you gonna wear?"

"I don't know. Jeans?"

"Absolutely not. Want to borrow my black skirt?"

"Your leather skirt?" The skirt in question was in the new long style, but it fit like a second skin.

"Uh-huh."

"That's not me, Brooke. If you don't think I should wear jeans, I'll wear my gray skirt and sweater."

The outfit, smoky gray cashmere and the nicest Natalie owned, had been a gift from her older sister Rose the previous Christmas. In giving it to her, Rose had said, "You work so hard, sweetie, and every girl needs to have one outfit that's beautiful. Besides, it matches your eyes exactly." Ever since, whenever Natalie had worn it, she'd felt special.

"Perfect," Brooke said happily, now that she'd gotten her way. "Well, guess I'd better get going. I'll pick you up at eight, okay?"

"Okay." Brooke had a car, a secondhand Camaro that had belonged to her older brother, whereas Natalie relied on her legs, her bike, and public transportation to get her wherever she needed to go.

Brooke left, smiling, and Natalie decided she'd use the time until she had to get ready for the party to clean her tiny apartment. The apartment was her only extravagance, but it was one she was determined to manage. Last year she'd lived in one of the dorms. That was how she and Brooke had met. They were assigned to rooms across the hall from one another. By the second semester, they had traded roommates and were rooming together.

Yet as much as Natalie liked Brooke, it drove her crazy to live in constant chaos. The trouble was, Natalie was obsessively neat and organized, and Brooke was a slob.

But even more importantly, Natalie knew if she were going to keep her grades up, she had to have some privacy and quiet time to study. So she'd worked two jobs over the summer and saved every possible penny, earmarking it for a place of her own this year.

Affordable small apartments in New Haven weren't easy to find, and Natalie knew she'd been extraordinarily lucky. Hers was owned by an eighty-year-old widow who lived in the small shotgun house in the front of the narrow property. Most days Natalie rode her bike to school and work; she worked two days and two nights a week for a textbook supplier, doing typing and general clerical work. On bad-weather days, she caught a city bus at the corner, which deposited her at the southern entrance to the campus.

The widow, Mrs. Buckley, had said, "I don't hold with noisy parties and shenanigans like dope and drinking."

"I don't drink, and I don't do drugs," Natalie had assured her.

The woman's stern expression gradually softened. "I think I believe you," she finally said, and the apartment was Natalie's.

Natalie had been elated. She still was. This was the first time in her life she'd ever lived alone, and she loved it. She kept the place spotlessly clean and neat, with a place for everything and everything in its place. And even though an apartment of her own meant there was no way she could afford a car, she didn't mind. The biking and walking she did were good exercise, the only exercise she got.

The studio apartment was less than three hundred square feet and consisted of the combination living room/bedroom, a minuscule kitchen with a tiny extension into which a table and two chairs just barely fit, and a bathroom. But it was enough. More than enough, in fact.

In addition to the futon, Natalie had filled the main room with a cheap bookcase and desk, a dresser, a small color TV set, which had been her parents' gift when she'd started college, two lamps, and a hand-me-down maple coffee table and end table donated by her brother Tony. The walls were decorated with posters of New York. Her favorite was one of Central Park at night, with the New York skyline in the background. Every time Natalie looked at it, she smiled and thought how she would be there someday.

The table and two chairs in her eating area were the only items she'd purchased. She'd bought them at Pier One, and they reminded her of the old-fashioned ice cream parlor in her hometown.

The small refrigerator and gas stove had come with the apartment, and although Mrs. Buckley had made previous tenants go to the Laundromat to do their laundry, she'd given Natalie permission to use the washer and dryer in the basement of the main house.

"Just as long as you buy your own soap and bleach," the older woman had said. Her voice was stern, but her eyes were kind.

Natalie knew she was lucky. Mrs. Buckley had taken a liking to her; that was clear. In fact, Natalie hadn't lived there a week before Mrs. Buckley was bringing over "half a loaf of bread I baked today" or "a couple of slices of my meat loaf, it's too much for me" or "just a bit of my stew, I've got way too much." At first Natalie protested, but when she realized it was giving the older woman pleasure to help her out, she stopped feeling guilty about accepting the welcome offerings. One day, she promised herself, when she was out of school and had some money, she would do something nice for Mrs. Buckley. In the meantime, she showed her gratitude by helping out with chores.

She made a mental note to ask her landlady if she wanted Natalie to rake the leaves in the front yard sometime this weekend.

After cleaning the apartment, Natalie took a quick

shower, changed into the cashmere outfit, and was ready and waiting when Brooke tooted the horn a few minutes before eight.

The wind whipped her hair into her face as Natalie descended the outside stairs, and she was glad she'd grabbed her trench coat. She could already feel winter in the air, but she didn't mind. She'd always liked winter, maybe because there was nothing quite so nice as being warm and snug inside when it was freezing outside.

Brooke chattered gaily as she drove to the slightly seedy area near the Yale campus where the party was being held. Even the fact she had to park three blocks away couldn't dampen her spirits.

"We're going to have a *great* time tonight!" Brooke predicted as they walked arm in arm toward the house.

Two

Adam Osgood Forrester had been named after his two grandfathers, Adam Turner Forrester and Osgood Henry Walters. As the oldest child and only son of parents Franklin and Phyllis, pillars of Westchester County society for six generations, much was expected of Adam, and he knew it, but the high expectations didn't bother him. On the contrary, they had always served to motivate him.

After all, he had led a charmed life—a life made possible by his parents and the other Forresters—and they deserved no less than his best efforts. Adam knew his ideas were old-fashioned, that most of his generation felt their parents lived in a world that was no longer relevant. Adam didn't agree. He was certain that having high standards and always doing your best would never go out of style. Unfortunately, his sister did not share his opinion.

Two years younger than Adam, Vanessa had been out of control since her teens. At fourteen, she'd started smoking. At fifteen, Adam's mother had been forced to get Vanessa a prescription for birth control pills when it was clear she had every intention of having sex whenever and wherever she pleased. At seventeen she'd been picked up in a raid at a local club, and it was only through Adam's father's influence with the local police that she'd avoided a formal arrest record. At nineteen she'd dropped out of college, saying it was archaic. Since then, she'd been working in New York and somehow managing to support herself. How, Adam had no idea. Mostly, he didn't want to know.

Now twenty-three, she delighted in taunting him about his "hang-ups" and his seeming need to please their parents. "What is your *problem*?" she'd said only last week when the two were both at home for their mother's fiftieth birthday. "Don't you want to *live*?" Because she knew he hated her cigarette habit, she'd blown smoke in his face.

"Oh, you mean drink too much, party too much, and constantly get into situations I can't handle and then expect Dad to bail me out like you do? No, I guess I don't want to *live*."

She'd made a face. "Perfect Adam. Always doing the right thing. Why, it wouldn't surprise me if you were still a virgin!" Her laugh was derisive. "God, you're so fucking boring! How can you stand yourself?"

He'd had to bite his tongue to keep from lashing back at her—something that he'd learned from experience would do no good. Besides, he had no intention of discussing his sex life with her.

"I suppose you'll even marry Julia to please them," Vanessa had continued in that same disdainful voice. Julia Hammond was the daughter of Adam's parents' best friends, Julius and Margarethe Hammond, and it was no secret that both sets of parents hoped Adam and Julia would get together.

Adam didn't answer. If he did, he knew he would eventually lose his temper, and he would not give his sister that satisfaction.

She'd grinned. "Well, if you're so spineless you'll allow them to pick your wife, you deserve to end up with someone as mousy and dull as Julia."

"Julia's not dull. And she's not mousy, either. She's sensible and thoughtful. And, you know, it's pretty rotten of you to say such nasty things about her." His earlier determination not to allow Vanessa to goad him into anger deserted him, but he still managed to keep his voice even. "Especially when she's always been nice to you."

"Nice to me! She tolerates me because I'm your sister, but the truth is, she can't stand me."

Adam would have continued to argue the point, but Julia *had* made several remarks about his sister that tended to support Vanessa's claim. "Did you ever stop to think that maybe she just disapproves of the way you behave?"

"As if I care." To underline this point, she gave him the finger.

Ignoring her crude gesture, he said, "That's the problem. You don't care what *anyone* thinks, do you?"

"No, I don't! You might be willing to throw *your* life away trying to make everybody else happy, but I'm not," she'd retorted.

"Don't worry, Van. You'll never be accused of trying to make *anyone* happy."

At that, she glared at him.

Thinking back on that conversation, Adam wondered if Vanessa would ever find what she seemed to be so desperately searching for. She'd had any number of lovers; like her jobs, none had lasted more than a few months. Nothing satisfied her for long. She was always moving on to bigger and better things. More excitement. More thrills. More danger. She'd lived on the edge for so long, she couldn't find any pleasure in normal, everyday life, which Adam found exasperating, and his parents found frightening. Adam had once hoped Vanessa might change. Now he only hoped she didn't cause herself or anyone else permanent damage with her increasingly risky lifestyle.

Adam might have grown up in comparative luxury, but he found great pleasure in simple things: a beautiful sunset, reading a good book, his first cup of coffee in the morning, the pristine appearance of a new legal pad. Even the short walk from his apartment to the law school each morning afforded him pleasure.

Vanessa might make fun of Julia, but Adam knew he could do worse than to marry her. It didn't matter to him that Julia wasn't exciting. She was pretty and sweet and kind and, even though she was almost four years younger, they had been good friends since they were children. They liked the same things, had grown up the same way. In short, she spoke his language. He might not be passionately in love with Julia, but he did love her. Anyway, Adam wasn't sure he believed in romantic love. He'd always thought that if he and Julia ended up together, they would probably have a good life.

As these thoughts and others had been running through Adam's head, he had been showering and shaving and was now rummaging through his closet while he tried to decide what he wanted to wear that night. He and his best buddy, Sam Berry, were going to a party given by a couple of the first-year law students. Adam hadn't really wanted to go. He'd have preferred to stay home and watch game three of the World Series. His beloved Yankees were two games down, but they were playing at home tonight and were favored to win. But Sam had twisted his arm, saying, "You can keep an eye on the game at the party. You know they'll have it on."

Yes, Adam thought now, they'd have the game on, but it would be noisy, and everybody would be drinking too much, and music would be blaring from the other rooms. Adam frowned at himself in the bathroom mirror. Why had he agreed to go? He didn't even like parties. Maybe he'd call Sam and tell him he'd changed his mind.

But just then the doorbell rang. Too late. That was probably Sam now. Giving a last whack of the hairbrush at a cowlick that refused to behave, Adam grimaced and walked out to the living room.

"Hey," Sam said when Adam opened the door. As always, his buddy wore jeans, but tonight's pair was at least clean, obviously Sam's concession to the fact he was going to a party. Sam was the first to admit he was a slob. "You ready?" he added.

"Yeah, I guess so." Adam still wished he could back out and stay home, but he knew Sam would argue with him until he gave in, so he compromised. "I've decided to drive, too, though."

Sam frowned. "Why? You know what the parking will be like."

"I don't care. I might want to leave earlier than you do."

Sam shrugged. "Suit yourself."

Fifteen minutes later, Sam managed to wedge his Corvette next to a Cutlass in the driveway at the house where the party was being held, which didn't surprise Adam. Sam always managed to find a choice parking place for his beloved sports car. The Corvette was almost new, a gift from Sam's father when he'd gotten his undergraduate degree. Adam, on the other hand, still drove the Mustang he'd gotten when he'd graduated from high school. Not that he minded. Cars were not important to him. Besides, like everything else he owned, he took good care of the Mustang.

Sam waited outside the house until Adam had parked and walked back to join him. Pink Floyd blasted them when they entered the front door. The house was already jammed; people spilled out of every room. Making his way through the throng, Adam grabbed a cold beer, said "See you later" to Sam, who had no interest in baseball, then headed for the TV room at the back of the house. As he entered the room, he grimaced at the sweetish smell of pot. Adam didn't do drugs. He'd tried pot once or twice, but he didn't like the way it made him feel. He liked being in control. Ignoring the smell, he looked around. All the chairs were occupied, so Adam found a spot on the floor and settled in to watch the game.

It was the top of the third, with two out and one on.

Reggie Smith was up to bat and hit a smashing line drive down the third base line, and all the Yankee fans in the room moaned. But Craig Nettles, the Yankees third baseman, made a sensational diving stop for the third out. Adam and the other Yankee fans erupted into cheers. The few Los Angeles fans who didn't were heckled good-naturedly.

"Why don't you traitors go back to La La Land?" somebody said, followed by others who echoed the sentiment.

During this exchange, Adam's stomach growled; he hadn't eaten any dinner. So during the next commercial, he went searching for food. He found it laid out on the dining room table. Grabbing a paper plate, he fixed a couple of ham sandwiches, added chips and a pickle, fished another cold beer out of the cooler in the corner, then turned to head back to the game. He reached the doorway just as a girl he'd never seen before was coming through from the opposite direction. They each turned sideways to let the other one pass, and in so doing, their eyes met.

Later, Adam knew he would always remember that exact moment when he first gazed down into Natalie's eyes—eyes that were a delicate blend of blue and gray, a shade that made him think of heather, even though he'd never seen heather in his life and had no idea what color it was. Fantastic eyes that reminded him of the soft, misty rain that fell in the spring. Wonderful eyes a man could happily drown in. Adam couldn't have torn his gaze away even if he'd wanted to; he was mesmerized by those eyes.

"I've never seen eyes that color," he blurted out.

"Excuse me?"

Shit. What had he just said? She probably thought he was a complete idiot. "Uh, can we start again? Let's pretend I said something normal like, *Nice party, isn't it?*"

After a moment—during which Adam held his breath—she smiled. "Okay."

"And then *you'd* say . . ."

The smile expanded. "Yes, it is."

If Adam hadn't already been captivated, her smile—accompanied as it was by a tiny dimple at the left-hand corner of her mouth—would have sealed his fate.

Giving him another smile, she began to move away, toward the food. The game he'd been so eager to return to now forgotten, he followed her. He couldn't let her get away; he had to know who she was.

Watching her fix a turkey sandwich, Adam decided she was one of the most intriguing girls he'd ever seen. In addition to those incredible eyes and that terrific smile, she had beautiful dark, curly hair and . . . Adam's gaze traveled down . . . a slender figure that curved in all the right places and a pair of really great ankles that he was sure were attached to equally great legs. Not for the first time, he rued the day short skirts had gone out of style and these long ones had become popular.

Because he couldn't just stand there ogling her, he took another handful of chips and tossed them onto his plate. "I'm Adam Forrester. I don't think I've seen you at one of these parties before."

"No," she said in a friendly voice, "this is my first." She put a few chips on her plate, then looked around.

Damn, he thought. *She's with someone.* "Aren't you going to tell me *your* name?"

"Oh. I'm sorry. I, um, was looking for my friend. She seems to have deserted me."

She. Relief flooded Adam. *She. Not he.* He grinned.

At his grin, she smiled again. Shifting her plate to her left hand, she held out her right. "I'm Natalie Ferrenzo."

After setting his bottle of beer on the table, Adam took her hand. Her handshake was firm. Her skin felt cool and smooth. He didn't want to let her hand go. He didn't want to let *her* go. "Want to find a place to sit and eat?" He had to raise his voice because music was once again blasting from the living room. Adam recognized the Bee Gees' "How Deep Is Your Love."

She hesitated, but only for a moment. "Sure."

After a fruitless search through the main rooms, they joined several dozen others who were sitting on the stairs leading to the second story.

"So what year are you?" Adam said when they were seated side by side near the top of the stairwell. He knew she was younger than he was, but it was hard to tell how much younger.

"I'm a sophomore. But I don't go to Yale. I go to Southern." Her eyes twinkled. "Still want to eat with me?"

"Why wouldn't I?"

"Oh, you know. Yale. Southern. Oil and water, right?"

"Come on. You don't really think that."

"Isn't it true?"

"No, it's not true." Even if someone had threatened to cut off his arm, he never would have admitted that most of the guys he knew wouldn't be caught dead with a girl from Southern.

She studied him thoughtfully for a moment, then smiled. "Okay."

"So what are you majoring in?" he asked.

"English."

He nodded. "My mother was an English major."

"Was she? What did she end up doing?"

"Getting married."

She smiled. "What about you?"

"Me? I'm not married."

The smile turned into a laugh. "I meant, what are you studying?"

"I'm in my last year of law school."

"A lawyer, huh? Yes, I can see that. You have a sort of lawyerly look."

Adam smiled ruefully. "I'm not sure that's a compliment."

She laughed again. The sound was infectious and made him want to laugh, too. "I just meant you have a serious, mature appearance. Which is a good thing to have if you're going to be a lawyer." She took a bite of her sandwich. "What kind of law are you interested in?"

"Well, if I could do exactly what I wanted to do, I'd probably go to work for the DA's office. However, what I'm actually going to do is work in the litigation department of Hammond, Crowley in Manhattan."

"Why? I mean, if you want to work as a prosecutor, why don't you?"

"Because this job was offered to me by a friend of my father's and, well, it's a good job."

"I guess you're lucky. I mean, having a job lined up already, when you still have a ways to go before you finish school."

He shrugged. "I've clerked there two summers already, so they know my work." He could have said he'd had several other offers from firms where he had no connections at all. The offers had come because he'd made law review, but explaining this might have sounded as if he were bragging.

For a while, they ate in silence. Then Adam said, "What about you? What do you want to do when you're finished with school?"

"I'm going to work in publishing. You know, be an editor."

"Are you?" She sure sounded confident.

"Yes. And I know what you're thinking."

"What am I thinking?"

"You're thinking that's what most English majors want. Like journalism majors want to be syndicated columnists and drama majors want to be Dustin Hoffman, English majors at East Coast schools almost always want to be editors for a big publishing house."

He grinned. "Even if I was thinking that, which I wasn't, it's obvious you're determined to reach your goal."

"Yes, I am."

Gradually, the conversation veered from school and careers to more personal areas. Natalie told him that she came from a large family. "I have three sisters and two brothers," she said.

"Six kids. Wow. I only have one sister. Are you the oldest? Youngest?"

"I'm next to the youngest. Tony's the oldest. He's thirty. Then comes John, who's twenty-seven. Then Rose, twenty-five. Then Carol, who's twenty-two. Then me. And last of all, Grace, who's just seventeen."

"I can't imagine having so many brothers and sisters. Do you get along?"

Natalie smiled. "We've had our share of fights, but down deep, we're very close. My sisters and I all slept in the same bedroom. Believe me, when four girls share a bedroom, you're close!" At his expression, she added, "We had to share a bedroom. There were only three, and the boys had one and my parents the other. At one time, my dad thought about putting a bedroom over the garage and putting the boys out there, but it would have cost so much, and we really couldn't afford it."

Adam thought of the big house he'd grown up in. There'd been six bedrooms. And only two kids.

As they continued to talk, he discovered that she worked twenty hours a week in addition to carrying almost a full load at school. It wasn't hard to figure out she needed to work, not after what she'd told him about sharing that bedroom. She was probably paying her own way through school. He admired that. He admired it a lot, even as he realized how lucky he was to be able to concentrate all of his energies on his studies.

They talked a long time, sitting there on the stairs. He could see Natalie wasn't sophisticated, but she was intelligent and well-read, and she had a natural empathy that was evident in the way she listened and commented. Adam found himself telling her things he rarely told anyone. About Vanessa and the grief she'd given his parents. About their mother and the heart problems that had been discovered a couple of years ago and how they worried Adam. About the dog he'd had since he was a kid and how broken up he'd been when Shep had died the year before.

Adam was shocked when he finally looked at his watch and saw it was nearly eleven-thirty. They'd been talking for more than two hours! He knew he should say good-bye to her and go find Sam. But he didn't want to. He couldn't bear to. He was just getting to know her. "Do you want to get out of here?" he blurted.

"I'd love to."

He smiled. "Great."

"First, though, I have to find my friend and tell her I'm leaving," Natalie said.

There was that smile again. Did she have any idea what that smile did to him? "Okay. You go find your friend, then we'll meet by the front door."

"All right."

As he watched her walk down the steps, Adam experienced a momentary twinge of guilt, almost as if he were being disloyal to Julia, but that was ridiculous. He wasn't engaged to Julia. They'd never even really *dated*. Sure, he'd been her escort at her debut, and she'd asked him to a couple of dances, and occasionally, when they were both home in Westchester, they'd gone to a movie or played tennis at the club, but their relationship was more sisterly and brotherly than anything else. Yeah, he knew his parents and hers hoped they would end up together. But he and Julia had certainly never discussed anything serious. He'd never done more than give her a good night kiss, for crying out loud, and he knew for a fact that she'd dated a lot of guys in the past few years. She'd even *told* him about some of them.

He cast aside the suspicion that Julia had mentioned those guys because she wanted to make him jealous. That had probably just been his ego causing him to think so.

So there was absolutely no reason he couldn't see another girl if he wanted to.

And he'd be damned if he'd feel guilty about it when he did.

Three

~~~~~

After retrieving her trench coat, Natalie found Brooke dancing. "I'm leaving," Natalie yelled over the music.

"What?" Brooke shouted back.

"I'm leaving. I'll call you tomorrow." Natalie waved good-bye and started to walk away.

"Wait!" Brooke ran after her. Once they were out of the room where it was a bit quieter, she said, "What do you mean, you're leaving? You're not going to *walk* home, I hope?"

"No. I'm getting a ride."

"You mean you *met* somebody? A guy?"

Natalie smiled.

"Well, well, well," Brooke said thoughtfully. "This is a first. Any guy who can get you to go home with him must be something pretty special."

Natalie knew her expression gave her away, because just thinking about Adam Forrester made her feel all warm inside.

"Aha! I was right. Where is he? I want to meet him."

Natalie didn't want to introduce Adam to Brooke. Not yet. After all, this might be a one-night thing. She might never see Adam again. Yet she knew it would be useless to argue, so she contented herself with saying, "Look, don't make a big deal out of this, okay? Don't embarrass me in front of him."

"Would I do that?"

"Yes, you would."

Brooke crossed her hands over her chest. "I promise I'll behave. In fact, you don't even have to introduce me. I just want to see what he looks like."

Just then, Natalie saw Adam approaching. Under her breath she said, "Here he comes now."

Brooke slid her gaze in the direction Natalie indicated. "That one? The preppy-looking guy in the loafers and khaki pants and green sweater?"

"Yes," Natalie hissed.

Brooke grinned. "Gee, this is just like *Love Story*, Nat. Preppy guy, Italian girl, New England school."

"Oh, good grief! Go away. I'll call you tomorrow."

But Brooke couldn't resist a parting shot. "All right, I'm going." Her smile turned sly. "Don't do anything I wouldn't do. Of course, that leaves a wide-open field."

Natalie pretended she hadn't heard that last bit as she watched Adam approach. She couldn't help smiling inwardly at Brooke's dead-on description of Adam. He did look like a preppy, with his all-American good looks, his neatly combed light brown hair, his nice smile, and his obviously expensive clothes. Not to mention those grave brown eyes.

All you had to do was look at him to know he hadn't spent his summers working at the local supermarket or gas station the way her brothers had. Natalie was sure Adam was the product of private schools, had spent most summers on the tennis court or at the country club pool, and had never had to worry about money in his life.

Out of your league, in other words.

The thought was unwelcome, and she pushed it away. She wasn't going to marry him, for heaven's sake. He was just a cute guy who was going to take her home from a party. Nothing more. Besides, she was just as good as he was. Hadn't her parents emphasized that very thing more times than she could count? She remembered how her dad had always told her she could do anything or be anything she wanted to.

"It's not like when I was a kid with immigrant parents who didn't speak good English," he'd said. "You've had all the advantages, Nat. Make the most of them."

All the advantages. Well, in his eyes, she guessed she had. After all, she hadn't had to quit school after eighth grade to help support the family the way her father'd had to. She'd finished high school, graduating with honors, and here she was in college, something her parents hadn't even thought about doing because it was entirely out of their realm of possibilities.

"What's the matter?" Adam said, reaching her side. "You're frowning."

Shaking off her thoughts, she smiled. "Nothing's the matter. I was just thinking about home. How different it is here."

"Yes," he agreed. "Home is the real world." A shadow briefly crossed his face, but as he reached for her coat and helped her into it, then put on his own brown leather jacket, it disappeared, and Natalie wondered if she'd imagined it.

Outside, the cold air was a shock after the warmth of the house, but it felt good to Natalie. It was a beautiful night, clear, so that the stars stood out brilliantly against the navy sky.

Adam held her arm as they walked down the stairs. The small courtesy impressed her.

"My car's parked a couple of blocks away. You want to wait here while I go get it?"

"I don't mind walking with you."

They walked along silently for a while, then he said, "I almost didn't come tonight."

She looked up. "I almost didn't come, either."

"Why not?"

She shrugged. "I don't really like parties."

"I don't, either." After a moment, he added, "We're a lot alike, I think."

"Are we?" But she thought so, too. The way he'd talked about his family—it was easy to see he loved and respected them and, like her, wanted them to be proud of him. That alone was very important to Natalie. So many people their age didn't feel that way. And she had the sense that he tried to be a good person, something that was also important to her.

A few more silent moments passed. Then he said, "I'm glad I came tonight."

There was something about the way his voice softened that caused her heart to skitter as it hadn't done since she'd been in high school and had a crush on the most popular boy in her class, who hadn't even known she was alive. "Me, too."

With unspoken accord, they stopped walking. He looked down. She looked up. His face was in shadow. "Natalie." His voice sounded rough.

Her heart began to pound. And then she was in his arms, and he was kissing her. He tasted of beer and peppermint toothpaste. As his tongue parted her lips, delving and exploring, Natalie's head spun. She clung to him in wonder, her senses reeling.

They stood there, in the middle of that decaying downtown neighborhood, oblivious to the cars passing by, oblivious to everything except each other.

In some part of his mind, Adam knew he was doing something rash, something totally out of character for someone like him, something that might have far-reaching consequences, but he was powerless to stop. The only thing that mattered to him right now was this girl, a girl he wanted more than he'd ever wanted anything in his life.

And she wanted him. The way she responded to his

kisses, the way she didn't pull back when he pressed her close, told him all he needed to know.

Afterward, he wasn't sure what would have happened or how long they would have stood there kissing each other if that horn hadn't sounded. A bunch of guys—Yale undergraduates, Adam was sure—honked and hooted at them as they drove by.

Reluctantly, Adam released her. "We'd better find the car." His voice was ragged as he fought to get his emotions and his body under control.

She nodded. In the moonlight, her eyes shone. Damn, she was beautiful! Not wanting to let her go, he kept his arm around her as they walked the rest of the way to his car. He felt dazed, almost as if he'd been struck by lightning. Was this what people meant when they said they had fallen in love at first sight? He swallowed. *In love? In love?* Where the hell had that come from?

When they got to the car, he opened the passenger door and helped her inside. Then he walked around to his own side and climbed in. "Where . . ." He cleared his throat. "Where do you live?"

In a subdued voice, she told him the address. *What is she thinking?* he wondered as he started the car and pulled away from the curb. Did she feel as stunned and awkward and confused as he did?

They didn't talk on the short drive to her place. He was afraid to say anything, because he knew he wasn't thinking logically. Even after he'd parked in front of the house, helped Natalie out of the car, and walked her down the driveway toward the garage, they were silent. He wished he knew what was going on in her mind. Would she ask him in?

At the foot of the stairwell leading up to her apartment, she finally broke the silence. "I had fun tonight, Adam. Thanks for bringing me home." She turned as if to start up the stairs.

"Natalie, wait." He put his hands on her shoulders. "Do you have a roommate?"

She shook her head.

His heart hammered. "Can I come up?"

"I . . ." She looked down. "I don't think that's a good idea," she said in a small voice.

She was right. He knew she was right. Things were happening too fast. He needed to think about this, decide if this was a smart thing to do or if it would just complicate his life. Yet he couldn't help the disappointment that settled like a weight on his chest.

"Things are moving a little too fast for me," she added softly. Rising on tiptoe, she gave him a quick kiss. "You can call me if you want, though."

She was halfway up the stairs before he remembered he didn't have her phone number. "Are you listed in the book?"

She stopped. "No." She gave him her number.

He repeated it, saying, "I'll call you tomorrow," then watched until she was safely inside.

All the way home, he kept saying her number out loud so he wouldn't forget it. And the first thing he did when he entered his apartment was go to his telephone book and write it down. Just seeing it there gave him a rush. Suddenly, he couldn't wait until tomorrow. Smiling, he headed for his bedroom, but he'd barely taken three steps when the phone rang.

It startled him. He didn't get many phone calls, and the ones he did get rarely came after midnight. He grabbed the receiver. "Hello?"

"Adam?" It was his father.

"Dad?" Alarm caused his voice to squeak. "Is something wrong?"

"I'm afraid so, son."

"Mom? Is it Mom?"

"Yes. It's your mother. She's had another heart attack."

Fear nearly paralyzed Adam. Two years ago, his mother

had suffered her first heart attack. Since then, they'd all hoped there wouldn't be another. "Is . . . is she okay?"

"She's alive, but . . ." His father's voice broke. "She . . . she's in the Critical Care Unit. They said it was a bad one."

Adam swallowed. He could hardly get the question out. "Is . . . is she going to make it?"

"I don't know. The doctors won't commit themselves. They say if she can make it through the first twenty-four hours, she'll probably live."

"W-when did it happen?"

"A couple of hours ago."

"Where are you now? At the hospital?"

"Yes. I'll probably stay through the night."

"What about Vanessa?"

"I haven't been able to reach her."

Adam's sister had an apartment in Manhattan. "Well, it's Friday night. She's probably out with someone."

"Yes." His father sounded weary. "I'll keep trying."

"Listen, Dad, I'm going to come down there."

"Yes. I thought you might."

"I'll be there in a couple of hours."

His father told him exactly where he'd be, then added, "Be careful, son."

"I will."

Thirty minutes later, all else driven from his mind, Adam was on the road, heading for home.

Four

Adam rubbed his eyes wearily, then glanced over at his father, who stood staring out the window of the third-floor waiting area outside the CCU.

Adam admired his father and wasn't ashamed to admit it. Franklin Forrester was the kind of man Adam aspired to be: a good man, a strong man, someone you could depend on, someone who was dignified and respected, someone who had always made the people around him feel secure. Even now, when Adam knew his father had to be extremely worried about his mother, Franklin was refusing to show any doubt that she would pull through just fine, that this latest attack was anything but a temporary setback.

Adam couldn't help an inward smile. This refusal to believe anything but what he wanted to believe was so typical of his father. Sometimes this trait could be frustrating, but most of the time, Adam understood that his father's positive thinking was the main reason he had been so successful, not only in his business dealings but in his personal relationships, as well.

Except for Vanessa.

Sighing, Adam looked at his watch. It was eight o'clock in the morning. He'd only been there six hours, but in some ways it felt as if he and his father had been waiting there for days.

"Dad?" he said.

His father turned to look at him.

"Do you want me to try to reach Vanessa again?"

His father shrugged. "If you want to."

They'd called Vanessa's apartment periodically through the night with no success.

"I don't think it'll do any good. She's probably away for the weekend," his father added.

Adam nodded. He was sure his father was right. Still, walking down the hall to the pay phones and attempting to reach Vanessa would give Adam something positive to do. Anything was better than just sitting there.

Five minutes later, he rejoined his father. "Still no answer," he said.

Franklin nodded. Adam thought about going down to the cafeteria, maybe getting some coffee and a sweet roll. Since they had just come from seeing his mother about fifteen minutes ago, he knew they had plenty of time before they'd be called into the CCU again. She was only allowed to have visitors once each hour. They weren't sure if she was aware of their visits or not. Mostly she slept.

So far, thank God, she was holding her own. Even though Adam knew this, it was tough to see her looking so pale and weak and hooked up to so many machines. Phyllis Forrester was much too young to have such a bad heart. Of course, Adam knew age had nothing to do with illness. If you didn't believe that, all you had to do was look around you. He thought about all the children who were stricken with cancer and other catastrophic diseases every day. He guessed he should be glad he'd had his mother this long, but it was hard to think that way. He loved his mother. They'd always been close. It would be devastating to lose her.

Just then, the elevator dinged. A few seconds later, Julius and Margarethe Hammond emerged.

Adam knew his father had called Julius last night, so it didn't surprise him that he and his wife had shown up at the hospital so early. In fact, he wouldn't have been surprised if they'd been here last night when he arrived.

As they walked down the hall, Adam studied them: Julius, tall, big, handsome, with thick gray hair and intense dark eyes; and Margarethe, tall, slender, and athletic-looking, with blond Scandinavian good looks. Adam knew if Julia had been at home, she'd have come this morning, too, but she was spending her final year of college in Stockholm, where Margarethe had been born and raised.

"Franklin!" Margarethe Hammond said. She hurried over to Adam's father and hugged him. Heavy winter coat slung over one arm, she wore dark tailored pants and a turtleneck sweater, the sort of casual outfit she had always favored.

Julius grasped Adam's hand, saying, "Sorry about your mother, Adam."

"Thank you, sir."

Once the first greetings were over, the Hammonds sat down, and Adam's father answered their questions.

Margarethe sat next to Adam, and once his father had updated them on his mother's condition, she said, "I called Julia to tell her about your mother. She was so upset."

He nodded.

"She loves your mother so much," Margarethe continued.

"I know."

"She started to cry and said how much she wished she could be here with you."

Her words made him uncomfortable. "How . . ." He cleared his throat. "How's Julia doing?"

Margarethe frowned. "Haven't you heard from her?"

"Yes, I had a letter last week." He didn't add that he hadn't answered it yet.

"Well, then you know she's homesick."

Adam nodded. That had been obvious from what she'd written.

"But Julius and I both feel this year away will be good for her. Besides, I want her to perfect her Swedish and get to know my family better. I told her this would probably be her last opportunity to spend any amount of time with them, because once she graduates from college . . . and gets married . . ." She paused significantly. "She'll have too many responsibilities here. Don't you agree?"

Adam avoided her eyes. "You're probably right."

"Well, you wouldn't want *your* wife to be gone for long periods of time, would you?"

This last was said coyly, and Adam's mind raced for an answer. "I can't even imagine being *married*," he finally said.

She smiled indulgently. "Oh, I know. But that will change. You'll see." Reaching out, she squeezed his hand. "Your mother and I can't *wait* to be grandmothers."

"Margarethe, leave the poor boy alone," Julius said. "He's worried about his mother, and you're badgering him about having babies!"

After that, no more was said about Julia or marriage, but for the rest of the day, Margarethe's words haunted Adam, because it was clear to him that they not only hoped he and Julia would marry, they fully expected it to happen. One of these days very soon, he was going to have to decide what it was he really wanted, and if Julia wasn't part of his plans for the future, then he'd have to figure out how to extricate himself from a sticky situation without causing hurt feelings.

Yet, even as he told himself this, he realized that down deep, he already knew the answer. He'd known the answer from the moment he'd looked into a beautiful pair of blue gray eyes the night before.

• • •

Natalie rushed home from work Saturday afternoon. What an idiot she was! She had forgotten to tell Adam she had to work today. Oh, she hoped if he'd called her and hadn't gotten an answer, he'd have figured out that she was working. Surely he would have. Surely he'd call again.

As she turned the key in the lock, she heard her phone ringing. Smiling broadly, she rushed inside and grabbed the receiver.

"Nat?"

Natalie's heart sank as she recognized her sister Rose's voice. Normally, she was happy to hear from Rose, but today . . . She sighed.

"What's wrong, honey?" Rose said.

"Oh, nothing. I just got home from work, that's all. I'm out of breath."

"Want me to call you back a little later?" Rose always called Natalie, because she knew Natalie had to watch her pennies.

"No, that's okay." Natalie told herself if Adam tried to call now and got a busy signal, he'd call back.

"So what kind of week did you have?" Rose said.

"It was good. I think I aced my psych test."

"Great. I knew you would."

"What about you? How're the kids doing? Jenny over her ear infection?" Jenny was Rose's two-year-old.

Now it was Rose's turn to sigh. "I hope so. Her doctor said if she keeps getting them, they'll probably need to put tubes in her ears."

"Oh, dear. Poor thing."

"It's really not *that* bad. Lots of kids have to have it done."

"Are you trying to persuade me or yourself?"

"Me," Rose answered ruefully.

"What about the baby? How's he doing?"

"Oh, Nat, you should see him. In the last month, he's

gained three pounds. It's no wonder, though. He eats like a little lumberjack."

Natalie smiled. Reagan was six months old and a much-adored addition to Rose's family. "Send me some new pictures."

"Okay, I will. And you're coming home for Thanksgiving, so you'll see him then."

Natalie smiled. "Yes." Thanksgiving was always a big deal at the Ferrenzos'. Natalie's mother Connie loved to cook, and she went all out for the holidays. The entire clan would be there, including several of Natalie's aunts and uncles and numerous cousins.

They talked awhile more, then Rose said, "I have something to tell you."

From her tone, Natalie knew whatever it was, it was serious. "You're not pregnant again!"

"God, no," Rose said, laughing. "Much as I love mine, if I was pregnant, I'd shoot myself."

"Well, what then?"

"Chris has been transferred."

"Transferred! Where to?"

"Ohio."

"Ohio!"

"Yes. His company has built a new plant in this little town about fifty miles north of Columbus."

"Oh, no! You mean you're moving?"

"Of course, silly. He can't commute."

"I know. I just . . . *wow* . . . Ohio. That's so far away! When are you going? Not before Christmas, I hope."

"Actually, yes. We're going to move the week after Thanksgiving. We don't want to wait, because you know how bad the weather can get in January."

"But what about a house? Where will you live?"

"Well, Chris is in Crandall now—that's the name of the town where the plant is located—and he called a little while ago to say he'd found us a house to rent. We thought we'd wait awhile before we buy anything."

"I can't believe this. Oh, Rose, I'm going to miss you."

"But honey, you're hardly ever here, anyway. And you told me you wanted to try for a job in New York after you graduate."

"I do, but when I come home to visit, I count on seeing you and Chris and the kids."

"You'll still see us. We'll come back for holidays, and I'm sure I'll come and stay for a while every summer. Plus you can come and visit us. This is a terrific opportunity for Chris, and to tell you the truth, I'm kind of excited about moving somewhere new."

Natalie knew she should be happy for her sister, but she hated the thought that Rose would be leaving Connecticut.

"This is the way it is when you marry, Nat. You go wherever your guy goes."

Natalie wondered how she'd feel if she loved a guy and married him and then he wanted her to move away from all the people and things that were important to her. Somehow she couldn't see herself marrying anyone who *would* want that. Nor could she see herself giving up her career in the publishing world—a career she was determined to have—to accommodate someone else. Rose was different. Rose didn't work, so for her, moving wouldn't be a huge sacrifice. Maybe it would even be an adventure.

"You know what, Rose? I met a guy last night." Now where had that come from? Natalie hadn't intended to tell her sister about Adam. It had just kind of popped out.

"Oh?"

"Yes. I went to this party," she said, continuing happily. Now that she'd started, she wanted to tell Rose everything about Adam and what had happened between them. She held nothing back, not even the kiss on the street. When she finished, she felt almost as giddy as she had last night. "And he said he'd call me today, but of course, I've been at work."

"Wow, Nat, he sounds great. A lawyer. And going to

Yale." She said it reverently. "I always knew you'd end up with someone special."

Natalie laughed. "Now don't get carried away. I may never hear from him again."

"Oh, you'll hear from him. I'm sure of that. I'll bet he's trying to call you right now."

But if he had been, Natalie thought later, he hadn't made any attempt to call back, because her line was free all night. She stayed up until eleven, but the phone remained silent. Nor did he call on Sunday, and the only time Natalie was away from the phone was the hour and a half it took her to go to church and get back.

On Monday, she found herself unable to concentrate in her English lit class, even though it was her favorite of all her courses this semester. Angry with herself, she tried to stop thinking about Adam and why he hadn't called, but her traitorous mind kept veering back to the forbidden subject. Over and over, she replayed Friday night's events. The way he'd kissed her. How he'd asked to come up to her apartment. How he'd seemed to understand when she'd said no. And how he'd asked for her phone number and said he'd call.

She hadn't forced him to do anything.

So why hadn't he called?

And why do you care?

The question kept her awake that night. Why *did* she care? She'd had other disappointments in the guy department, but they'd never bothered her for long. What was so different about Adam?

He was nice-looking, yes, but that wasn't it. Looks had never been that important to Natalie. She truly believed it was what was inside a person that counted. No, it wasn't the way he looked that was so special. Maybe they'd only spent one evening together, but in those few hours, he had revealed himself to her. And in so doing, she had known he had the same beliefs and values and morals she had. Adam had integrity. It shone in his eyes. He was the kind of person you could depend upon, the kind of person who would always do what was right rather than what was easy.

And don't forget the physical attraction. Yes, there was that. There was definitely that. The way he made her stomach feel hollow when he kissed her and the way the kisses had left her wanting more. In the end, maybe the physical attraction was the most important element of all, because without it, none of Adam's great qualities would have mattered. It was the combination of the two that kept her looking at the phone and willing it to ring.

When several more days went by, and she still hadn't heard from him, she finally accepted that she wasn't going to.

Forget him, she told herself. *You've wasted enough time mooning over him. Remember, you're not in college to find a husband. You're here to get an education.*

Besides, no matter how much she'd liked him, down deep she knew they came from different worlds. Seeing him again would probably only be setting her up for a future letdown.

Maybe not hearing from him was for the best. Now she could focus on her goals without any distractions.

So, although she was disappointed and even a bit hurt, she would get over it. Determinedly, she pushed any remaining thoughts of Adam Forrester out of her mind.

Five

Adam missed more than a week of school, and he knew when he got back to class he would be swamped with work. He wasn't sorry about the lost time, though. His mother had rallied and was doing much better, but if she hadn't, if she'd died and he hadn't been there, he never would have forgiven himself.

All the way back to New Haven he thought about Natalie. He couldn't wait to see her again. So even though he had no business focusing on anything other than getting caught up with his missed course work, the first thing he did when he arrived at his apartment Tuesday evening was call her. The phone rang and rang with no answer.

Damn. Where was she? He couldn't remember if she'd told him when she worked, but he doubted it would be at night. And yet, how would she get twenty hours in each week if she *didn't* work at night?

Maybe she's out with some other guy. The thought caused a hot stab of envy.

He kept trying her number, but at nine-thirty, when she still hadn't answered, he decided to give it up for the night and call her in the morning.

On Wednesday, it was after four before he finally got home, and he brought a stack of work with him. Still, he was barely in the door when he dumped the books and papers and headed for the phone.

Once again there was no answer. Frustrated, he stood looking at the phone for a long moment. He knew he'd never be able to settle down and study until he had talked to her. He at least wanted her to know he was trying to get in touch with her. Finally, he wrote her a quick note, then grabbed his jacket and car keys. Five minutes later, he was on his way to her apartment.

When he arrived, he parked in front and walked to the back and up the stairs. Before leaving the note, he knocked, but there was still no answer. Taking the note out of his pocket, he shoved it under the door.

He was halfway down the stairs when she suddenly appeared in the driveway. His heart leaped at the sight of her. She wore a red knit cap pulled low on her head, a white down jacket, and jeans, and she was riding a ten-speed. By the time she realized he was there, they were only a few feet apart. For one unguarded moment, she looked as glad to see him as he was to see her, but the emotion was quickly masked, and her eyes and her greeting were both cool. "Hello, Adam."

"Hi. I just left you a note. I've been trying to call you since last night."

"Have you?" She got down off her bike and propped it against the stairs.

Man, she was giving off enough ice to freeze the tropics. She was obviously pissed, probably because he hadn't called her when he'd said he would. "Yes. I wanted to explain about why—"

"You know, Adam," she said, interrupting him. "I don't have the time or energy to play games. You said you were going to call me a week and a half ago. You didn't. I got the message. Why don't we just leave it at that?"

"Look, after I left you that night? I got a call from my dad. My mother had had a heart attack, and I had to go home to Westchester. I left immediately, and was there since yesterday. That's what I started to tell you. I just got back yesterday afternoon."

She studied him for a long moment. Then, in a softer voice, she said, "I'm sorry about your mother. How is she?"

"She's doing better."

"I'm glad."

For a minute, he didn't know what else to say, because she wasn't giving him any encouragement. But he couldn't just give up and walk away, so he continued on doggedly. "I was thinking maybe we could go get something to drink. Or if you don't have any other plans, we could grab a pizza or something."

She didn't answer immediately. And when she did, there was regret in her voice. "I appreciate the invitation, but I don't think so."

"Why not?"

She sighed and looked down at her feet.

"Why not?" he said more insistently. He had an almost irresistible urge to reach out and touch her cheek, which was rosy from the cold. "I thought you liked me," he added in a softer voice. "Was I wrong?"

Another sigh. Finally, she looked up. "I do like you. That's the problem."

"I don't understand."

"Look . . . I know how this is going to sound—"

"What?"

"The thing is, I like you too much. And when you didn't call me—" She held up her hand to ward off his rejoinder. "When you didn't call me, I was hurt. And for days afterward, I kept wondering why you hadn't called. I spent far too much time thinking about you and wondering what I'd done wrong. I don't like feeling that way. I don't have time for it. I know you had a good reason for not calling, but I just think it's better if we forget about anything further between us."

He knew she was probably being sensible, but he didn't

want to be sensible. Seeing her again had only reinforced all those earlier feelings he'd had about her. He had no intention of saying good-bye to her. "I don't want to forget about it."

"Well, maybe you—"

"Tell you what. I'll make you a deal. Just have dinner with me tonight. Then, if you still don't want to see me again, I won't bother you."

She shook her head. "I don't know." But her tone said she was wavering.

"I know a great Italian place. Do you like Italian food?"

For a long moment he was sure she was going to tell him to get lost. And then, suddenly, she smiled. "Of course I like Italian food. I *am* Italian."

"I knew that," Adam said in a burst of happiness, even though he hadn't. "So you'll come?"

The smile slowly faded, and she looked away.

"Please don't say no."

She looked at him again. In her eyes he saw confusion. He also saw something else. Something that caused his blood to flow faster. His gaze drifted to her mouth. He remembered how sweet that mouth was, how kissing her had made him dizzy with longing. And he knew if they hadn't been standing outdoors, in plain view of her neighbors, he wouldn't have been able to stop himself from pulling her into his arms and kissing her again. The desire was so great, it was a physical ache.

"Don't say no," he repeated softly.

She hesitated.

He held his breath.

"All right. But first I have to put my stuff in the apartment." She locked up her bike. "I'll just be a minute."

He grinned. "I'll wait."

Afterward, he couldn't remember anything they said to each other. Nor could he remember what they'd eaten. All he remembered was Natalie. How her eyes glowed in the light of the flickering candle that sat in the middle of the table. How her mouth looked as she enthusiastically ate her food. How her laugh sounded, soft and throaty and delightful, whenever he said something that amused her. And he'd tried hard to amuse her, because every time she did laugh, he felt as if he'd been given a gift.

And later, when he'd finally taken her home, how it had felt to kiss her again. How she'd clung to him and returned his kisses eagerly. If she'd have let him, he'd have taken her to bed, but she had gently pushed him away when things started to get too heavy.

"I'm sorry," she said. "I-I think we need to slow down. Think about this. Okay?"

"Okay." He'd have agreed with anything she said, given her anything she wanted.

After that night, they were inseparable. Every free moment was spent together. And when they weren't together, they were thinking about each other.

Adam was crazy about her. Sometimes he still felt guilty, but not often. Julia, her parents, his, what they wanted, what they hoped would happen, became less and less important. Natalie was all that mattered.

Even the plaintive letter he received from Julia early in November didn't deter him, although it *did* disturb him, because Julia said she wasn't sure she would stay on in Sweden after the first of the year.

I'm so homesick for Mother and Daddy and all my friends, especially you, Adam. I told Mother that I couldn't bear the thought of you being finished with school and starting your new life in New York and me not being there to share it all with you. I was so looking forward to helping you furnish an apartment and hearing all about your first days at the firm. You think I'm right, don't you, Adam?

He'd answered immediately, saying he would never forgive himself if she cut short her stay on his account.

I'm going to be awfully busy those first few months after graduation, Julia. You forget, I'll have to spend most of my free time studying for the bar.

After the letter was sent, he wondered if he should have been more blunt. Just come right out and told her he had met someone. But how could he do that? If she really *was* thinking of him as a future husband the way their parents seemed to be, then didn't she deserve to be let down face-to-face?

When he didn't receive an answer to the letter, he decided he'd been borrowing trouble. Obviously, Julia thought of him as a friend and nothing more. She had probably read his letter and decided he was right. Maybe she'd even gotten over her homesickness by now.

The week before Thanksgiving, his and Natalie's feelings for each other had reached the point where they both knew they could no longer deny what they felt. That Saturday night, Adam picked Natalie up from work. Leaning across the seat, he opened the passenger-side door for her, and she got into the car, bringing with her the light, flowery fragrance of her perfume and the fresh, cold air of the November evening. She slid close to him. As always, when seeing her after even a short absence, his heart quickened. Smiling, he gave her a quick, hard kiss before pulling out into traffic.

"Do you want to stop and get something to eat, or do you want to go home first?" he asked.

She put her hand on his thigh. "Home first." Her voice sounded odd.

Adam swallowed. He met her eyes for a brief moment. And there, in their depths, he saw what he'd been waiting for. His heart lurched. "Are . . ." He cleared his throat. "Are you sure?"

"Yes," she whispered. "Very sure."

His thigh burned where her hand lay, and his heart started playing leapfrog. His excitement almost caused him to rear-end the car in front of him, which had stopped for a red light.

After that, he drove carefully, but his mind was chaotic. Did he have any condoms with him? He couldn't remember, even though he'd been carrying one for the past week. But what if he'd forgotten to put it in the pocket of these pants? Maybe he should stop at the pharmacy just in case. Holding on to the wheel with his right hand, he shoved his left hand into his pants pocket, not an easy feat while driving. Relief coursed through him as he felt the foil packet.

Somehow he made it to her apartment without getting into an accident.

Five minutes later, the door to her apartment securely closed and locked behind them, they stood facing each other. As the darkness of evening crept through the windows and shut out the rest of the world, Adam reached for her.

Smiling, she walked into his arms.

Six

Natalie had known since early that morning that today would be the day she and Adam would make love for the first time. She had prepared for it by putting fresh sheets on the futon and making sure the small apartment was in perfect readiness. She had thought about what would happen all day long, and she hadn't had a single reservation. She had believed she was ready.

But now, even though she was in love with him, and even though she wanted him, she couldn't help feeling nervous, even a bit scared. And Adam sensed it.

"What's wrong?" he asked gently. "Have you changed your mind?"

"No, no, it's just that . . ."

"What?" His lips trailed from her mouth to her neck. As he nuzzled, his hands stroked her back, then moved lower to cup her bottom.

Her breath caught as she felt how hard he was. "I-I'm scared." Then, in a rush, before she lost her nerve, she whispered, "This is my first time. And I don't want to disappoint you."

For a moment, he froze. "You mean—?" Then his arms tightened around her. "You could never disappoint me. I'm honored to be the first."

Of all the things he could have said, this touched her deeply. She lifted her face to look into his eyes. "Thank you for saying that. I-I'm so glad it's you."

He kissed her then—a long, deep kiss that shook her to her core. After that, she forgot her fears and let her body's needs and wants take over.

Later, she never remembered them undressing. One moment they still had all their clothes on. The next, they were skin to skin, and their clothing lay in a jumble wherever they'd tossed it.

Natalie couldn't believe how glorious it felt to lay naked with Adam. She closed her eyes and reveled in the feelings that cascaded through her as his hands and lips paid homage to her body. And gradually she lost her shyness and began to touch him, too. She loved the way he felt, so strong and hard, so different from her, and when he groaned, it made her feel powerful to know she had the ability to affect him this way.

"I can't wait any longer," he finally gasped.

She was more than ready for him. There was some initial pain when he entered her, but it was quickly forgotten as passion and desire built. She knew he was trying to hold back, but she didn't want him to; she wanted to feel both his urgency and his strength.

Yes, she thought, pushing against him as he thrust deep and hard. *Yes. Yes.* This connection, this taking and giving, this *sharing*, this was what she'd dreamed about. This was what she'd wanted. This was where she belonged.

I love you. I love you.

It was a song in her heart as he brought her higher and higher and then higher still. And then, just before his own shuddering release, she fell apart in a shattering series of such intense sensations—an exquisite combination of pleasure and pain—she thought she might die of it.

When their hearts calmed and their breathing slowed, he pulled her close, fitting her body to his, spoon fashion.

"Next time will be better," he said huskily.

"I'm not sure I could take it," she teased.

She could feel his smile. "Mine, either, but what a way to die." He lazily stroked her breast.

Yes, Natalie thought. If she were to die right this minute, she didn't think she'd mind.

"Before we try it again, though," he added, chuckling and abandoning her breast, "I'd better build up my strength. Give myself a fighting chance."

"What do you mean?"

"I was thinking about pizza."

Natalie pretended mock indignation. "Food? You want *food*? Now I know what's *really* important to you." She started to pull away. "Okay, fine. I'll go call for a pizza."

Laughing, he drew her back, and then they were kissing again, and soon all thought of anything except each other was wiped from their minds.

"Tell me something," Adam said. He'd just finished his fourth slice of pizza and felt happily full. He and Natalie, both wrapped in blankets, were sitting cross-legged on the floor, the open pizza box between them.

She smiled. "What?"

God, she was beautiful, he thought for at least the thousandth time. Tonight she looked even more beautiful to him than she usually did, with her hair all tousled and her lips swollen from his kisses and her eyes soft from their lovemaking. "What's wrong with the guys you've known up to now?"

She didn't answer for a moment. "The truth is, I haven't dated that many guys."

"That had to have been your choice, right?" Hell, he couldn't imagine *any* guy who wouldn't want to date her.

She nodded, but there was a trace of something in her eyes, some emotion Adam couldn't identify. "Since I've been at Southern, it *has* pretty much been my choice, I guess. I mean, I don't encourage . . ." She smiled. "Let me rephrase that. Until I met you, I *didn't* encourage guys to ask me out, so not many did, and when they did, I usually turned them down. That wasn't the case when I was in high school. . . . I was pudgy and a bookworm. Boys didn't ask me out."

Adam was incredulous. "That's hard for me to believe."

Now her smile turned bittersweet. "It's true. Let's put it this way. I was not the kind of girl whose initials would ever be carved into a tree."

Adam remembered how one day the past week they'd walked by a big elm tree and she'd pointed out how someone had carved a heart around two sets of initials in the bark.

He could see she was pretending she didn't care that she hadn't been popular back then, but it was obvious to him that the memory was painful.

"My mother kept telling me my time would come, that I was just a late bloomer, but that's difficult to believe when you're sixteen and you haven't been invited to the prom. When your sister has gotten an orchid corsage and a beautiful blue formal dress and you haven't." Her eyes met his. "I would have given anything to be sent one of those orchids."

Adam couldn't stand it anymore. Reaching over, he took her face in his hands and kissed her. "Those boys were stupid," he murmured against her mouth. "Stupid. And their loss is my gain."

The next morning, Natalie woke up to discover Adam quietly dressing.

"What time is it?" she said, sleepily stretching. She felt wonderful.

"Five o'clock." Sitting on the edge of the futon, he leaned over and kissed her. "I have to go, but don't you get up. Go back to sleep, and I'll call you later, okay?"

She smiled. "Okay."

Natalie slept through her first class, something she never did. When she finally awakened, it was after ten, and she knew she'd have to really hurry to make her eleven o'clock class.

She probably shouldn't have bothered, because she had a nearly impossible time paying attention. All she could think about was Adam and last night. She kept wanting to pinch herself to make sure everything had really happened, and she couldn't wait to get home so she could talk to him and find out when she would see him again.

She pedaled furiously on the way home, and when she turned into the driveway, she was going so fast, she nearly missed it. When she saw it, she screeched to a halt and just stared.

There, right in the middle of the fattest part of the trunk of the maple tree that stood in the corner of the yard closest to the driveway, in a fresh carving that really stood out, was a big heart. And in the middle of the heart were two sets of initials. Hers and Adam's.

Tears filled her eyes. That carving was the sweetest, most wonderful thing anyone had ever done for her, and she knew that no matter how many gifts she received in the future, nothing would ever compare to this.

For days afterward, Natalie was in another world. A world in which everything and everyone was wonderful. All her senses were fine tuned. The sky had never looked so blue, the air had never smelled so sweet, the sun had never shone so brightly. She floated through the days, bemused by love and the physical awakening of her body.

She loved Adam so much. He was so sweet, so thoughtful, so romantic. She still couldn't get over what he'd done after their first night together. Thinking of the maple tree always brought a smile to her face. If she hadn't been in love with Adam before he'd carved that heart with their initials, she certainly would have fallen in love with him when she discovered it.

"Geez," Brooke said after several days of nonstop smiling on Natalie's part. "You were enough of a pain in the

cheerful butt before you met Adam, but now you're pos-
itively revolting!"

"You're just jealous," Natalie retorted, sighing dreamily
as she remembered the way Adam had kissed her the night
before, starting with her mouth and working his way
down all the way to her toes. The things they did brought
a blush to her face every time she thought about them,
yet they excited her, too, and she couldn't wait until they
could do them again.

"Yeah," Brooke said dryly. "I am. I really need to get
laid. Doesn't Wonderful Adam have any wonderful
friends?"

Natalie grinned. Brooke had taken to calling Adam
"Wonderful Adam" after Natalie had gushed about him
for the dozenth time. "It's funny you should mention that,
because the other day Adam said his friend Sam had asked
if *I* had any friends."

Brooke sat up straighter. "Really? What's Sam like?
Have you met him?"

"Yes, I've met him. He's really nice. A lot of fun. He
and Adam have been friends for years. You might have
seen him at that party where I met Adam."

"Is he a law student, too?"

"Yes."

"What does he look like?" The way a guy looked was
really important to Brooke, and she'd be the first to admit
it.

"Don't worry. He's cute. He has blond hair and blue
eyes."

"I don't normally like blonds," Brooke said doubtfully.

"You're always drooling over Robert Redford," Natalie
pointed out, for ever since Brooke had seen the actor in
The Way We Were, she hadn't missed one of his movies.
Most she'd seen three or four times.

"True. Okay, then. Fix me up!"

The following Saturday night, the two couples double-
dated. They went to see *Coming Home* with Jon Voight,

then headed for Viva Zapata's—a favorite hangout of students—a dark, noisy place with sawdust on the floor, where they had incredibly cheap nachos and pitchers of beer. It was fun, Natalie thought, although if she were completely honest with herself, she had to admit she preferred to be alone with Adam, either at his place or hers. Just thinking about being alone and making love caused her heart to beat faster. As her mother would say, she had it bad.

Later, after Sam and Brooke had gone their separate way, Natalie and Adam talked about the evening.

"How did you and Brooke ever get to be friends?" he asked. "You're nothing alike."

"I know. We talk about that all the time. Actually, I think that's the reason we get along so well. We complement each other." Natalie chuckled. "I think I fascinate her. She's always calling me a Goody Two-shoes. She couldn't believe I was still a virgin."

His arms tightened around her, and he buried his face in her neck. "I'm such a lucky man."

Natalie sighed as his mouth moved lower, to the crevice between her breasts. She helped him unbutton her blouse, then unhook the front fastener of her bra. Closing her eyes, she gave herself up to the delicious warmth that spread through her body as Adam's hands and mouth worked their magic.

"You're so beautiful," he said later. They were lying facing each other on the futon, naked under a quilt that had been made by Natalie's grandmother.

"I'm not really, you know."

"Yes, you are."

"You're prejudiced."

He kissed the tip of her nose and pulled her closer.

Natalie sighed with happiness. Was there anything in the world that compared to this? And to think she hadn't known, hadn't a clue, how wonderful making love could be. She couldn't believe how much her life had changed.

Before Adam, she had thought she was happy and that her life was full. But she hadn't known what true happiness was. *I'm a woman now,* she thought. *A woman who is complete in every way.* Oh, she loved him so much.

He was everything she'd ever wanted in a man: kind, thoughtful, funny, loyal, intelligent, fun-loving, ambitious, courteous, honest . . . He was *so* honest. One day, as they were leaving Luigi's, their favorite Italian restaurant, Adam had spied a fifty-dollar bill lying on the sidewalk. Anyone else would have happily pocketed it, but not Adam. He went back inside the restaurant and asked Luigi to see if any of his other customers were missing any money. No one was, but Adam still wasn't satisfied and had insisted on leaving the money with Luigi in case someone should come back looking for it.

He also loved kids, which was very important to Natalie, because she definitely wanted a family.

Adam loved her, too. She was sure of it, even though he hadn't yet said the words. Sometimes that fact bothered her, but not often. Adam was cautious, the kind of man who wanted to be sure before he acted, the kind of man whose word meant something. A lot of guys, they would say they loved a girl because they'd had sex or they wanted to have sex. But Adam wasn't like that. When he said the words, Natalie would know he meant them.

"Nat."

"Hmm?" She cuddled closer.

"What are you thinking about?"

She smiled. "You."

"What about me?"

"Oh," she said playfully, "you're just fishing for compliments."

"No, seriously. What about me?"

Sighing, she raised her face to look at him. "Okay. I was thinking how happy I am. How you've changed my life."

"Oh, Nat." He buried his face in her hair. "Sometimes

I can't even remember what it was like before I met you. I think about you all the time. When we're not together, I count the hours until we will be."

"I'm the same way," she said with a catch in her throat.

They were silent for a while, each lost in their own thoughts. Natalie closed her eyes, nearly falling asleep, when Adam spoke again. "I'm going to hate being away from you this week."

"Me, too." Thanksgiving was Thursday. They were both leaving Wednesday afternoon to go to their respective homes. "It's not too late to change your mind. My mom would love for me to bring you home with me."

His arms tightened around her. "There's nothing I'd like better, but with my mother being sick so recently . . ." His voice trailed off.

Natalie told herself not to feel disappointed because he hadn't reciprocated with an invitation to *his* parents' home, and yet she couldn't help a twinge. She told herself the absence of an invitation was just another facet of Adam's cautious nature, nothing more. "It's okay. Don't worry about it."

Later, though, after he'd reluctantly climbed out of her bed and gone home to his own place, saying, "I'd better go, I've got a test Monday, and I have to study," she wondered if there was another reason why he hadn't invited her to go home with him over Thanksgiving. Maybe he was ashamed of her. After all, she wasn't exactly in the same social class as his family. Then she told herself she was being ridiculous. Adam wasn't like that. He wasn't a snob. The reason he hadn't asked her home to meet his family was because he would want to be perfectly sure about the two of them before he did anything of that nature. And that was fine with her. She didn't believe in jumping into things, either. The kind of commitment she wanted from Adam wasn't anything to be taken lightly, by either of them.

Still, it was hard saying good-bye to him on Tuesday

night. After he'd gone, Natalie told herself it was silly to feel so bereft. After all, it wasn't as if he were going away forever. He was coming back. They would be together again.

But not for long.

The thought was unwelcome. She had been trying not to think about how little time was left in the semester. How, in January, Adam would graduate and leave New Haven. How he'd be in New York, and she'd be here.

What if he forgot about her? What if he got to New York and became so wrapped up in this new phase of his life that she faded away, became just a pleasant memory and nothing more?

No. That would never happen. Never. Adam loved her just as much as she loved him. And very soon he would tell her so.

Seven

Wednesday morning, as Adam packed for the trip home, he thought about the upcoming weekend. He had decided it was time to tell his parents they would have to give up their ideas about a marriage between him and Julia.

This wasn't the greatest time to break the news, because the two families traditionally spent the holiday together. His mother and Julia's mother alternated as hostesses, and this year it was Margarethe Hammond's turn to do the honors. Still, it had to be done.

Adam knew he couldn't tell his parents before they went to the Hammonds, because if he did, it would ruin the day for everyone. He couldn't imagine his mother and father being able to pretend that everything was the same in front of Julia's parents when everything *wasn't* the same. Which meant *he'd* have to do the pretending.

He was dreading it.

Well, he had no choice. Somehow he would get through the day. But Friday morning, first thing, he would talk to his parents. After that, he would call Julia in Stockholm and tell her his news, saying something about how long they'd been friends and how he'd wanted her to be the first to know, just as he hoped he'd be the first to know when *she* fell in love. That way, even if she had been harboring a secret dream that eventually the two of them would end up together, she would have a face-saving way to react.

Adam hoped his news wouldn't hurt her. That she'd be genuinely happy for him. But even if it did hurt her, in the end, she'd be better off. Surely she wouldn't want to marry someone who didn't love her the way she deserved to be loved.

Reassuring himself that everything would work out, he folded a sweater and put it on top of the other clothes in his suitcase.

He'd have loved to have gone home with Natalie this weekend, and he knew after he told her he couldn't, she had wondered why he hadn't invited her to come home with him. He'd wanted to. But that was impossible. Jesus, he could just imagine the expressions on the faces of Julia's parents if, without any preparation at all, he walked into their home with another girl.

He smiled as he thought about Natalie. His parents would be disappointed about Julia, of course, but once they met Natalie, they would love her. How could they help but love her? She was wonderful.

Natalie made him feel as if he could do anything, be anything. When he was with her, he felt ten feet tall. Invincible. He knew it sounded corny, but it was true. When they were together, nothing else, no one else, existed. And when they were apart, she was all he thought about. When he'd told her he counted the hours until they'd be together again, he'd meant it.

How could he have ever imagined he could marry Julia? *I must have been crazy.*

Suddenly, he couldn't wait to get home. Couldn't wait to see his parents and tell them everything. Couldn't wait to lay everything on the table with Julia. Because once those chores were over, he could come back to New Haven and get started on the rest of his life.

A life with Natalie.

• • •

"Bless us, oh, Lord, and these Thy gifts, which we are about to receive from Thy bounty . . ." Ralph Ferrenzo looked around slowly, smiling at the members of his family. "And thank you for bringing us all together again and for all the blessings you've given us this past year, through Christ, our Lord, Amen."

"Amen," everyone echoed.

Natalie added her own silent Thanksgiving prayer. *Thank you, Lord, for bringing Adam into my life.* Earlier, they'd taken turns giving thanks for the things that were important to them individually, but she hadn't felt she could say anything about Adam yet.

As her father began to carve the turkey, and her mother started passing the side dishes, Natalie wondered if Adam and his family ate early the way her family did—it was only two o'clock—or if they had a later dinner. She wondered if his sister would be there. Adam had said he wasn't sure if Vanessa would show up. "She hates holidays," he'd said with a grimace. But he hadn't elaborated.

Natalie frowned. For some reason, he'd seemed reticent about discussing the holiday. Natalie had told him all about how the Ferrenzos celebrated, how her mother started cooking days ahead of time and how her aunts and sisters and sister-in-law all brought their individual specialties and how her father made a big production out of carving the turkey and knew exactly what kind of meat each one of them liked the best. She told him how they all went to Mass together in the morning and how, after dinner, the women handled the cleanup and the men kept one eye on the kids and the other eye on the TV screen and whatever football game was on. She told him how, after dessert and coffee, a bunch of them would play Uno around the kitchen table and how her sister Grace always played the piano for a singalong.

But Adam had told her practically nothing, only that they normally celebrated the holiday with some friends of his parents. She'd waited, but he hadn't continued. In fact, she remembered now with a slight frown, he had changed the subject.

"Mashed potatoes, Natalie?"

Natalie blinked. She'd been so lost in her thoughts she hadn't realized her uncle Bill was trying to hand her the bowl of potatoes. "Oh, sorry. Yes, thank you." She put a spoonful on her plate, then passed the serving bowl. After that, she forced herself to pay attention to the conversation.

"You're looking good, Natalie," her aunt Tess said after a bit. "College life must agree with you."

Natalie smiled. She liked her aunt Tess, who was her mother's younger sister. "Thanks."

"Whenever I see that kind of bloom on a girl's cheeks, I figure she's in love," her uncle said, winking.

Natalie's eyes met Rose's across the table.

"Is that right?" her oldest brother, Tony, said. "You met a guy? Who is he? He better treat you right, or we'll break his legs."

"Tony!" Her mother looked pained.

"Got the name, might as well have the game," Tony said unrepentantly.

"Just what do you mean by that?"

"Come on, Ma." He grinned at his father, who ducked his head to hide his own smile. "You know how we *Eye-talians* are. We don't put up with any horse manure. You breaka her heart, we breaka you face."

"I don't know why you're always saying such awful things about Italians. Italians are wonderful people. Some of the greatest art and music in the world was created by Italians. Why, you should be *proud* to be an Italian. Your great-grandfather—" The burst of laughter from the others caused Natalie's mother to break off her spirited defense. She smiled sheepishly. "You're pulling my leg again, aren't you?"

Tony grinned. He loved to tease her about their shared

heritage, although he was just as proud of it as she was.

If Natalie had thought the exchange between Tony and her mother would make him forget about her, she was mistaken. A few moments later, he turned his attention her way again. "So what about this guy, Nat? Do I hafta get after him or not?"

"Tony, will you behave?" his wife, Alicia, said. She gave Natalie a sympathetic look. "You're embarrassing your sister."

Everyone was looking at her now, and no matter how she tried not to, Natalie knew she was blushing.

"*Have* you met somebody?" Carol asked. At twenty-two, she was unattached but unabashedly looking.

"Well, I am dating someone, but—"

"Aha!" Tony said. "Uncle Bill was right. So who—"

"Oh, leave her alone," Rose said, interrupting him. "If she's met someone special, she'll tell us about him when she's good and ready."

"That's right," Natalie's mother said, "so can we please change the subject?" Looking around the table, she smiled lovingly at her children and grandchildren. "I haven't had a chance to say it, but it's so nice to have us all together." Her gaze moved to Rose. "Especially since we might not always be able to be."

"Oh, Ma," Rose said. "It's only Ohio, not Siberia."

Relieved to have the spotlight removed, Natalie gave her mother a grateful smile. At fifty-three, Connie Ferrenzo still retained much of her youthful energy and charm. A petite woman, she had large dark eyes and thick, salt-and-pepper hair worn in the same short hairstyle she'd preferred ever since Natalie could remember. She worked as a clerk in the office at the local high school, a job she'd held for twelve years, ever since Grace, the youngest of her six children, had started kindergarten. She didn't make a lot of money, but her job gave her free summers and two weeks at Christmas, which both she and Natalie's dad seemed to think was more important than a fatter pay-check.

"I like being able to do things with my grandkids," she'd said, "and if I had to work all the time, I wouldn't be able to."

Natalie wondered if her mother would still feel that way by the time Natalie and Grace had children. And then, forgetting her vow not to think about Adam again, she began to daydream about what their children would look like if they were to marry. She could just see a sturdy little boy with Adam's dark eyes and later a little girl that looked like her family. Natalie knew this kind of thinking was dangerous. Adam had never so much as breathed a hint of marriage, just as he'd never said he loved her. Yet she couldn't seem to help herself.

It was scary to realize how important to her Adam was, for what if she was wrong? The worrisome thoughts she'd had before she left school returned with a vengeance. What if he *didn't* feel the same way? What if she *was* just a pleasant diversion? What if, when he finished law school, he left her and never looked back?

The thought caused an actual physical pain in her stomach. *Oh, God, how would I bear it?* And yet women through the ages had borne even greater losses and managed to continue on, hadn't they? Her aunt Maria was a perfect example. She'd only been married six months and was pregnant when her high school sweetheart went off to fight in World War II. He'd been killed at Omaha Beach. Her aunt had been brokenhearted, but somehow she'd survived. She'd even married again and now had four grown children and several grandchildren.

Remembering her aunt's resiliency and strength, Natalie told herself Ferrenzo women were tough. She could and would handle whatever the future held. But even as she reassured herself, she sent another silent prayer heavenward.

Please, God, if you'll only give me Adam, I'll never ask

you for anything else again. Then, realizing how ridiculous it was to think she could actually bargain with God, she smiled sheepishly and turned her attention back to her family.

"Adam, you look even more handsome than usual," Margarethe said. She hugged him, then turned to his mother and beamed. "Phyllis, that's a beautiful dress. Such a becoming color. Where *ever* did you find it?"

His mother smiled happily. "Lord & Taylor, on sale."

His mother *did* look nice, Adam thought. Better than he'd imagined. But he was still concerned about her. She just didn't seem to have any strength and tired so easily. Last night, for instance, she'd gone up to bed at eight. He and his father had sat in the study and talked for a couple of hours after she left them, and in the comfortable camaraderie between them, Adam had been sorely tempted to bring up the subject of Julia. But he hadn't, and now he was glad. It really would have been too awkward for his parents today.

"So, Adam," Julius said, "what do you think of Professor Braun?"

Professor Braun taught torts and had a formidable reputation. "I like him."

"Thought you would. He's a tough old bird, but he knows what he's talking about."

"Yes. I've learned a lot from him."

By now they'd all gone into the living room, and the maid was serving the hors d'oeuvres. Julius took drink orders and walked over to the bar, beckoning to Adam to follow him.

"Everyone at the firm is looking forward to you coming on board," he said as he mixed the drinks.

"I'm looking forward to it, too, sir." But Adam wondered if he would still be going to work for Hammond, Crowley once Julius knew Adam was involved with someone other than Julia. Somehow he doubted it.

Adam wasn't sure he cared. Yes, Hammond, Crowley was one of the most prestigious firms in Manhattan and most young lawyers would jump at the chance to work for them, but they weren't the only firm. Without being falsely modest, Adam knew there were plenty of other firms that would be only too happy to have him.

But if he married Natalie, maybe he wouldn't go to work for a big firm at all. Maybe he'd do what he had secretly dreamed of doing: get a job as an assistant DA, either in New York or New Haven, depending on where Natalie wanted to finish school. He wouldn't make a lot of money, but they wouldn't need a lot. Natalie wasn't like Julia. She wouldn't require an expensive apartment and equally expensive clothes and entertainment.

Julius handed him the vodka tonic he'd asked for as well as the scotch his father wanted. As they walked over to rejoin the others, Julius said, "You know, Adam, I'd always hoped to have a son follow in my footsteps." Then he smiled. "But this is just as good. Yes, sir, just as good. Maybe even better." He winked. "Guess I'll just have to wait on a grandson or two, eh?"

There was no mistaking his meaning. Adam felt about two inches tall right then. Here he was, daydreaming about a life with Natalie, and Julius was thinking of him as a son-in-law. And even though Adam knew most of what Julia's parents and his own parents believed was simply wishful thinking and not based on fact at all, he still felt terrible because he had not corrected them long ago.

I didn't know any better before. I really did think I might marry Julia.

Maybe so. But suddenly he couldn't wait until tomorrow. Because the sooner he got this off his chest, the sooner they all knew the truth, the better for everyone.

Eight

A noise awakened Adam. Heart pounding, he sat up and looked at the bedside clock. Three-thirty. All he could hear right now was a tree branch scraping against the window. Was that what woke him up? Or had he been dreaming?

Then he heard the noise again. Voices. Coming from his parents' room. Something was wrong. Bounding out of bed, he grabbed his sweats, pulled them on, then hurried down the hall. His parents were just coming out of their bedroom. His father had his arm around his mother's shoulders and was half supporting her as they walked toward him.

"Dad? What is it?"

"Your mother's having chest pains. I'm taking her to emergency." His father's voice was calm, but when his eyes met Adam's, Adam saw the concern.

"I'm going, too." Racing back to his room, Adam thrust his feet into his loafers, grabbed his jacket, and rejoined his parents.

This couldn't be good, Adam thought as he helped his father get his mother downstairs and out to the garage and into the car. It had been less than two months since her last attack. She'd only been out of the hospital for five weeks.

The fifteen-minute trip to the hospital seemed to last forever, but finally they pulled into the emergency entrance. "You go in with her, Dad, and I'll park the car," Adam said.

When Adam arrived inside, his mother had already been taken to one of the treatment rooms. The resident cardiologist had been called in, and Adam was told to wait in the waiting area.

It seemed an eternity before his father came out. "The EKG looks normal. They don't think it was another heart attack."

Adam felt weak with relief. "I was scared."

"She scared the hell out of me, too."

His dad's admission surprised Adam. As far as he could remember, his father had never admitted to weakness of any kind. "Can we take her home?"

"Not yet. They want to keep her for a few hours. Make sure she's okay. After all, the pain was caused by *something*, and with her history . . ."

Adam swallowed. So she wasn't out of the woods yet.

"But you go on home, Adam. I'll stay here with your mother."

"No, Dad. That's okay. I'll—"

"I mean it. There's no reason for both of us to be here. There's nothing you can do. I'll just call you when they're ready to release her, and you can come back and get us."

"But what if . . . ?" Adam couldn't finish.

"The doctors would tell us if there was any real danger right now," his father said firmly.

Adam knew there was no sense arguing with his father, who rarely took no for an answer. Besides, his father was right. There *was* nothing for him to do there.

So he left and went back to the house. He was no longer sleepy, so he didn't go back to bed. Instead, he put on a pot of coffee, then headed upstairs, where he shaved and showered and dressed. Then he drank his coffee and read the morning paper. While he was fixing himself breakfast, the phone rang. It was his father.

"The doctor's decided he wants to run some more tests today, so your mother probably won't come home until tomorrow morning."

"I'm coming back there, then."

Adam got back to the hospital at eight. He insisted his father take the car and go home to get cleaned up.

After protesting for a while, his father finally gave in, saying, "I'll be back by ten."

"There's no hurry. As you said, she's fine right now."

After his father left, Adam went into his mother's room. Her eyes were closed, her breathing even and deep. But the rosy color she'd had yesterday at the Hammonds' was gone. Now she looked pale and small and much older than fifty.

Damn. Life was so unfair sometimes.

Adam sat down in the chair next to her bed. He put his head back and closed his eyes, too.

Funny how the best laid plans could go wrong, he thought. By now, he'd expected to have a heart-to-heart talk with his parents. Instead, here he was, in the hospital, keeping a vigil at his mother's bedside.

He wondered if he dared bring up the subject of Julia today. He sure didn't want to say anything that might upset his mother. He guessed he'd have to play it by ear. It looked like he might have to stay until Sunday, anyway, now that this had happened, so he could always talk to them tomorrow.

It was nearly ten before his mother stirred, and at least ten more minutes before she opened her eyes. When she turned and saw him, she gave him a weak smile. "Hi."

With a lump in his throat, he reached for her hand. "Hi. How're you feeling?"

"Foolish."

"Foolish? Why?"

"For making such a fuss. The pain was probably just heartburn or something."

"You don't know that. What would have been foolish is *not* coming to the hospital. With your history, you should never take any chances."

"I know. I just . . ." Tears filled her eyes. "Oh, I'm so tired of this. I just want to be well."

He squeezed her hand. "That's what we all want."

"I'm so glad you're here, Adam. I only wish—"

"I know. You wish Vanessa was here, too." That damn sister of his. He should have called her when he was at the house earlier. Given her a piece of his mind for not making it home for Thanksgiving.

"Well, yes, that, too . . . but what I meant was, I wish Julia could have been here, too. I know you must miss her a lot."

Adam squirmed. "Well, sure, I miss her. Heck, she's more of a sister than Van is."

"Oh, Adam, she's more than that. You don't have to be shy about saying it. We all know how you two feel about each other."

"Mom—"

"Your father and I are so happy about it, too. You must know that. We couldn't love Julia more if she were our very own daughter."

"I—" He stopped. What could he say? What *should* he say? Was she in any shape to hear the truth?

"You know what I think?"

He shook his head. "No. What?"

"I think, after graduation, you should take some time off. Go to Stockholm and stay for a while."

"Look, Mom, this is probably not the best time, but I really don't feel the way you seem—"

"Well," his father's hearty voice said from behind him, "it looks like you're feeling better, Phyllis."

In the wake of his father's entrance, the subject of Julia was abandoned, and Adam knew it was probably a good thing, because he'd been on the verge of doing something foolhardy. No matter what his mother had said, and no matter how much he wanted to correct her, she was obviously in no shape right now to hear the truth.

For the rest of the day, Adam debated whether to bring up the subject with his father, but he finally decided he'd wait until they got back home. This really wasn't the time or the place for a disclosure that was probably going to be upsetting, maybe even cause an argument.

Late that afternoon, Dr. DeAngelo, his mother's long-time cardiologist, came to talk to Adam and his father. "I'm going to let her go home in the morning," he said, "but I want to warn you . . . no stress. No more holiday parties, no more big meals. She needs rest and quiet and calm." He went on to explain the pain she'd felt was definitely angina, and he was putting her on some new medication. "But we'll keep a close watch on her. If she continues to have these episodes, we'll look into surgical possibilities."

Adam's father frowned. "I thought you said she wasn't a good candidate for bypass surgery."

"I did, but that was before. Circumstances change."

Suddenly Adam knew what the cardiologist was really saying, and all the fear he'd managed to bury came rushing back. He wondered if his father understood the underlying message the doctor had just given them. A quick glance at his father's face revealed nothing.

After Dr. DeAngelo left them, Adam's father said he was staying with Adam's mother that night and once more insisted that Adam go back to the house. "In fact," he said, "you should probably head on back to school. You were going to leave tomorrow, anyway."

"But, Dad—"

"You heard what DeAngelo said. Your mother's to have complete quiet and calm. If she knows you're here instead of back at school, she'll fret. We don't want that."

Adam sighed. His father was right. It would be better

to go back. It was clear now that the talk about Julia was going to have to wait. His father was too concerned about his mother for Adam to want to burden him further. There would be a better time for a heart-to-heart after his mother was home and settled down again.

So Adam went into his mother's room and kissed her good-bye and explained why he was going back tonight instead of tomorrow. She got teary-eyed again and apologized for ruining his weekend.

"Mom, that's ridiculous. You didn't ruin anything. Do you think I care about anything but you? Dad and I both just want you to get well and stay well."

"So are you still dating Adam?" Rose asked. It was Saturday night. Everyone else had gone home or gone to bed, and Rose and Natalie were alone in the kitchen together. Rose had made hot chocolate.

Natalie nodded. "Yes."

"By the look on your face, I'd say Uncle Bill was right. You're in love."

Natalie knew her smile was probably goofy. "I'm crazy about him."

"And what about him?"

"I think he feels the same way."

"Is it serious?"

Natalie spooned some of her melted marshmallow into her mouth. "I don't know."

Rose sipped some of her hot chocolate. Her dark eyes, so like their father's, studied Natalie over the rim of her cup. "Are you sleeping with him?" she asked softly.

"Yes," Natalie murmured, staring into her own cup.

Rose sighed.

"I know what you're thinking."

"No, you don't."

Natalie raised her eyes to meet her sister's. Rose's smile was affectionate, understanding. "Did you sleep with Chris before you married him?" Natalie asked.

Rose nodded.

Natalie suddenly relaxed. "It's so hard not to when you love someone."

"Are you sure you love him, hon?"

"Oh, Rose, I love him more than I ever thought I could love anyone. I love him so much, it hurts."

Rose smiled.

"You know what he did?"

"No, what?"

"He carved our initials in a tree." Natalie went on to explain how this had happened. "And last week, out of the blue, he sent me orchids because one time, in talking about how miserable I was in high school, I'd said that I'd never been given flowers."

"That's so sweet."

"It *is*, isn't it? I'm telling you, Rose, Adam is wonderful. In fact, he's perfect."

Rose chuckled. "No man is perfect, Nat."

"Adam is."

"There's nothing about him you would change?"

"Nothing." But maybe that wasn't true. Maybe, if Natalie could magically make Adam's background closer to hers, she would.

"I see just a trace of doubt in your face," Rose said.

"Am I that transparent?"

"It's just that I know you so well." Rose drank some more of her hot chocolate. "So what is it you'd change?"

Natalie shrugged. "I don't know. This is probably silly, but sometimes I feel just a bit insecure about the kind of world Adam comes from. It's very different from mine."

"Is his family wealthy?"

"From what he's said, I think so. They live in one of the wealthiest areas of Westchester County."

Rose didn't say anything for a long moment. She toyed with her cup, which was now empty. Finally she spoke. "Nat, sweetie, just be careful, okay?"

"I'm careful."

"I don't mean about birth control or anything like that. I mean be careful of your heart. I don't want to see you get hurt."

"Rose, I know what you're saying, but please . . . don't worry about me, okay? I'm a big girl. I can take care of myself."

Rose nodded, but she didn't seem convinced.

Later, as Natalie lay in bed and tried to go to sleep, she thought about Rose's warning. And as much as she wanted to tell herself her sister was just being that—a concerned and loving older sibling—she couldn't completely dismiss the tiny seed of doubt she'd been feeling for a while.

If only Adam would say something about the future.

Then she told herself it was ridiculous to worry, that Adam would say something when he was ready. After all, it had only been about six weeks since they'd first set eyes on each other. Hadn't she already decided Adam was cautious and would want to be completely sure before he declared himself?

Banishing her doubts once again, she finally fell asleep.

Nine

Adam couldn't wait to see Natalie again. He had decided that even though he hadn't been able to come clean with his parents, he was going to tell Natalie all about Julia. He probably should have told her before this. But once he explained the situation, she would understand why he hadn't.

His reason for needing to be back in New Haven on Saturday was so he'd have enough time to prepare the closing arguments for a mock trial that would take place the following week. He was the primary counsel for the defense. Normally, he enjoyed this kind of assignment immensely, but he had a hard time concentrating on Sunday. He kept looking at the clock and wondering what time Natalie would return.

He started calling her about two. When five o'clock came and went and she still didn't answer, he put the receiver down in frustration.

He thought about driving over to her place and waiting for her, but that was stupid. It might be hours before she got back. Expelling a noisy breath, he turned his attention back to his books.

It started snowing at six. He tried her number again.

Still no answer. Walking to the window, he looked out. The snow was sticking.

It worried him that she wasn't back yet. He couldn't even remember the name of the girl she'd bummed a ride home with. She'd told him, but he'd forgotten. Why hadn't he thought to ask what kind of car the girl drove? Did Natalie even *know* the girl or had she gotten her name from one of the bulletin boards?

By seven-thirty, when there was still no answer at Natalie's, Adam started to worry. The snow was coming down fast and furious. He'd bet the streets were slippery.

When the phone rang, he jumped. He was almost disappointed to hear his father's voice; then he immediately felt guilty. His father had promised to call him once he'd gotten Adam's mother home and settled in.

"How's Mom doing?" he asked.

"Good. She's upstairs in bed. She has a new novel, so she's happy."

"Did the doctors have anything else to say after I left?"

"Nothing new. Just emphasized how important it was to let nothing disturb her. DeAngelo even suggested we not let her watch the evening news or read the newspapers."

Adam couldn't imagine how his father would prevent his mother from doing either of those things. Phyllis Forrester had once described herself as a "news junkie." She had complained bitterly about the New York area newspaper strike earlier in the year, saying she couldn't seem to get her day started without her daily fix of coffee and the *Times*.

"Good luck," Adam said.

His father laughed. "Yes, that's what I told DeAngelo. He doesn't realize how stubborn your mother can be."

Adam grinned. He wondered if his father realized how what he'd just said was a perfect example of the pot calling the kettle black.

"So how was your trip back?" his father said. "Any problems?"

"No. The roads were clear. It's snowing here now, though."

"Yes, it's started snowing here, too. Well, son, I'd better let you go. I'm sure you have a lot of work to do. I just wanted to let you know your mother was home and everything was okay. I'll call you again in a few days, keep you posted on how things are going."

"All right. And, Dad?"

"Yes?"

"Next time I'm home? There's something I want to talk to you about."

"Oh? Is it something serious?"

"Uh, not really *serious.* But important to me."

"Well, sure, son. You know I'm always ready to listen."

Adam looked at the phone thoughtfully after he'd hung up. *Always ready to listen.* He knew his father thought he listened, but mostly Franklin only heard what he chose to hear. This time, though, he would *have* to hear Adam, like it or not.

Grimacing, Adam picked up the phone again. This time, when he dialed Natalie's number, she answered on the third ring.

"You sound out of breath." Suddenly, the concerns he had over his mother and telling his parents the truth about his feelings for Julia were all wiped from his mind. Natalie did that for him—made him feel happy and worry-free just by the sound of her voice.

"I just got back about ten minutes ago and I was in the bathroom."

"Sorry."

"No, that's okay. When did you get home?"

"Yesterday."

"Oh, that's right. I'd forgotten you were coming back early. So how was your Thanksgiving?"

"Eventful."

"Eventful? Did something happen?"

"Yes. But listen, I don't want to talk over the phone. Can I come over?"

"Sure. If you want to. Just be careful. It's slippery out there."

Adam smiled. Now she was worrying about *him.* "I will." His voice softened. "I can't wait to see you, Nat. I missed you."

There was a catch in her voice when she answered. "Oh, Adam, I missed you, too."

He almost added, *I love you,* but stopped himself just in time. When he said the words, he wanted to be with her. He wanted to see her face. Instead he said, "I'll be there in twenty minutes."

"I'll be waiting."

Natalie picked a pillow up from the futon and hugged it. He'd missed her! He couldn't wait to see her! Maybe it was true what they said, that absence made the heart grow fonder. Throwing down the pillow, she went back to the bathroom where she washed her face, put on fresh lipstick and mascara. Then she reached into her duffel bag, which she still hadn't unpacked, and dabbed on some perfume. She thought about changing her clothes but decided she probably wouldn't be wearing them very long anyway, so what was the point? Lastly, she ran a brush through her hair. Then, while she waited for Adam to arrive, she unpacked and put things away.

Almost exactly twenty minutes after they'd hung up, Adam was at the door. She'd barely shut it behind him before he crushed her to him. His lips were cold, but they warmed up fast as he kissed her over and over again.

And then, in a moment Natalie knew she would never forget, he took her face in his hands, looked down into her eyes, and said huskily, "I love you, Natalie. I love you with all my heart, and if you'll have me, I want to marry you."

Natalie's heart zoomed as his words sank in. "Oh, Adam! I love you, too. And marrying you would make me the happiest girl on earth!"

Later, after they'd made love and told each other again and again how much they loved each other, Adam held her close and said, "There's something I need to tell you."

Now that she knew Adam loved her and wanted to marry her, nothing could shake Natalie's happiness, not even the somber note that had crept into his voice. "Okay."

"I know you wondered why I didn't ask you to come home with me for Thanksgiving."

"Well, actually, I *did* kind of wonder."

"I wanted to, but I had to talk to my parents about something before I could tell them about you or bring you home to meet them."

Natalie waited.

"The thing is, there's this girl."

Natalie stiffened. *Girl?* The first warning bell of alarm sounded in her brain. *What girl?*

"She's the daughter of my parents' best friends. I've mentioned them. The Hammonds? Her father is the managing partner at Hammond, Crowley, the firm I'm supposed to go to work for after graduation."

Swallowing, Natalie said, "What about her?"

He sighed heavily. "Well, for years both my parents and hers have kind of assumed Julia and I would end up together."

Natalie forced herself to listen without comment as he explained how he and Julia Hammond had been friends since they were kids, how he loved her but had never been *in* love with her, and how he'd stupidly gone along with their parents' assumptions without putting up objections because he had actually thought that maybe he *would* marry Julia.

"I had no clue," he added dryly. "Because I'd never been in love. I really thought being friends and having a lot in common would be enough to make a good marriage. Now I know better."

"Did you and Julia ever talk about marriage?"

"No. We never even really *dated.* I was her escort when she made her debut, and we've danced together at the club and she invited me to a couple of dances at her school and in the summers we've seen a few movies and played tennis together. Things like that. Stuff that friends do."

"That sounds like dating to me."

"It wasn't like that. It's just that our families are close. We were together a lot, so it was kind of natural for us to do things together. But our relationship was always more like brother and sister than anything else. I mean, she's told me about her boyfriends and even asked my advice a couple of times."

"And have you told her about the girls you've dated? Have you told her about *me*?"

"Nat, I haven't even talked to Julia since August. We've written a couple of letters, that's all. And, no, I didn't say anything about you because at first there was nothing to tell, and then, once there was, I knew I needed to talk to my parents first."

"Did . . ." Natalie licked dry lips. "Did you ever sleep with her?"

"No. I swear I didn't. Hell, I barely even kissed her. Just gave her a couple of good night pecks when I dropped her off at home, and that was it."

"You said you haven't talked to her since August. Didn't you see her when you were home this time?"

"No. She's spending her last year of college in Stockholm with her mother's family. That's why I mentioned writing to her. I won't actually see her again until May." He hesitated. "At least I don't think I will. She mentioned that she was hoping to come home in January, but her parents didn't say anything about it when I saw them on Thanksgiving, so hopefully she's settled down now. She was homesick."

"She's not coming home for *Christmas*?"

"No. The Hammonds are planning to go to Sweden for Christmas. They're having a big family reunion there."

"Oh." Natalie couldn't help it. It really bothered her that Adam hadn't told her about Julia before now.

"Nat . . ." He kissed her softly. "Don't be mad. Please."

"So what did your parents say when you told them about me?" She wanted to know, yet was half afraid to hear.

"I haven't told them yet."

"But I thought you said that was the reason you didn't ask me to come home with you this time. Because you were *going* to talk to them."

"I was, but something happened. My mom had another episode. We took her to the hospital in the middle of the night after Thanksgiving."

All Natalie's irritation disappeared as she listened to the events of the weekend and realized how worried he was about his mother.

"I'm sorry, Natalie. I wanted to get this all behind me. I *intended* to get it behind me."

"You did the right thing," she said softly.

"I hope to tell them soon." He held her closer, his breath warm against her forehead. "You understand, don't you? I have to do this right. I can't take a chance with my mother's health. The doctor was adamant about not upsetting her."

"Yes, I understand. But there is one thing that bothers me."

"What?"

"Why did you take so long to tell *me* about all this?"

"Well, at first, just like there was no reason to tell Julia about you, there was no reason to tell you about her. Then, by the time I knew I was in love with you, I didn't want to say anything that would make you attach more importance to this than there actually is."

"But, Adam, I've told you everything about my life. It

hurts me that you'd hold something like this back. It makes me think maybe there really *is* more importance to the situation with Julia than you're willing to admit."

"I swear, Natalie, there isn't. You've got to believe me. The only thing I'm guilty of in this whole thing is stupidity for not realizing long ago that a future with Julia would never work. As soon as I realized I could never marry her, I resolved to set my parents straight." He lifted her chin and gazed down into her eyes. "I love you, Natalie. I love you more than I ever believed it was possible to love anyone. I promise you, I will clear this up, and then I will acknowledge you to the world."

They kissed then, but some of Natalie's happiness had faded.

"What is it?" he said when the kiss ended. "I can tell something is still bothering you."

"It's just that your parents are going to be so unhappy when you tell them that the girl they've counted on you marrying all these years is not going to be their daughter-in-law. And that it's *my* fault."

"It's not your fault. It's mine. They'll see that."

"Oh, Adam, I know that's what you want to believe, but I'm afraid that's not the way it will be. They'll resent me. It'll be awful. Every time we're with them, they'll be wishing I were Julia." Although Natalie rarely cried, she felt on the verge of tears now.

"Sweetheart, that's not true. My parents aren't like that. They're going to love you."

But no matter how many assurances he gave her, Natalie couldn't rid herself of her fears for the future.

"Natalie, trust me," Adam said. "It's going to be okay."

Much later, after they'd talked and talked and made love again, and Adam had fallen asleep, Natalie lay awake thinking over everything he'd said. Adam seemed so confident that he could smooth things over. That his parents would not only understand but accept her and love her.

But what if they didn't? Could she still marry him if his family blamed her?

Her family was so important to her. She couldn't imagine being alienated from them. And she didn't want Adam to be alienated from his, either. Not because of her.

But what could she do? She was helpless. Whatever happened, happened. She had no control over it. All she could do was pray that Adam was right and that, in the end, all would be well.

Ten

The weeks between Thanksgiving and Christmas were so busy, Natalie didn't have much time to brood or worry. The semester was winding down, finals were looming, plus she had all her Christmas shopping to take care of.

The Christmas break would begin on Monday the eighteenth, but Natalie wasn't going home until the end of that week. Her boss had offered her a week of work because so many of his full-time employees were taking vacation, and as an added incentive to her, he'd promised to pay her for the following week, as well.

Natalie couldn't pass up the chance to make that much extra money, so she'd agreed.

Adam would be leaving on Sunday, the seventeenth, and they were having their Christmas celebration the night before.

Natalie was determined to make the night special. She didn't want to think about anything that might happen or not happen in the future. She just wanted to be happy and make the most of their first Christmas together.

After hours of looking, she'd found the perfect gift for Adam: a beautiful soft leather folder that would hold a letter-sized yellow tablet on one side and business correspondence or notes on the other.

Thrilled with her find, she had his initials embossed in gold on the cover. She could see him carrying the folder in his briefcase next year and knew that each time he handled it, he would think of her. She wrapped the box lovingly, in green foil paper tied with gossamer gold ribbon. She couldn't wait to see his face when he opened it, even though part of her didn't want Saturday to arrive at all, since it would be their last night together until after the new year.

Once she'd found his gift, she turned her energies to making her little apartment look Christmasy. She wished she had a Christmas tree, but that kind of expenditure would have been foolish, for not only would she have had to pay for a tree, but she would have had to buy ornaments, too. Capping her decision was the fact that she would have so little time to enjoy the tree before leaving for Emerson.

She settled on a wreath for her window and several scented Christmas candles. She also found a festive red tablecloth for her little table and hung a sprig of mistletoe over the doorway.

On Saturday she dressed carefully in the dark green velvet dress she'd gotten two Christmases ago. Humming "Silent Night," she checked on the chicken casserole in her tiny oven. Satisfied that everything was ready, she poured herself a glass of the port Adam had given her earlier in the week and settled in to wait for him. She'd managed to find Christmas carols on the radio, and the music played softly in the background. It was snowing outside—the first snowfall in weeks. *A perfect night,* she thought happily.

When she heard Adam's footsteps on the outside stairs, she ran to the door and threw it open.

As soon as the door closed behind him, he pulled her into his arms and gave her a long, hungry kiss, which left them both wanting more. It was always like this between them. Their need for each other seemed to grow stronger every day.

When the kiss finally ended, Adam smiled down into her eyes. "Merry Christmas."

"Merry Christmas," she answered breathlessly.

He held her at arm's length. "Wow. You look spectacular." He smiled. "I have good taste."

As she looked into his eyes, the love she felt for him nearly overwhelmed her. But she kept her voice light. "I was just having a glass of the port you gave me. Would you like some?"

"Sounds good." He shrugged out of his overcoat and laid it over the back of her rocking chair. He was wearing dark wool pants and a soft burgundy cashmere sweater and was so handsome it almost hurt to look at him.

After getting Adam his drink, she joined him on the futon. Once she was settled next to him, he withdrew a small box from his pocket. It was wrapped in silver paper and a matching ribbon. "Merry Christmas." Smiling, he handed her the box.

Her hands trembled as she held it. All she could think was, *Is this a ring?*

"Aren't you going to open it?" There was amusement as well as tenderness in his voice.

"Let me get your present first." She started to get up, but he took her arm and stopped her.

"You can get mine after you open yours."

"All right," she said softly. Her heart was beating too fast, and she was so nervous, she couldn't get the ribbon untied at first, but finally she managed it. Inside was a dark blue velvet jeweler's box. Slowly, she opened the lid. In the box, nestled against white satin, lay a tiny gold heart on a delicate gold chain. The face of the heart was covered with pavé diamonds. "Oh," she breathed. The necklace was so lovely, she forgot to be disappointed that it wasn't a ring. "Oh, Adam. This is so beautiful. I just love it."

"Not half as beautiful as you are," he murmured, lifting her face to look into her eyes. "I love you, Natalie."

"I love you, too."

"I wanted to give you a ring."

She smiled tremulously. "Did you?"

"Yes. And just as soon as I've talked to my parents, I will. I hope you're not disappointed."

"Oh, Adam." She touched the heart. "I don't need a ring to know you love me." And at that moment, she didn't.

"Put the heart on," he said softly.

Giving him a brilliant smile, she nodded. But her fingers didn't want to cooperate, and she felt as if she were all thumbs when she tried to take the necklace out of the box. So in the end, Adam did it, fastening it around her neck, then kissing her neck, which led to kissing her mouth.

Flustered and laughing, she finally pushed him away, saying, "I slaved over our dinner, and if we keep on like this, it'll be ruined by the time we eat it."

"Okay, okay," he said, letting her go reluctantly.

She fingered her necklace. It was so lovely. She had never owned a piece of jewelry so beautiful. She was sure he'd spent far too much money on it, but she couldn't help being thrilled to have it. "Now it's your turn," she said.

She could see by the expression on his face that he loved the leather folder. "It's wonderful. I feel important just looking at it," he said, grinning.

"You don't have anything like this, do you?"

"No." He rubbed the initials on the front. "Every time I use this, I'll think of you."

"That was my plan."

"Little schemer." He reached for her, but she twisted out of his grasp.

"Dinner," she reminded him.

While they ate, they talked about the future. Adam told

her that he had decided he wanted to pursue a career as a prosecutor, preferably in New York. "How would you feel about transferring to Columbia?"

Natalie smiled. "I'd love it if I could get in."

"You'd get in."

"It costs a lot to live in New York, and you won't be making much money at first. But I can find a part-time job."

"I don't want you to have to work. I want you to be able to concentrate on school."

"But I work now," she pointed out.

"Yes, but you're not married to me now. A man should be able to take care of his wife."

"This is the seventies, not the fifties," she said, amused that he had such old-fashioned ideas. "I don't need to be taken care of. I think marriage should be a partnership where both people contribute."

"I do, too. But first you need to finish your education."

"There's no reason I can't do both."

He started to answer back, then laughed. "Are we having our first argument?"

She grinned. "I think we are."

Leaning across the table, he planted a kiss on her nose. "You can't win, you know. As a future prosecutor, I can shoot down any line of defense you present."

After that, the subject of whether or not she would work once they were married was dropped, and they finished their meal.

When dinner was over, Adam helped her clean up the kitchen. Afterward, he turned off all the lights as Natalie readied the futon. Then, by the glow of the Christmas candles, they slowly undressed one another. Their love-making was unhurried and exquisitely tender, with a long, slow buildup of passion.

Later, sated and happy, they lay entwined in each other's arms, and Natalie knew that no matter how many years they were together or how many times they made love to each other, nothing would ever surpass this perfect night.

All the way home Adam rehearsed what he would say to his parents. Although he had told Natalie everything would be all right, he wasn't as convinced as he'd led her to believe. It was just that he hadn't wanted her to worry. It was bad enough he was worried. Not about his father's reaction. His father might bluster and argue, but in the end, he would come around. He would have to. No, it was his mother and her feelings that concerned Adam. Above all, he had to find a way to tell her that her dreams about him and Julia weren't going to come true without upsetting her too badly.

By the time he pulled into the circular drive of his parents' large colonial home, he was nervous. He had decided to break the news to his father first. Then together they could decide when and how to tell Adam's mother.

His mother had obviously been watching for him, because the door opened when he was only halfway up the front steps. She threw her arms around him and hugged him. The scent of Joy, her favorite fragrance, enveloped him. "Oh, I'm so glad to see you. I was worried about you driving in this weather."

She seemed thinner to him than she had the last time he'd been home. "Hi, Mom. Are you doing okay?"

She shrugged. "Oh, you know. Just a little tired, that's all."

Adam put his arm around her shoulders. She felt so frail. "Where's Dad?"

"In the library. Why don't you go in and say hello? I'll get us something to drink. What would you like? Beer? Coffee? A soft drink?"

"A beer would be nice."

"How about something to eat? Are you hungry?"

"No, thanks. I had a cheeseburger on the road."

She smiled. "You and your cheeseburgers." Still smiling, she went off in the direction of the kitchen, and Adam, after removing his coat and gloves and putting his suitcase at the foot of the stairs, headed for the library. The double walnut doors were closed, and he could hear his father talking on the phone. He knocked softly, then opened the door. His father smiled at him and beckoned him in.

"All right, George," he was saying. "Sounds good. So you'll have that report ready next week and we'll plan to get together and discuss it. Okay. See you then." Hanging up, he said, "You made good time."

"Yes, I did. The roads were clear, and the traffic wasn't as bad as it usually is."

"Car holding up okay?"

"No problems." Adam cleared his throat. "Um, Dad, remember when I told you I had something I needed to discuss with you? Something that's important to me?"

"Yes."

"Do you think we could talk about it now?"

"Sure. Your mother and I don't have anything planned for today."

"The thing is, I'd like to keep this just between you and me. At least for right now."

His father's eyes narrowed. "What's going on, Adam? Is this something that will upset your mother?"

Adam grimaced. "I hope not."

Just then, Adam's mother walked in, bearing a small silver tray upon which were two bottles of beer, two mugs, and a cup of coffee. Beaming at Adam, she handed first him, then his father, a beer and a mug. Taking the cup of coffee for herself, she started to sit on the leather sofa when his father said, "Phyllis, Adam and I need to talk in private for a few minutes. Do you mind?"

"Oh! No. Of course not." She gave Adam a curious look. "There's nothing wrong, I hope."

"No, there's nothing wrong," Franklin answered before Adam could. Once she was gone, he got up from behind his desk and walked over to shut the door. "Now," he said, "what's on your mind, son?" Although the words were mild, the look in his eyes was not.

"Dad, I know how you and Mom feel about Julia. And that the two of you as well as her parents have been hoping she and I would end up together. For a long time, I even thought that was a possibility myself. But now I know it's not."

"What do you mean, it's not? Has Julia turned you down?"

"No. I haven't even talked to her in months. The problem is, I don't love her. And I don't want to marry her."

"You don't love her," his father repeated.

"No."

"Adam, that's the most ridiculous thing you've ever said. Of course, you love her. I've seen the two of you together."

Adam shook his head. "I didn't explain myself well. Yes, I care about Julia, the same way I care about Vanessa. But I'm not *in love* with her. I'm in love with someone else, someone I met this year, someone I want to marry."

"What? Are you crazy? You *can't* marry anyone else!"

Adam stared at his father. "Look, I know this is a shock to you, but—"

"A shock! That's not the half of it. Adam, you have no idea what you're saying. Why, if Julius got wind of this, he'd have a stroke."

"I hardly think—"

"And what about your mother? She's supposed to be avoiding stress of any kind. Why, this will kill her!" Franklin shook his head. "No. Impossible."

"Dad, would you stop interrupting and *listen* to me for a minute?"

Just as if Adam hadn't spoken, his father barreled on. "I don't know who this other woman is that you've met, and to tell you the truth, I don't care. You can just forget about her." Franklin's eyes blazed as he glared at Adam.

"Dad," Adam said patiently. The last thing he wanted was a shouting match. "Have you heard anything I've said? I don't love Julia. How can I marry her if I'm in love with someone else?"

"In love! What do you know about being in love? You're still wet behind the ears!"

Adam told himself not to lose his temper. It wouldn't solve anything. "I'm twenty-five years old and perfectly capable of knowing my own feelings," he said evenly.

"Who is this woman, anyway?" his father demanded.

"She's a student at Southern Connecticut. An undergraduate who—"

"Are you sleeping with her?"

As Adam debated how he wanted to answer this question—which his father had no right to ask—his father forestalled him by saying, "Okay. Fine. So you're sleeping with her. Good. Get it out of your system. And then, when you've had your fill, come home to Julia, where you belong."

"Stop it! Just because you want something to be a certain way doesn't mean it's going to be that way. Now listen to me, Dad. Please. I'm not going to get her *out of my system*, as you put it. I love Natalie, and I intend to marry her."

"Where is this girl from?"

"What difference does it make where she's from?"

"Just answer me. Where is she from?"

Adam sighed. "She's from Emerson."

"Emerson." Franklin said it as if it were a bad word. "Where the hell is Emerson?"

"It's in the northern part of Connecticut."

"What about her family? Who are they?"

"You . . ." Adam wet his lips. "You wouldn't know her family."

"Try me. What's this Natalie person's last name?"

Adam hesitated. "Ferrenzo."

"Ferrenzo," Adam's father repeated. "And what does her father do?"

"He's in the delivery business."

"*Delivery* business? What is he, a mailman?"

"No." Shit. What was the use? He might as well tell his father the truth. Franklin would eventually find out the truth, anyway. "He drives a delivery truck for UPS."

The look on his father's face told Adam exactly what he was thinking. "It's honest work," Adam said. Why was his father acting like this? He wasn't a snob. At least Adam had never thought he was.

"I never said it wasn't. But her father's occupation ought to clearly point out that this woman and her family aren't our kind of people. You're not looking at this thing realistically. I know you think you're in love with her. But you're confusing love with lust."

Adam stiffened. "I know the difference between love and lust. Look, I'm sorry. I know you're disappointed, but I *do* love Natalie, and although I'd like your blessing, I don't have to have it. I'm still going to marry her."

Franklin stared at him. When he spoke, his voice was colder than Adam had ever heard it. "If you do this thing, you will completely ruin our family."

"Come on, Dad, don't you think you're exaggerating? I know Julia's parents will probably be disappointed, too, but I doubt they'll stop speaking to us."

"You don't know what you're talking about! They'll never forgive you. You're *jilting* their daughter!"

"I'm not jilting her. We're not engaged."

"You might as well have been. It's been understood, by everyone, that you and Julia would eventually marry. All that was left was the formality."

"That's not true. You *hoped* we'd marry. Hell, I'm not even sure Julia *wants* to marry me. We've certainly never talked about it. For all I know, she's not the least bit interested. And as far as her parents are concerned, I can't believe they'd want their daughter to marry someone who doesn't love her." Gentling his voice, he said, "You're making too much of this. If you want me to, I'll go and see Julia's parents myself. Explain everything. I don't expect you to do it."

Suddenly, shocking Adam, his father, who had always seemed like a rock, crumpled before his eyes. He began to shake, and his face turned gray. "Adam, please," he begged. "Don't do this. You don't understand. Julius will crucify me. He'll call in my notes, and we'll lose everything."

"What notes? What are you talking about?"

Slumping into his chair, Franklin's voice deteriorated to an anguished whisper. "The notes for all the money he's given me." At that, he started to cry.

Adam stared at his father. His mind was whirling. "I-I don't understand. Why did he give you money?"

For a long moment, his father couldn't answer. Finally, he seemed to get himself under control, although he couldn't meet Adam's eyes. "About six years ago, I had some financial reversals. I stood to lose the business, the house, everything. He bailed me out. We owe everything to him. Even your education's been paid for by him."

"My education? Grandfather left money for my education."

"That money was used up long ago," his father said wearily. "If not for Julius, I'd have had to declare bankruptcy. He saved my hide, and he did it because of you. You and Julia. He said what was his would be hers one day, anyway. But if you marry someone else, everything will change."

"I-I can't believe this."

"Now you understand why you can't go through with this, don't you, Adam? Because if you do, if you marry someone else, instead of tearing up those notes I signed, Julius will demand payment. We'll lose the house. We'll lose everything. Think about what the shock and shame will do to your mother, Adam. You can't do it. You *have* to marry Julia. Our lives depend on it."

Adam was numb. Frozen.

He just sat there, trying to absorb what his father had said. How could this have happened? How could his father have done this to him? The disappointment and disillusion he felt was acute. All of his life, he had respected his father and been proud of him. He'd wanted to be just like him. Now Adam wasn't sure he could ever respect his father again.

Finally, feeling as if he'd aged twenty years in the last twenty minutes, he stood. For a long moment, he looked down at his father.

"You do realize," he said numbly, "that you sold me for thirty pieces of silver."

Then, without another word, he turned and walked out of the library and up the stairs to his room. The sound of the door closing behind him echoed through the house.

Eleven

⁓

If Adam was grateful for anything over the holidays, it
was the fact that Julius and Margarethe Hammond were
in Sweden. If, on top of everything else, he'd had to con-
tend with seeing them and pretending nothing was different in front of them, he would have lost his mind.

It was bad enough he had to keep up a pretense for his
mother. Adam knew she suspected something was wrong,
but either she was afraid to ask what it was or she felt it
was none of her business, because she didn't say anything
to him except to tell him if he ever wanted to talk about
anything, she was ready to listen.

For three days after his father's revelation, Adam could
hardly bear to be in the same room with him, and he
avoided him whenever possible. But on Wednesday, his
father cornered him. "We have to talk," he said.

"Hasn't everything already been said?"

"Adam, please." His father's hand shook as he clutched
at Adam's arm.

Adam wanted to harden his heart. He didn't want to
feel sorry for his dad, but the agonized expression on his
father's face and the fear in his eyes were impossible to
ignore. How had this happened? How had his father,
who'd always been so strong and so proud, been reduced

to this weak, trembling old man? Heaving a sigh, he jerked his head in the direction of the library.

"What are you going to do?" his father said once they were alone with the door closed. Even his voice sounded old.

"I don't know." Adam had gone over and over the problem. And he still had no answer. In desperation, he said, "Couldn't we borrow the money to give Julius? I'll work the rest of my life to repay it." So he'd never be a prosecutor. So he'd have to go to work for some big law firm where he could make a lot of money. So what? At least he'd have Natalie. At least they'd have each other.

"Who'd give it to us?" his father said.

"The bank here in town? I know you've done business with them. You play golf with Mr. Hubbard, don't you?"

Franklin shook his head. "There's no collateral. Even Keith Hubbard won't give me a loan with no collateral."

"What about the house? This house must be worth a fortune. Couldn't we mortgage it?"

"It's already heavily mortgaged. I told you. I had some serious financial problems. The business was going under. That's why I needed Julius's help."

"But how did things get to that point? It wasn't that long ago that you expanded the business."

"What does it matter?" his father said almost defiantly. "I made some decisions that didn't work out. It happens."

"Just how much do you owe Julius?"

Adam was staggered when he heard the amount. The situation was far worse than he'd imagined. Jesus. It would take fifteen, maybe twenty years to make enough to pay it back.

"So now you see why," his father said, "there's no other choice. You have to marry Julia."

Adam didn't reply for a long time. When he did, his voice was resigned. "This whole thing is a nightmare. I'm still having trouble believing it's happened. But you know what's almost the worst part of the whole sorry mess?"

Franklin looked at him mutely.

"It's that you've never even said you're sorry."

That night Adam couldn't sleep. And for the remainder of the holidays, he could think of little else. It became more and more difficult to pretend in front of his mother, who kept darting worried glances his way.

Thank God Vanessa was only home for Christmas Day and then hurried off to go skiing with friends, so at least he was spared her almost uncanny ability to sense when he was trying to hide something from her. As it was, she managed to get him alone after dinner.

"What's eating you?" she said. "Did someone else get nominated for the Mr. Perfect award this year?"

Adam smiled grimly. "Very funny."

She grinned. "I thought it was."

"Not that it's any of your business, but nothing's eating me."

"Don't try to snow me, Adam. Did you and Dad have a fight?"

"No, we did not have a fight."

Her eyes narrowed. "I don't believe you."

"I don't really care whether you believe me or not."

She made a face. "Fuck you, Adam."

"My, my, such lovely language. Someone should wash your mouth out with soap."

"You're such a tight ass, you know that?" She flounced off and, after that, she left him alone. That night, remembering the exchange, he thought that if Vanessa had been a different kind of sister, if they'd had a different kind of relationship, maybe he wouldn't have ended up in this mess, because he'd never have turned to Julia for the companionship and friendship he missed. Immediately, he was ashamed of himself. The chaos his life had deteriorated into wasn't Vanessa's fault.

The days after Christmas seemed to crawl by, but finally it was time to go back to school. He wouldn't be there long. His graduation would take place in two weeks.

What would happen after that, he still didn't know. He kept thinking there had to be another way to solve this problem than marriage to Julia, some avenue he hadn't thought of yet, some miracle that would allow him to have the future he'd dreamed of instead of the one his father had bartered him into. He clung to his hope, because if he hadn't, he would not have been able to make it through the holidays.

Adam drove back to New Haven without even seeing the landscape rushing by. As each mile brought him closer to Natalie, his heart became heavier and heavier.

I can't lose her.

But what other choice did he have?

Natalie got back to New Haven early in the afternoon on the day before classes were to convene. Even though she'd worried about Adam and what his family would say when they found out about her, she'd still managed to have a wonderful Christmas. She loved being with her family, and Christmas had always been her favorite time of year. The only disappointing note had been her decision not to wear her diamond heart in front of her family, because she didn't want to answer questions about Adam until she had something concrete to tell them. And she knew if they saw the heart, they would flood her with questions.

She had missed Adam acutely, though, and couldn't wait to find out what had happened between him and his parents. As soon as she got to her apartment, she called him, but there was no answer. She told herself to be patient. It was early. He would call her when he got in.

She fixed some tuna salad because she hadn't had any lunch. While she ate, she read *The Thorn Birds*, a book she'd started while she was home and was thoroughly enjoying. She had just finished eating and was washing up the dishes when her phone rang. She hurriedly wiped her hands, then raced into the living room and grabbed the receiver. "Hello?"

"Natalie."

She broke into a delighted grin. "Adam! Hi! I was wondering when you'd get back."

"I just got in. Listen, Natalie, can I come over? I need to talk to you."

There was something ominous in his voice, and Natalie knew whatever it was he was going to tell her, it wasn't good news. Her heart sank, but she tried not to let her trepidation show in her voice. "Sure. Come on."

While she waited for him, she kept telling herself not to jump to conclusions. Maybe he was just tired. Maybe he just wanted to tell her how hard it had been to tell his parents how he really felt about Julia. Maybe . . .

But no amount of assurances helped her feel better. And when Adam did arrive a scant fifteen minutes later, she took one look at his face and knew she was right to be afraid. He looked terrible. There was a bleakness in his eyes she'd never seen before, an awful resignation that made her heart thump too hard, and when he took her into his arms and held her, she could feel his body trembling.

"Adam, what is it?" she cried.

"Nat." He sounded desperate, as if he was going to break down at any moment.

Swallowing hard, she disentangled herself from his arms. "Adam," she said softly. "Please come and sit down. Tell me what happened. Did . . . did you talk to your parents about us?"

"Yes," he said in a strangled whisper.

"And?" she prompted gently.

He began to talk. As Natalie listened to the death of all her hopes and dreams, she grew curiously stoic. It was almost as if she had always known Adam was beyond her reach, that what they'd shared had been too good and too perfect to last.

"I don't know what to do," he said when he'd finished

telling her everything. "I've thought of nothing else for days, and I can't find any solution."

"You do know what to do," she said softly, taking his hand. She raised it to her lips and kissed it. She loved his hands. She loved everything about him, and she always would.

"I love you, Nat. I can't stand the thought of a life without you."

There was a lump in her throat the size of Alaska, but Natalie knew she had to be strong. She couldn't break down in front of him. It would only make things harder for both of them. "I know you do. And I love you. But how could we be happy if we ruin your parents' lives? I can't live with that, and I know *you* can't."

Crushing her to him, he buried his face in her hair. "I hate him."

"No, you don't."

"Yes, I do, and I'll never forgive him for this."

"Adam . . ." She drew back and took his face between her hands. In a broken voice, she said, "Please don't hate your father. Hate is such a destructive emotion. I can't bear the thought of you living the rest of your life filled with hate. Not you, Adam."

The look on his face tore at her heart, and it was all she could do not to cry. But she knew if she gave in to the tumult inside of her, she would never be able to say good-bye to him. They would be lost.

"I'll never see you again, will I?" he said dully.

She shook her head, then said the hardest words she'd ever have to say. "No. If you're going to marry Julia, you have to commit to her wholeheartedly. That's only right."

He nodded, despair etched in every line of his body.

"This isn't her fault."

"No," he said hoarsely.

After that, there was nothing left to say except good-bye. As he turned to leave, Natalie thought he was going to kiss her, and she backed away. She only had a finite amount of willpower. If he kissed her, she was afraid she would weaken.

His eyes, those wonderful, serious eyes, met hers for a long, pregnant moment. In them she saw a gamut of emotions. "I'm so sorry, Natalie," he said. "You deserved better than this."

And then he opened the door. A minute later, he was gone. Natalie held herself together until she heard the sound of his car pulling away. Then, and only then, did she allow the tears to come. Sinking to the floor, she beat the carpet with her fists and sobbed her rage and heartbreak until there were no more tears left.

Part Two

Twelve

*"I just can't **wait** to see the actual book."*

Natalie smiled. She was on the phone with Tina Broland, a first-time author, and her unbridled excitement over the upcoming publication of her debut novel was refreshing.

"I'm praying the reviewers will like it," Tina continued anxiously.

So was Natalie, who wanted all her authors to do well. But she especially hoped Tina's book would make a splash, because she was one of the nicest and most deserving young authors Natalie had ever worked with. The book, *A Home for Benny*, had been a true labor of love; the story of a young boy who had lost his parents as well as his eyesight in a terrible fire, and Natalie knew it was based on an episode from Tina's own childhood. From the moment Natalie had read the first page, she'd known she had something truly special in her hands. Visions of the Newbery Medal had been tantalizing her dreams ever since. "Tina, you don't have a thing to worry about. The reviewers are going to love it."

"Oh, I hope you're right."

"I know I'm right."

"Well," Tina said, sighing, "I shouldn't keep you. I know how busy you are."

"I'm never too busy to talk to you," Natalie assured her, even as her gaze roamed over the stacks of manuscripts that covered every spare inch of space on her desk, the tops of her filing cabinets, a good bit of the floor, and several shelves of her bookcase. In all her ten years of employment at Bramwell Press, a small but prestigious publisher of children's books, she had never once been caught up.

After promising Tina she would call her the moment she had any news, they said good-bye. Natalie put the phone back into its cradle, laid her pencil down, and stretched. She'd been sitting too long; her muscles were all cramped. Pushing her chair back, she got up and touched her toes several times, then turned and peered out her tenth-floor office window. It was almost five o'clock, already dark. Snow swirled down, and the lights of Forty-ninth Street below and Fifth Avenue beyond looked cheerful and inviting. From her vantage point, she could almost see the tree at Rockefeller Center.

She smiled. Christmas was her favorite time of year in New York, a season when the dirty streets were less noticeable and the people, although hurried, were friendlier. She loved everything about it: the decorations, the Santas on every corner, the impromptu concerts given by street musicians, the hustle and bustle, the goodwill and general merriment. There were times she longed for the green lawns and unhurried pace of Emerson, where she'd grown up, but other times—like the winter holiday season—there was nowhere else she'd rather be than in Manhattan.

Of course, it helped that she loved her job. She didn't even mind the long hours. Normally, she worked until seven most nights because those quiet hours after five when there were no meetings and no telephone calls gave

her the longest stretch of uninterrupted time to read manuscripts. But tonight she planned to leave early. She
hadn't finished her Christmas shopping, and she was going home the day after tomorrow. She still needed to find
something for her sister Rose and for Jenny, Rose's
fifteen-year-old and Natalie's godchild.

She'd just about decided she was going to buy Jenny a
Fossil watch. She'd seen one in black and chrome that she
was sure the teenager would love. And maybe Rose would
like one of those tapestry vests Natalie had seen at Bloomingdale's the other day. She tried to picture her sister in it,
maybe paired with a pair of dark green slacks. Should she
go back and get it? Or should she try Lord & Taylor, which
was closer to the office? She loved Lord & Taylor, whose
windows at Christmas were a child's delight, filled with
dancing dolls and Santa's elves and sparkling lights.

"Hey, Natalie, you staying late tonight?"

Startled, Natalie whipped around. Standing in the doorway was Hilary Steinmetz, a fellow editor and Natalie's
closest friend in New York.

Hilary grinned. "Sorry. Didn't mean to scare you."

Natalie returned her friend's smile. "I guess I was lost
in my thoughts. And no, I'm not staying late. I've got
Christmas shopping to finish."

"Good. Want to get something to eat first? I'm starving.
I was thinking about going over to that new deli on Forty-
eighth. I've been having wet dreams about a Reuben sandwich all afternoon. Well, I *would* be having wet dreams
if I were a man."

"You're always starving," Natalie said with amusement. "I swear, I don't know how you stay so thin."

Hilary looked down at her bony frame. "Genes, what
else? Anyway . . . " She eyed Natalie's petite frame.
"You're not exactly fat."

"Yes, but I don't eat like you do."

"What're you two doing? Goofing off again?"

The baritone voice came from behind Hilary. Natalie recognized it as belonging to Ken Pinella, the head of their marketing department.

"What's it to ya?" Hilary said, grinning. "You writing a book?"

Ken rolled his eyes. "Don't you get tired of the same sorry lines?"

"Don't you get tired of keeping tabs on us?" she countered.

Natalie's eyes briefly met Hilary's. It was obvious to both of them that Ken had a gigantic crush on Natalie. Too bad, she thought for the hundredth time, that she wasn't interested. She knew most women—especially New York women—would think she was crazy. Read any newspaper or magazine article on the subject, and you would be quoted the statistics on how nearly impossible it was to find a good man in the city. And Ken was a very good man. He was single, smart, nice-looking, heterosexual, and had a good job.

But he didn't do a thing for her. She liked him, yes, but that was as far as it would ever go. Truth was, she hadn't had a serious relationship since Adam. Oh, she'd dated. She'd even slept with two of the guys she'd gone out with. But those had been disappointing episodes, never repeated. They had left her feeling empty and a bit dirty, that last a remnant of her Catholic upbringing, she was sure.

Natalie was no longer religious. In fact, the only time she went to church now was when she returned home to Emerson, and then only because it was less trouble to pretend to still believe than to upset her parents by letting them know she no longer did.

"Jeez, Hilary, give a guy a break."

Natalie turned her attention back to her coworkers, who were still good-naturedly ribbing one another.

"I was just trying to talk Natalie into going over to

Kipling's to get something to eat," Hilary said, finally taking pity on Ken.

His blue eyes brightened. "Want some company?"

"Hilary might," Natalie said. "I'm not really hungry." She opened her bottom desk drawer and took out her purse. "Besides, I don't have time. I still have Christmas shopping to do."

"Ah, Nat," Hilary said. "Come on. What'll it take? An hour at most? You'll have plenty of time to shop afterward."

"My treat," Ken said.

Natalie shook her head firmly and, after a few more minutes of trying to persuade her to change her mind, Hilary and Ken gave up and left.

Natalie eyed a manuscript that badly needed her attention. She thought about taking it home with her, then decided that tomorrow was soon enough to work on it. Fifteen minutes later, dressed warmly in fur-lined boots, long black wool coat, black leather gloves, and a black cashmere scarf, she was walking briskly south on Fifth Avenue, headed for Lord & Taylor.

Adam wearily rubbed his forehead. He had a headache, and he badly needed fresh air. He'd been in his office since seven this morning, and it was now six-thirty. Nearly twelve hours. He hadn't even gone out for lunch, just had Mary Beth, his secretary, bring him a sandwich that he ate at his desk while he read depositions.

For the past eight months, he and his staff had been working on a product liability case involving one of Hammond, Crowley's most important clients. A case this size generated reams of paperwork and involved thousands of man hours of investigation before trial. Adam wasn't worried about the progress of the case, though. He'd reviewed all the documents over the past couple of days and had determined they were in good shape.

Even if they hadn't been, right now he didn't care. No

matter how nice his office was—and as a senior partner, it was extremely nice—he was tired of being cooped up, and he was leaving.

Thirty minutes later, he walked slowly along Fifth Avenue, idly gazing into the brightly lit, beautifully decorated store windows. He was no longer thinking about work. Now his mind was preoccupied with thoughts of Julia, who was once more nursing a cold.

Julia was always sick, or at least it seemed that way to him. She was constantly getting colds and coughs, which almost inevitably led to bronchitis. A couple of times in the past eleven years she had even ended up with pneumonia. Maybe if she ate more, she wouldn't be so fragile. He thought about the way she'd looked this morning. Her silk robe had hung on her. Adam would be willing to bet she'd lost at least ten pounds since summer, and she hadn't had even a pound of extra weight to start with.

But at the breakfast table, where she'd insisted on joining him, even though he'd encouraged her to stay in bed, she had only taken a few bites of toast and a few sips of the orange juice Alma, their housekeeper, always squeezed fresh each morning. Adam had tried to get Julia to at least try some of the mushroom omelette Alma had concocted, but she'd shaken her head, saying, "I can't, Adam. Nothing tastes good to me right now."

Nothing tastes good to you, ever, he'd wanted to say, feeling some of his old frustration, but he hadn't. He'd learned a long time ago that Julia couldn't help being the way she was, just as he couldn't help being the way he was. His wife could be passionate when it came to art, music, or clothes, but if it had to do with more earthy pursuits like food or sex, she could only summon mild interest.

The winter was hard on her. Yet she refused to escape it, as many of her friends did, by spending the worst months in Palm Springs or the south of France. She insisted her place was with him. Guiltily, he thought about how she had asked him if he'd be home early tonight.

"I'll try to," he'd said, even as he knew he probably would work late once again. He couldn't seem to help himself. Even when he could have gone home early, he didn't, because when he was at home, Julia's clinging and her constant chatter and gossip about things and people that did not interest him got on his nerves. The trouble was, when she was well, she spent her time in such trivial ways. Shopping. Playing bridge. Going out to lunch. Going to plays and gallery openings. Haunting antique shops. And endlessly decorating and redecorating their brownstone. Pursuits without purpose or meaning.

Why hadn't he realized all this years ago? When they were kids, she hadn't seemed shallow. Had he just been too young to recognize her limitations? He remembered how he always thought they were alike because they'd been raised in the same environment. Nothing could be further from the truth.

Maybe things would be different if they'd ever had children. But no matter how many times they'd tried, Julia had failed to conceive. They had seen countless doctors. Had all the tests. All the doctors and tests said the same thing: There was nothing wrong with either of them.

Their inability to have a child was a great disappointment to Adam, but he'd tried to hide the depth of his feelings from Julia, because he knew how much her childless state bothered her. How could he not? The envy in her eyes when they were around their friends who had children was obvious. He would never want her to think he blamed her. It was bad enough that he didn't love her the way he knew she loved him. It was also unfair to criticize her for the ways in which she spent her time, even in his thoughts. After all, what else did she have but her friends and her bridge parties and her ceaseless redecorating to fill her empty days?

And yet, would she *really* have enjoyed children? This thought was one that nudged its way into his brain more and more often lately. Did she want a child because she loved children and wanted to be a mother, or did she want a child because she knew *he* did?

Somehow he couldn't picture Julia as a mother. Sticky hands and snotty noses weren't exactly Julia's cup of tea. If they *had* had a child, she would probably have wanted to hire a live-in nanny and leave most of the responsibility for the care of their child to her.

Lost in his dismal thoughts, Adam passed Cartier, St. Patrick's Cathedral, Saks Fifth Avenue. It was only when he reached Rockefeller Center that he roused himself to his surroundings. Drawn by the beautiful tree and the music, he crossed the street and joined the throngs of people standing at the railing looking down at the skaters below.

A girl in a short red skirt was doing a series of jumps. Adam smiled. The girl was good. Watching her brought back memories of childhood, when he and Vanessa and their friends had skated on the pond at the back of their parents' property. Vanessa had been the best skater of them all, although not as good as this girl tonight. He wondered if Vanessa ever skated anymore.

The girl in the red skirt finished her routine with a well-executed spin, and there was a burst of appreciative applause from the spectators.

Adam watched the skaters for a while longer but knew he couldn't put off going home forever, so as much as he would have liked to stay, he had better be on his way.

He turned to leave and collided with a woman who had also been watching the skaters, causing her to drop one of her packages.

"Oh, sorry," he said.

They both bent to pick up the package at the same time and nearly bumped their heads together.

"Here, let me," he said, laughing. He retrieved her package, and they both stood.

Adam started to apologize again for his clumsiness but stopped in midsentence. Stupefied, hardly able to believe what he was seeing, he stared into a face he had never forgotten, a face that had haunted his dreams for twelve years and that he had never thought he'd see again.

Natalie was stunned. How many times she had imagined seeing Adam again, yet in all the years she'd lived in New York, she never had. They might as well have been living thousands of miles apart. She'd known he was there, at least in the beginning, because when she first moved to the city, she had yielded to temptation and called the law firm where she was pretty certain he had gone to work. But she'd hung up once she found out what she'd wanted to know. And she'd never called the firm again. She hadn't known if he was still with his father-in-law's firm or worked somewhere else. She hadn't known if he lived in the city or commuted from Long Island or Westchester County or some other place. She hadn't wanted to know. Why torture herself? And when Brooke, who had married Sam Berry, who used to be Adam's best friend, had brought up Adam's name, Natalie told her—firmly and without equivocation—that she did not want to discuss him, then or ever.

"That part of my life is over," she'd said.

And now, when she'd least expected it, here he was standing right in front of her. Her heart was beating too fast as she drank him in. He was so handsome. Even more handsome than when he was younger. His face had more character, and the sprinkling of silver in his hair made him look distinguished and important. Yes, maturity suited him.

So many times she had imagined what she would say if she ever saw him again. It would be something friendly and kind or maybe something witty and sophisticated. At the very least, she would behave in a mature way. But now that their reunion was fact instead of fantasy, she was too shaken to form coherent thoughts, let alone words, so all she could do was stand there and stare at the only man she had ever loved.

Adam couldn't seem to find his voice. He couldn't believe it was really Natalie standing there. She was so beautiful! Older and thinner than he remembered—although it was hard to really tell when she was wearing so many layers of clothing—but so lovely.

Those eyes. He had never been able to forget her eyes. They were so clear and honest.

Turmoil, regret, sorrow . . .

He felt them all as he looked at her. But he also felt happiness, because it was obvious to him she was just as glad to see him as he was to see her.

"Natalie," he finally said, although his voice didn't sound like his at all. "I can't believe it. It's really you."

"Hello, Adam."

"What are you doing here? Do you live in New York?"

He had to bend down to hear her answer, because a group of street musicians had started playing a lively rendition of "Winter Wonderland" and between that and the music from the rink below and the cacophony of horns and cars and people, it was hard to carry on a conversation without shouting.

"Yes," she said. "I live here."

The snow was coming down harder now. Several flakes caught in her hair. Adam was suddenly reminded of all the times he'd buried his face in that wonderful hair. That memory brought forth others, images he had tried to forget because to remember was to invite a deep loneliness and yearning that could only be assuaged by the woman standing before him—a woman he thought he would never see again.

Taking her arm, he drew her away from the crowd at the rink. "I still can't believe it's you."

"I know. I'm kind of shocked myself," she said with a half smile.

"So you work here in Manhattan?"

"Yes. I've been here ten years now."

"Ten years!" How was it possible? All that time, she'd

been right here in New York, and he hadn't known. "Who are you working for?"

"Bramwell Press. Do you know them?"

"Bramwell Press," he repeated. "Children's publisher?"

"That's the one."

"So you realized your dream, did you?"

This time when she smiled, he saw the old Natalie, the one whose smile had so bewitched him. "Yes, I'm an editor there."

"And are you happy? Is the job what you thought it would be?"

"It's not quite what I thought it would be, but I do love it. I can't imagine doing anything else."

He nodded. "I'm glad."

"And you? Are you still working for your father-in-law?"

"No. He retired two years ago, and I was made a full partner in the firm last year."

"I always knew you'd do well."

She sounded sincere, but he wondered what she was really thinking. He wanted to tell her she was wrong if she thought the partnership had come to him because of who he was instead of what he'd accomplished. He wanted to explain how he'd worked his butt off, harder than anyone else, just because he *was* related to the former managing partner. He'd deserved that partnership. Paid for it in blood. No one had given him anything. But how could he say any of these things? She had a right to think whatever she wanted to think, and he had no rights at all. Not with her. Never with her.

"Well," she said, and now her smile was strained. "It's been really nice seeing you again, Adam, but it's getting late. I should go."

She reached for her parcel, and it was only then he realized he still held it. Instead of relinquishing the package, he held on tighter. He couldn't bear to have her leave when he'd only just found her. Looking down into her eyes, he said, "Please don't go. We've barely had a chance to talk. Have you eaten yet?"

For a moment he thought she was going to ignore his plea. He held his breath.

"No," she finally said. "I haven't eaten yet."

"I haven't, either." Then, heedless of consequences, heedless of everything except this woman and the way she could grab onto his heart like no one else in the world, he said recklessly, "Why don't we go into the Sea Grill?"

This was the restaurant that overlooked the skating rink. It was immensely popular because of its location and excellent food. Yet the suggestion wasn't really reckless, Adam thought. He wouldn't be seen there, not by anyone who knew him. The Sea Grill wasn't the kind of place his and Julia's friends frequented, since they were mostly old money New Yorkers who turned up their noses at any place tourists went.

But even if he and Natalie were seen, he didn't care. Right now, he didn't care about anything but preventing Natalie from leaving.

He simply wasn't ready to give her up again.

Thirteen

***

Natalie knew it was inviting trouble to go anywhere with Adam. She should not spend another minute with him, because he was dangerous to her well-being—a well-being she'd fought long and hard to achieve. She remembered those horrific weeks and months after they'd parted in New Haven, how she had barely managed to get out of bed each morning. She'd lost weight, her grades had fallen, she'd been a total wreck.

She remembered how Brooke had worried about her, to the point where she'd threatened to call Natalie's parents and tell them what was going on.

Did she want to chance a relapse by opening all those old wounds?

She'd only been in his company for ten minutes, and already all the old feelings were stirring in her again. She opened her mouth to say no. But somehow what came out instead was, "All right."

His smile went straight to her heart.

She told herself she was just curious. Didn't she have a right to be curious? After all, this was the man she had thought she would marry, the man who would father her children, the man who would be there in sickness and in health till death did them part. She had given up so much.

Was it too much to ask that she at least have this one evening with him?

Ten minutes later, thanks to the twenty-dollar bill Adam had slipped the hostess, they were seated across from each other at a small rink-side table. Natalie was absurdly glad she'd worn her new raspberry wool dress to work today instead of her standard uniform of black skirt and sweater or black skirt and blouse. She knew the rosy color was becoming and could tell by the way Adam was looking at her that he thought so, too.

Oh, God, she thought, her heart beating too fast. *Those eyes of his.* They were so warm, so wonderfully warm, and when he looked at her the way he was looking now, they made her feel beautiful and desirable and special. She swallowed and looked away, pretending to study the skaters. She'd been right to think she shouldn't have come. It frightened her to realize that after all these years, he still had the ability to stir her so profoundly.

They didn't talk while studying the menu or placing their orders, but once that was done, and their wine had been poured, Adam sat back in his chair and said, "You look wonderful, Natalie."

"Thank you. So do you."

He shrugged her comment off with a self-deprecating grimace. "Tell me about your job."

She settled back, too, told herself to calm down. They were only having dinner. After tonight, she would never see him again, and that would be okay. "I've worked for Bramwell ever since graduating from college. I started as an assistant editor, was promoted after two years to an associate editor, and two years later, I was made a full editor. Now I'm in charge of acquisitions for our middle-grade fiction line."

"Three promotions in ten years. Sounds like you're doing well."

She smiled. "I'm grossly underpaid, of course, but aside

from that, yes, I guess I have done well. Now, what about you? Are you a litigation attorney?"

"Yes, corporate litigation."

"And do you like *your* work?"

"Most of the time."

"You don't sound certain of that."

"I'm sure you remember I once entertained dreams of criminal law. Saving the world and all that rose-colored glasses kind of stuff. But we all lose our starry eyes sooner or later."

He tempered his words with a smile, but he didn't fool Natalie. It was clear he would much rather have followed those early dreams. It hurt her to know that. She had hoped he would be happy in his profession, since he'd had to compromise with his personal life, and yet in a deep, dark part of her soul, a part of her she wasn't proud of, his ambivalence with its hint of discontent was some-how validating to the importance he had played in *her* life.

Startling her, he reached across the table and lifted her left hand. "No ring?"

"No." The touch of his hand caused her insides to shudder, but she didn't dare wrench it away, because she didn't want him to know how fragile her equilibrium was. He rubbed her fingers with his thumb, and suddenly it was hard to breathe. Memories flickered, and her skin tingled as it remembered all those nights when those sensitive fingers had played against her body. She wet her lips. *Stop it. You'll make yourself crazy.*

Just then, their waitress appeared, and Adam released her hand. Grateful for the interruption, Natalie took a deep breath and fought to control her wayward emotions. The waitress set their salads in front of them. When she turned to leave, Natalie picked up her salad fork and took a small bite of hers, a concoction of spinach, shiitake mushrooms, and warm bacon dressing. "This is delicious."

"Yes, mine's good, too," Adam said. He'd ordered the Caesar salad.

For a while they ate quietly. Then, feeling calmer and more in control of herself, Natalie said, "How is your mother doing?"

Sadness flickered in his eyes. "She died seven years ago," he said quietly.

"Oh, I'm sorry. Her heart?"

He nodded. "Yes."

"What about your father? Is he still alive?"

Adam shook his head. "No. He died last year."

She wondered if they'd ever patched things up between them, but it was a question better left unasked. "And your sister? Vanessa? How is she doing?"

He smiled, shaking his head. "Vanessa has finally settled down, sort of. She's married and has two kids, but she's still a hell-raiser. Except now she's turned her energies to women's rights."

"Really? From the things you told me about her, she didn't seem like that type."

"I know. Shocked everyone."

"So what is it she does?"

"She's working for a nonprofit group that concentrates on women's health issues."

"Good for her."

"Yes. That's what I say, too."

"Does she live here still?" Natalie remembered that his sister had had an apartment in the city.

"Since the birth of her second child, she and her family have moved out to the island. Massapequa."

"Do you see them often?"

"Not often enough." He made a face. "My wife isn't fond of her kids. They are a bit on the wild side." Now the grimace turned into a smile. "Van never did believe in discipline."

Natalie made herself smile. *My wife.* The words had cut deep. "What about you? Do you have any children?"

"No." Sadness shadowed his eyes for a moment. "It's been a big disappointment to us."

She nodded. Yes, she understood those feelings. She wanted children, too, and at the rate she was going, she would probably never have them. But that wasn't something she could say. Not to Adam. As she was casting about for another safer topic, their waitress appeared to clear their salad plates and bring their entrées.

Both of them had ordered the Maryland crab cakes, a specialty of the house. Once the food was set before them and the waitress had gone, Natalie decided it was silly to try to avoid anything too personal. After all, it wasn't as if she and Adam were simply casual acquaintances. Once they had been as close as two people could be.

"I'm sorry about the children. But are you happy otherwise, Adam?" And this time, she told herself she sincerely wanted him to say yes.

For a moment, he hesitated. "We're happy enough, I suppose. Julia's busy with her clubs and her friends, and I have my work. We get along as well as any couple married as long as we've been."

Despite his words, Natalie knew he wasn't telling her the truth.

"What about you?" he said softly. "Are you happy, Natalie?"

"Yes. I am. I love my job, I have some good friends, a nice little apartment, two cats. It's a good life."

"I'm glad. You deserve to be happy."

Suddenly she remembered the last words he'd ever said to her. *You deserved better.* The memory brought tears to her eyes, and she quickly looked out at the skaters. *Please, God, don't let me fall apart.* If she hadn't been so shaken, she might have laughed. Natalie Ferrenzo, fallen-away Catholic who professed to no longer believe in God, was constantly calling on him for help.

"What about your family? Parents still alive?"

Back in control, Natalie turned to him again. She

smiled. "Oh, yes, and still going strong. In fact, my dad is still working. I don't think he's ever going to retire. Not unless they force him to. Which they might very well do. They *have* put him at a desk job, though. And he constantly complains about it. Says he's still strong as an ox and can do whatever the younger guys can do . . . and better."

Adam reached for a roll, broke it, and buttered half. "How old is your father?"

"Sixty-seven, and my mom's sixty-six. But neither one looks it."

"Good genes."

Seeing the soft look in his eyes, Natalie's heart betrayed her again. Being here with him was like walking through a field of land mines. You never knew when one might explode.

"Actually," he continued, "they're not that old."

Natalie nodded. "It's funny, isn't it? When I was a kid, I thought people in their forties were old. Now that I'm thirty-two, even the sixties seem young."

"Yes, your perspective changes."

They continued to talk about their families. She brought him up to date on her siblings, he told her more about Vanessa's kids and how much he enjoyed them, despite their wild tendencies.

"Even though I don't see her as much as I'd like to, Vanessa and I are closer now than we ever were before," he said.

"Kids have a way of making that happen."

He nodded. "I just wish my parents could have lived longer. My mother never got a chance to know either of her grandchildren."

"That's a shame. My mother dotes on her grandchildren. She says they keep her young."

A few minutes later, their waitress reappeared to clear away their plates and ask if they'd like coffee or dessert. Natalie saw Adam glance at his watch.

"None for me, thanks," she said. Then, to Adam, "It's getting late. I need to get going."

"Yes," he said, "I do, too." He smiled at the waitress. "Just the check, please."

While he dealt with the check, Natalie excused herself and hunted out the ladies' room. By the time she returned, he had paid the bill and was ready to go.

They didn't talk in the elevator going up to the street level, but once they were outside, she said, "Thank you for dinner, Adam. It was really nice. I hope—"

"Can I call you, Natalie?"

She had been going to say she hoped he had a good Christmas. Their eyes met for a long moment. "Is that really wise?" she asked softly.

"Just to talk."

She knew she should say no. Nothing good could come of seeing him again. *Oh, God.* But it had been so good to see him again. It couldn't do any harm just to talk to him occasionally, could it? "All right."

He wrote her home number and her office number in a small leather notebook he took out of the inside pocket of his overcoat. And then he asked for the address of her apartment and office, and wrote those down, too.

"I'm leaving the city day after tomorrow," she said. "I'm going home for Christmas and won't be back until after New Year's."

They wished each other a Merry Christmas, and when she would have turned to walk away, he insisted on getting her a cab. She told him it wasn't necessary, she always took the bus home. She said it was no big deal, she wasn't nervous, the bus let her off down the street from her apartment, and she only had to walk a little over a block.

"You're not taking the bus this late," he said. Paying no attention to her protests, he flagged down a cab, saw that she was comfortably installed in the backseat, then gave the driver instructions and paid him.

"Have a good trip," he said.

"I will."

Natalie didn't look back, but she knew if she did, Adam would still be there, standing and watching as the cab pulled away into traffic.

Fourteen

It was nine-thirty before Adam unlocked the front door of the three-story brownstone on West Sixty-ninth Street. A gift to his daughter from her father, it had been Adam and Julia's home since their marriage.

Built at the turn of the century, the house was both charming and solidly constructed. Because of its prime location near the park, it had more than tripled in value since Julius Hammond had purchased it. On his own, Adam could not have afforded to buy it—not then, not now—and because it was Julia's, he had never felt any proprietary fondness for the place. He enjoyed living there, yes, but he was always aware that the house did not belong to him.

The bottom floor, which was partway below street level, was Alma's domain. It contained the laundry room, the storage room, Alma's bedroom and sitting room, and a bathroom. The second floor, just a few steps above street level, contained the kitchen, dining room, living room, a small powder room, and a library, which doubled as Adam's study.

The third story held the master bedroom suite of bedroom and dressing room, the master bath, a guest bedroom and bath, and a small room with a bay window that faced the street, which Julia used as an office.

In addition, there was a small walled garden and patio out back. The only amenity missing was a garage, an unheard-of luxury for most New Yorkers.

Adam and Julia did keep a car, but it was garaged a few blocks away, and they mainly used it for weekend getaways. During the week, Adam walked to work unless the weather was inclement, in which case he took a cab. The office was only eighteen blocks away, no more than a forty-minute walk, which he enjoyed. Some days, his walk to and from work was the only exercise he got, although he did belong to a gym and tried to get there a couple of evenings a week.

Julia rarely walked anywhere and relied on cabs or friends. Lately, she'd been hinting about hiring a driver, but Adam had discouraged her. He considered it a waste to keep a driver on call. To Julia's credit, she hadn't yet thrown into Adam's face the fact that she had more money than she knew what to do with and could hire ten drivers if she so fancied.

She understood it was a point of pride with him that he provide the money for the maintenance of their home and for the day-to-day expenses of their household. He didn't object when she used her own money to indulge herself in a new fur or a designer dress, but he drew the line when it came to areas he felt were his responsibility.

Even that might have bothered him if Julia's money had been coming from her father, but it wasn't. She had inherited a sizable estate from her grandfather, which had been invested wisely and continued to grow.

It had taken a lot of planning and work, but Adam had almost completely repaid Julius Hammond every cent he'd spent on both Adam's education and his father's poor business judgment. At first, Julius had protested, saying he'd torn up the notes on Adam and Julia's wedding day.

But Adam had insisted a debt was a debt. "I don't feel right about us taking that money," he said. He didn't add that he couldn't have lived with himself if he'd been under that kind of obligation to Julia's father. Bad enough he'd unknowingly benefited from Julius's charity all those years. At least now Adam had regained his self-respect.

Soon, he thought, he would be entirely free from financial obligation to his father-in-law. His year-end bonus would be distributed at the end of January. There would be more than enough money to liquidate the remainder of the debt.

As Adam walked into the foyer, the twin scents of lemon wax and roses greeted him. Alma kept the furniture polished to a high sheen, and on the bachelor chest that stood to the left of the front door, there was always an arrangement of fresh-cut roses in the Limoges vase that had been a wedding present from Julia's aunt Hester.

After carefully relocking the door, Adam took off his overcoat and hung it in the small coat closet under the stairs. Then he slowly headed up to the third floor. Although only a small lamp was lit in the foyer, it was enough for him to see his way.

"Adam? Darling? Is that you?" Julia called when he was halfway up.

"Yes, it's me."

Their bedroom was at the back of the house, and Adam saw that it was still brightly lit. As he'd expected, he found Julia propped up in bed under a thick coverlet, a book lying open across her legs. Her nose was red, and a box of tissues lay within reach.

"I was beginning to get worried," she said. "I called your office, but there was no answer."

Pushing away his irritation—after all, she had a right to call him if she wanted to—he said, "I took a client to dinner. I'm sorry. I should have called you." He could hardly look her in the eye when he said *client.*

"Oh, it's okay. I wasn't *really* worried. It's just that I

miss you so when you're not here. The house seems so empty." She lifted her arms.

Dutifully, Adam bent to give her the embrace she expected. Holding her thin body gently, he placed a soft kiss on her cheek. "Are you feeling any better?" he asked as he released her. As always, his feelings for her were a complicated mixture of pity, love, and exasperation.

"A little." She patted the bed. "Sit by me, darling. Tell me all about your day."

He shook his head. "You don't want to hear about my day. It was boring."

"You can at least tell me about this client you had to entertain," she said, pouting a little.

Adam suppressed a sigh. He knew she wasn't the least bit interested. But she was doing what she thought she should do: expressing an interest in her husband's work. "He was boring, too." He had taken off his tie and was unbuttoning his shirt. "What about your day?"

She frowned. "Liz came over this afternoon. She wanted to gloat about being chosen to chair the league benefit." Liz Wainright was Julia's oldest friend. There was a long-standing rivalry between them.

Adam sat down on the edge of the bed and removed his shoes. "Did you call Dr. Fisher?"

"Yes." She reached for his hand.

"And?" Her fingers felt like a vise. A velvet vise from which there was no escape.

"He called in a prescription for me." She rubbed her thumb over his knuckles.

All Adam could think about was how he'd held Natalie's hand earlier in just this way. "Did the pharmacy deliver it?" His voice sounded strained, even to his ears.

But Julia didn't seem to notice. "Yes," she said tiredly.

"That's good." He knew she did not want this cold to turn into anything more serious, because it was very important to her that she be well enough to attend the dinner party her parents were having Christmas Day, not to mention the party the firm always hosted New Year's Eve and the open house Julia always insisted on having New Year's Day. The thought of all those obligations depressed Adam more than they ever had before.

Abruptly, he pulled his hand away and stood. "I'm exhausted," he said. "I'm going to take a shower."

"Poor baby, I'm sure you are. You work too hard. Perhaps I should speak to Winston about it." Winston Crowley, who was Julia's godfather, had taken over as managing partner when Julia's father retired.

"Julia," he said warningly.

"Oh, I know," she said. "You're a full partner in the firm, you make your own decisions, and you fight your own battles." She smiled indulgently. "I've heard it all before."

"Yes, well, make sure you don't forget."

"Now, don't get all worked up, darling. I didn't mean it. You know I'd never say anything to Winston."

"I hope not." Adam gathered up his shirt and shoes and headed for the dressing room.

"You're not mad at me, are you?" she said in a small voice.

He stopped. Suppressed another sigh. "No, I'm not mad at you."

"Because Julia can't stand when Adam is mad at her."

Adam gritted his teeth. He despised her little-girl act, and he particularly despised when she referred to herself in the third person. He couldn't understand how she could talk and act like a mature woman one minute—even a *bossy* woman—and then revert to baby talk in the next. Why did she do it? If he thought it would do any good, he would tell her how much it bothered him for her to behave this way, but the one time he had, she had started to cry, and then he'd felt terrible. He wasn't up for that kind of scene tonight.

A few minutes later, as he stood under the spray of hot water, Adam thought about how he had lied to Julia. He thought about all the nights he worked late, nights he could have come home if he'd wanted to. He thought about their marriage and how lusterless it was. He thought about how guilty he always felt when confronted with Julia's devotion and dependence and how unfair their situation was to her. But mostly he thought about Natalie and all the feelings that he had buried for so long but that had come back with such a vengeance tonight.

She was so different from Julia. She was strong and vital and in the time he'd known her, she had never been ill, whereas Julia was frail and always seemed to be fighting off something.

Natalie was comfortable with her physical side. She was a warm, passionate woman who liked sex and wasn't afraid to show it. Adam didn't think Julia had ever liked sex.

Natalie's attitude toward life was different, too. She was filled with optimism and looked forward to the future. She never whined or complained. Julia, on the other hand, seemed to find fault with just about everything.

Natalie was independent; she had goals. Julia's only goal in life seemed to be how she could one-up her friends, either by the parties she gave or the clothes she bought or the committees she served on.

If Julia had had even some of Natalie's qualities, he thought sadly, their marriage might have had a fighting chance. But her clinging and neediness were smothering. At times he thought he would go nuts if he had to endure his marriage one more day.

These unkind thoughts, which he had been having more and more often lately, made him feel even more guilty than he did already.

After all, Julia couldn't help the way she was. It wasn't as if she had ever pretended to be anything else. He was the one who had changed, not her. So if he was unhappy, it was his fault. He reminded himself that, when he'd married her, he had vowed he would be a good husband. That he would forget about what might have been and be content with what was.

But tonight, seeing Natalie again, seeing what he'd given up and what he'd gotten in return, he knew he had been fooling himself.

His marriage had been doomed from the start.

Natalie couldn't sleep. Over and over, she rehashed the evening, from the moment she had set eyes upon Adam until the moment the cab pulled away from the curb at Rockefeller Center.

If she had entertained the notion that she was over him, she now knew she was wrong.

Tonight had proven she would never be over him.

Fifteen

The Hammond family always attended the Christmas Eve service at St. Mark's Episcopal, where Julius and Margarethe had been members for years. Adam had been raised a Methodist, but he always deferred to Julia when it came to church attendance. She cared where they went; he didn't. After the service, they headed home where they had a late supper, traditionally Virginia ham and corn soufflé and sweet potatoes and popover rolls that Margarethe had made herself.

Once supper was over, they moved into the mammoth living room where Christmas carols played softly and the hundreds of twinkling white lights on the eight-foot spruce tree provided an appropriate backdrop for the exchanging of gifts. This year, as always, there was a roaring fire in the fireplace and Janet, their housekeeper, had put out the brandy and eggnog along with a plate of Christmas cookies.

Anyone looking through the huge picture window and seeing the four of them sitting around the fireplace would have thought they were an ideal family, Adam thought wryly, a family who had everything.

That year, again as always, the gifts were expensive and plentiful. Embarrassingly so, Adam thought, but he knew better than to say anything. He'd done that once, the first year after he and Julia were married, and afterward, he'd been taken to task by Julius.

"My girls look forward to Christmas," he'd said. "And I like indulging them." His manner was mild, but his eyes were hard. "Now don't you spoil their fun."

Ever since, Adam had gone along with the inevitable. It wasn't hard to figure out what to give Julia. He simply went to Cartier and selected a tasteful piece of jewelry for his wife who, like her mother, felt a woman could never have enough jewels. Julia always picked out the gifts for her parents, so that was no problem, although Adam insisted on paying for whatever it was they gave them. Once the gift giving was over, they sat over their drinks until it was time for bed.

That was Christmas Eve.

On Christmas Day, the Hammonds entertained with a lavish dinner, something Adam didn't really enjoy but had learned to endure. This year's gathering was just as much of a strain as Adam had feared, mostly because Winston Crowley and his family made up the lion's share of the guest list. The only other guests in attendance were the Hammonds' longtime friend and family physician, Peter Bendel, and his wife, Trudy, both of whom Adam genuinely liked. He also liked Cynthia Crowley, Winston's wife. She was a nice woman, with a cheerful disposition, and Adam knew she liked him.

Matthew Crowley, Winston's oldest son and a coworker of Adam's, was another story. From the day Adam had started with the firm, Matt Crowley had despised him. Adam was sure the reason was envy. Matt was a pedestrian lawyer at best, and he had been stuck in the firm's tax department for years. He resented Adam's elevation to a full partnership and never missed an opportunity to bad-mouth him. Matt's animosity hadn't hurt Adam's career, but it was awkward to deal with the man, especially in a social situation such as this one.

Exacerbating the work situation, Matt had once entertained notions about Julia. Adam was sure his interest had more to do with Julia's wealth and social position than any romantic feelings, but that didn't make Adam's conquest any easier for Matt to bear. He had eventually married Victoria Van Horn, a girl with a flawless pedigree but no money. Adam couldn't stand Victoria, either. She was a snob of the first order. Julia was a snob, too, but Julia wasn't mean. Victoria was. Adam had seen her cut dead anyone she considered her social inferior.

As he sat at his in-laws' beautifully appointed dinner table, he wondered what Natalie would think of this crowd. Somehow he didn't think she'd be impressed, even though every person there was well-educated, intelligent, as attractive as money could make them, and of impeccable lineage.

Natalie. What was she doing right now? he wondered. He remembered what she'd told him years ago about the kind of Christmas her family always had. He smiled as he pictured a big, noisy, happy family sitting around a big dining room table. It wouldn't be a fancy table like this one, but it would be loaded with good food, and everyone would be having a great time.

"How's Vanessa doing these days, Adam? I haven't seen her in ages."

The question came from Victoria, who had gone to school with Vanessa.

Adam shook free of his thoughts and turned his attention her way. "She's doing great."

"Still involved with her women's rights causes?" The question held just a hint of disdain.

Adam kept his voice even. "Oh, yes. She's passionate on the subject."

"You must be so relieved."

"I'm not sure what you mean."

"Well . . ." Victoria laughed. "We all know how wild

your sister was. It must have been a huge concern when she was so involved in the drug scene."

Had to get at least one dig in, didn't you, you little bitch? Adam would have liked to say just that, but in polite company, men did not call women bitches to their faces. Keeping his smile in place, he said mildly, "It just takes some of us longer to grow up than others. I've seen some who never grow up at all."

"Vanessa has turned out to be a lovely young woman," said Margarethe Hammond, her voice cool.

Although sometimes his mother-in-law grated on his nerves, Adam appreciated her loyalty. In Margarethe's code, if you belonged to her family, she would stick up for you and yours until her dying breath.

"Oh, I certainly didn't mean she *wasn't*," Victoria said in a falsely sweet voice. "If I offended you, Adam, I didn't mean to."

"No offense taken."

"We invited Vanessa and her family," Julia said as she passed the platter of roast beef to Dr. Bendel. "But they were going to Pennsylvania for the holidays to be with her husband's family."

Adam was inwardly amused by Julia's comment. She had no more wanted Vanessa and John and their kids there today than she'd have wanted some homeless person off the street. She'd only asked them because it was the thing to do, but she'd been highly relieved when Vanessa had declined the invitation. Still, Adam appreciated the fact Julia had asked.

"It must be hard for you now," Cynthia Crowley said softly, giving Adam a kind smile, "with both your parents gone."

"Yes." Adam missed his mother in particular. His feelings about his father were mixed. On the surface, at least, they had patched up their differences by the time his father died, but down deep, Adam had never really forgiven Franklin.

"They're always with us in spirit, though," Margarethe said.

Her statement elicited some sympathetic murmurings, then the conversation turned to more general topics. Glad to be removed from the spotlight, Adam let his thoughts wander again. As they had for the past three days, they headed straight for Natalie. Had she thought of him at all since they'd met the other night? He knew, if he were wise, he would put her out of his mind. It was foolish, dangerous even, to call her or try to see her again. Yet the thought of not doing so was unbearable.

For the first time since he and Julia married, he was glad they'd had no children. If they did, he knew he could not even consider leaving her. Even thinking the words *leaving her* made his heart beat faster.

He looked at his wife. Today she looked lovely in a powder blue wool dress trimmed in sequins and seed pearls. The color was flattering to her, but more than that, she seemed healthy, for a change. Her eyes sparkled, and she smiled a lot. How he wished he loved her the way she wanted him to love her. The way she needed to be loved.

Could he leave her? He had never before seriously considered it, but that was because he had believed Natalie was forever lost to him. So what would have been the point in hurting Julia?

He still couldn't believe that Natalie had never married. That maybe, just maybe, they could have a second chance. Other than not wanting to hurt Julia, there was no longer any reason he had to stay married to her. The money Julius had lent his father was almost paid back, and Adam's mother was dead.

How would Julia react if he asked for a divorce? Would she understand? Be reasonable? Surely she knew, down deep, that theirs was not a great marriage.

For the rest of the day, the possibility of a divorce and a new life with Natalie was all he could think about.

• • •

Natalie was so stuffed, she wasn't sure she could move. As usual, her mother had put out enough food for an army. Ham, turkey, dressing, lasagne, breads, salads, and all kinds of vegetables—it was a veritable feast. "Oh," she groaned, holding her stomach. "I ate too much."

"Me, too," echoed her sister Carol.

"We *all* ate too much," Rose said. "We always eat too much when we're here."

"Speak for yourself," Tony said. "I'm not through eating." To prove his point, he speared another slab of turkey, then reached for the bowl of stuffing.

His wife reached over and smacked his hand. "You're going to make yourself sick, Tony."

"Spouse abuse!" Giving his siblings an exaggerated look of alarm, Tony cringed away from his wife. "Did you see that? She hit me."

Natalie's mother rolled her eyes.

Natalie laughed, but a few seconds later, she tuned out as her family continued their good-natured banter. As they had several times already today, her thoughts turned to Adam. Absently, she fingered the diamond heart he had given her twelve Christmases ago.

"Natalie," her aunt Tess said, "I don't believe I've seen that heart necklace before. Is it new?"

Natalie dropped her hand as if she'd been burned. "I, um, no, it's not new." She avoided Rose's eyes. Her older sister was the only member of her family who knew about the necklace, and she was sure Rose was wondering why Natalie was wearing it now after all these years.

"Well, it's beautiful," her aunt said.

"Thank you."

"I noticed it, too," Natalie's mother said. "Are those real diamonds?"

"Yes." Oh, God. Why had she worn it today? She braced herself for more questions.

But her mother surprised her. "Well, I think it's wonderful that young women today can buy themselves diamonds if they want to," she said, beaming at Natalie.

Natalie felt terrible about misleading her mother, but she certainly wasn't going to explain that a former boyfriend had given her the necklace and that it had been hidden away in her underwear drawer until just the other day when she had decided she might want to wear it after all.

"Yeah," Grace added. "Believe me, if I could afford it, I'd buy some for myself, too."

"Maybe you won't have to," Carol said. "Maybe that good-looking firefighter you're dating will come through."

Grace grimaced. "Firefighters don't make any money, you know that."

"Where *is* Rick today?" Carol asked. "I thought he'd be here."

"Unfortunately, he had to work."

"I thought you weren't interested in marriage," Tony said, grinning. For years Grace had sworn she'd never marry.

Grace blushed.

Natalie could have kissed her sister for inadvertently moving the spotlight away from her and the subject of the diamond heart. After a few more minutes of the family teasing Grace about her boyfriend, Natalie's mother rose, saying, "I don't know about the rest of you, but I've got to move around a bit."

Natalie got up and began stacking plates. Following her lead, her sisters and sister-in-law began to help her.

But once the kitchen was cleaned up and Natalie's mother had put on coffee, Rose took Natalie by the arm, saying, "Come upstairs with me. There's something I wanted to show you," and Natalie knew her reprieve was over.

Once they were in the guest room with the door shut behind them, Rose said, "Okay, what's going on?"

"What do you mean?"

Rose pointed to the heart necklace. "That."

Natalie decided playing dumb was her best option. "What about it?"

"Natalie, come on. I wasn't born yesterday. I know that's the necklace Adam gave you. I also know you haven't worn it since he walked out of your life."

"So?"

"So what's happened to change things?"

"Maybe I just decided it was silly to let a beautiful piece of jewelry sit in a drawer gathering dust."

"Natalie . . ."

Natalie couldn't look her sister in the eye. The trouble was, she was no good at lying. And, if she were being *really* honest, she'd admit she wanted to tell Rose about seeing Adam again. She sighed. "All right. I ran into Adam the other night."

"You ran *into* him!"

"Well, actually, we bumped into each other." Natalie went on to explain exactly what the circumstances of the meeting were and then, figuring what the heck, told Rose how they'd had dinner together.

"Oh, Nat." Rose shook her head. "This isn't good. Honey, he's *married*!"

"I know that. Oh, come on, Rose. Don't look at me like that. All we did was talk."

"But he wants to see you again."

"I didn't say that."

"You didn't have to. I can see it in your eyes. And you want to see him, too. You're still in love with him, aren't you?"

"No!"

"Oh, Nat, I hope not. Because if you go down this road, it will only lead to more heartache for you."

Natalie felt as if she were going to cry. She hated seeing censure in her sister's eyes, and she was terribly afraid that's exactly what she did see. "There's nothing wrong in just talking to him occasionally, is there?"

"Even if that's all you did, yes, I think it would be wrong, because of your past, and because both of you would be *wanting* more. You know you would. And that's dangerous, sweetie. That's real dangerous."

Natalie bowed her head. Rose was right.

"Nat." Rose touched her shoulder.

Swallowing hard, Natalie willed herself not to cry.

"Sweetie, think about his wife. How would you feel if you were in her shoes?"

Natalie didn't want to think about the faceless Julia, because when she did, she felt ashamed. No, she hadn't done anything wrong in just having dinner with Adam, but Rose was right. She'd *wanted* to. Maybe she hadn't articulated the thought, even to herself, but it had been there.

Rose put her arm around Natalie's shoulders. "Are you okay?" she asked softly.

Natalie nodded. Finally, sighing deeply, she raised troubled eyes to meet her sister's. "You're right. I won't see him again."

Rose smiled sympathetically. "Good. That's the right decision."

Maybe it was, Natalie thought bleakly. But why was it that doing the right thing made you feel so bad?

Adam lay quietly, hoping Julia was asleep. He hadn't felt this guilty in a long time, not since he'd married her, in fact.

He'd known the minute he walked into the bedroom that she wanted him to make love to her tonight. At first, he'd considered stalling, pretending he'd only come upstairs to get a book or something, but when she'd patted the bed beside her and given him that special smile she reserved for nights like this one, and said, "I've been waiting for you, sweetheart," he'd known there would be no escape.

So he'd made love to her, and he'd tried his best not

to think about Natalie while he was doing so, but it quickly became apparent to him that if he didn't think about her, he would never be able to perform, because his body simply wouldn't cooperate.

And that was why he felt so awful now. Maybe he hadn't technically cheated on his wife, but tonight he had betrayed her in every important way.

Something had to change.

Even if Natalie didn't want him anymore, he couldn't go on like this.

Sixteen

Natalie decided to head back to New York two days earlier than she'd planned. Carol was disappointed. She and
her husband, Jeff, were having a New Year's Eve party
and she'd wanted Natalie to be there.

"I've told Mitch all about you, and he's been dying to
meet you," she said.

Mitch was their veterinarian and a golf buddy of Jeff's,
and Carol had been dropping hints about him for months.

"What's the point?"

"What do you mean?"

"Well, even if I liked Mitch, he lives here. And I live
in New York."

"So?"

"The logistics don't add up."

"Oh, come on, Natalie, surely if you met a guy you
really liked, you'd be willing to make some changes in
your life, wouldn't you?"

Her sister's question disturbed Natalie, because she
knew if the man in question were Adam, she'd make any
change necessary if it meant they could finally be together. Evading a direct answer, she said, "Look, I love
my job, and I love New York. I can't see myself ever

moving back here, so let's just forget about Mitchell, okay?"

Carol eventually gave up trying to persuade her to change her mind, and Natalie took the train back to Manhattan, arriving the day before New Year's Eve.

Although normally she took the bus, today, because she had so much to carry, she splurged on a cab from Grand Central to her East Twentieth Street apartment. Jim, the super, was in the lobby when she arrived, so she didn't have to hunt for her key. He gave her a big hug after buzzing her in. "Good to see you back, Natalie. Did you have a good Christmas?"

"Great, Jim. How was yours?"

"It was crazy. All the kids and grandkids were here."

She smiled. "Just the way you like it."

He grinned. "Yep."

Natalie's minuscule apartment was on the third floor, and usually she just climbed the stairs. Today, though, loaded down with luggage and Christmas presents, she waited for the ancient elevator.

Her cats, who during Natalie's absence had been tended by the elderly widow who lived across the hall, gave Natalie the cold shoulder for the first couple of hours after her return. Finally, though, they decided they'd spent long enough punishing her for leaving them for such a long time and allowed her to pet them.

"I'm sorry I was gone so long," Natalie told them later that night as both cats joined her in her bed. She scratched their heads in turn. "Do you forgive me?"

Isabella, a long-haired Siamese mix, purred contentedly and parked her overweight body as close to Natalie as she could get. Gabriel, a sleek black shorthair, pretended to still be miffed, but when she stopped scratching him, he butted her hand with his head.

Natalie was glad she'd come home early. And if she sat home alone tomorrow night, so be it. She'd spent other New Year's Eves alone and survived. She'd treat herself to a takeout dinner from Carmel's, a favorite neighborhood restaurant, and after dinner she'd luxuriate in a bubble bath, then she'd curl up on the sofa and read that Gail Godwin novel she'd been saving and watch the ball drop on TV.

But the next morning, when she called Hilary to tell her she was back in town, Hilary insisted she come and spend New Year's with her. "Isaiah is working, of course, but it's *Madame Butterfly*, which I know you love, and afterward the three of us will have a late supper. Now I won't take no for an answer." Hilary was referring to the program at the Met. Her husband was a cellist with the orchestra and he had two complimentary tickets to each performance.

"But didn't you plan to go with someone else?"

"Nope," Hilary said. "I asked my sister and a couple of other people, but they all had other plans."

So on New Year's Eve, Natalie, wearing her best black dress and her diamond heart, sat among a glittering audience enthralled by her favorite opera. Only once did she think about Adam, and that was because, during intermission, she saw a man who looked like him. But when she started to feel sad, she gave herself a stern lecture.

She had gotten along just fine without him for the past twelve years. And she would get along just fine without him again.

Julia always looked forward to the New Year's Eve party hosted by the firm. She had been attending the annual bash since her debut at eighteen. Because of her father's position, people had always made a fuss over her, and that hadn't changed.

In fact, now that Adam was a full partner, the other wives deferred to Julia more than ever. And Adam knew Julia liked being deferred to. She would never say so out loud, of course, but he could tell by the way her eyes gleamed with pleasure at their compliments and the way they hung onto her every word.

So even though Adam wasn't crazy about big bashes, he didn't mind going to this party the way he did others, because he never had to worry about Julia.

At her insistence, he had hired a limo for the evening. He thought it was a needless extravagance, but she said she wouldn't be caught dead arriving at the Waldorf in a smelly old cab.

"Now, aren't you glad you listened to me and ordered a custom-made tux instead of buying one off the rack?" she said as she walked into the bedroom and saw him knotting his black tie.

He just smiled. She'd asked him the same question the last time he'd had to wear a tux. He studied her. "Is that a new dress?"

"Yes. Do you like it?" She turned around slowly to show him the view from all angles. It was an elegant black crepe cut high in the front and low in the back. With it, she wore her grandmother's diamonds: a large starburst brooch and matching earrings. Her pale blond hair, normally worn in a smooth chignon, had been fashioned into an elaborate upsweep.

"It's beautiful. You look very nice."

She smiled and walked over to the mirror to stand beside him. "We make a handsome couple."

Adam looked at their reflection in the glass. She looked very pleased with herself.

She still had that cat-that-ate-the-canary look an hour later as they walked into the ballroom of the hotel. Adam left her talking to a fawning junior wife while he carried Julia's ermine wrap to the coatroom and checked it. As he headed back toward Julia, he spied his secretary and her husband.

"Mary Beth," he called, waving.

Mary Beth, a small, cheerful woman with salt-and-pepper hair and bright blue eyes, grinned and waved back.

Holding onto her husband's hand, she pulled him in Adam's direction.

Adam and Patrick Mahoney shook hands and exchanged pleasantries. "Did you just get here?" Adam asked.

"About ten minutes ago," Mary Beth said. "Isn't this a *gorgeous* room?"

They talked for a while, then Adam excused himself, saying he'd better find his wife. When he caught up with Julia, she was holding court with half a dozen wives and seemed perfectly happy. Deciding she was well taken care of, he began to circulate.

It was an hour or more before he sought her out again. She was standing with a group that included Victoria Crowley. As Adam approached, he heard Victoria say, with a smug smile in Julia's direction, that she and Matt had just found out they were expecting their third child.

After the initial exclamations, Julia said, "Congratulations, Victoria."

"Yes, congratulations," Adam added.

Julia swung around. "Oh. I didn't know you were there, Adam." She slipped her arm through his.

"Thank you," Victoria replied. She looked at Adam. "Matt's parents are so pleased. There's nothing quite like a new grandchild to make them happy."

He nodded and made some noncommittal comment. He wanted to give Victoria the benefit of the doubt and believe that she hadn't purposely tried to make Julia feel bad, but unfortunately, he knew better. Feeling bad for Julia, he said, "They're getting ready to serve dinner. Let's go find our table."

But Julia seemed fine during dinner. She laughed and talked and didn't act as if Victoria's announcement had bothered her in the slightest, so Adam forgot about it himself. Consequently, he was taken off guard when, later, as they were getting ready for bed, Julia brought up the subject, saying casually, "How did you feel about Victoria's news tonight?"

He stopped in the middle of removing the studs from his shirt. "How did *I* feel?"

Julia sat on the chaise and removed her shoes. "Yes. Did it bother you that she's expecting again?"

"Of course not. I'm happy for them."

"Adam, do you still want a child?"

He answered slowly. "Why are you asking?"

"Because I've been thinking. Maybe we *should* try to adopt."

He stared at her, completely taken aback. The one and only time he'd suggested adoption, she'd been adamantly opposed, so much so that he'd vowed never to bring up the subject again. "Are you serious?"

"Yes, I'm very serious."

"What brought on this change of heart?"

"I don't know. I've just been thinking about it for a while and . . . I guess I realized how unfair I was being. How unreasonable."

"I never thought you were being unreasonable. I've always respected the way you feel about adopting."

"But that's what I'm trying to tell you. I no longer feel that way." When he didn't immediately answer, she frowned in bewilderment. "I don't understand. Don't you *want* to adopt a child anymore?"

He shrugged. "I don't know. I've gotten used to things the way they are, I guess." He attempted a smile, but his heart wasn't in it. Why had she suggested this now? It was almost as if she sensed what had been going through his mind lately and was looking for a way to keep him tightly bound to her. "Look, Julia," he said as gently as he could, "I appreciate the offer. I know this wasn't an easy decision for you, but I don't think adopting a child is something you should do because of someone else."

"But I *said* I really wanted to now." Getting up, she walked over to him and slid her arms around his waist.

For a second, he was frozen; then he put his arms around her, too. She laid her head against his chest.

"Adam, I love you so much," she whispered. "I'd do anything for you."

He cleared his throat. "I know."

She raised her head. Her eyes held mute appeal. "If you want a child, I want you to have one."

What could he say? *No, I don't want a child.* That was a lie. *No, I don't want a child with you.* If he tried for a million years, he didn't think he could think of a more hurtful thing to say. *No, I'm happy the way we are.* Another lie. He didn't want to lie to her, and he couldn't tell her the truth. Finally he said, "I think we're past that stage of our lives."

She rubbed his back. "You're not angry with me, are you?"

"No, I'm not angry with you."

"I'm glad, because I couldn't bear it if you were." She tightened her arms around him. "I just want you to be happy, Adam."

He knew what she wanted in return, but the words simply would not come. He settled for, "I want you to be happy, too."

"Oh, Adam, I *am* happy. Tonight I was so proud. Everyone at the firm respects you and admires you so much. And their wives are all jealous of me because I'm married to you."

"Come on, Julia. They are not."

"Yes, they are. But it won't do them any good, will it? Because you're mine. All mine."

Adam closed his eyes.

"I don't know what I'd do without you, Adam."

"Julia . . ."

"It's true. I'd be so lost. Sometimes I even pray that we'll die together."

"Julia, for God's sake!"

"I mean it. I wouldn't want to live without you, Adam."

Suddenly he could no longer stand this conversation. Removing her arms, he said, "Julia, I'm very tired. And I've got a headache. I probably drank too much champagne. Let's not have any more talk about dying or anything else, all right?"

"I'm so sorry, my poor darling. How insensitive I can be sometimes. You go take some Advil and then come to bed. Do you want me to call down and have Alma fix you some warm milk or something?"

"Julia, it is two o'clock in the morning! No, I don't want you to disturb Alma, and I don't want warm milk. I just want some peace and quiet!"

Later, after she'd fallen asleep, Adam lay next to her in their big queen-sized bed and thought about what she'd said. He told himself she hadn't meant it when she'd said she wouldn't want to live without him.

She's not going to kill herself if you leave her.

But no matter how many times he told himself to forget what she'd said, that it had just been said for dramatic effect, he couldn't get rid of an ominous feeling in the pit of his stomach. A feeling that said the velvet vise was only going to get tighter and tighter and that if he didn't find a way to break free soon, he might as well be dead himself.

Adam's first day back at work after the holidays was spent with one eye on the phone and the other on his work.

At least a dozen times that morning he started to call Natalie. Each time, he replaced the receiver without dialing.

Five o'clock came, then six. At six-thirty, he couldn't stand it another minute. He knew he had no right to see her, not unless he was free, but he had to talk to her. Just talk, that was all.

He picked up the phone. Punched in her office number. He'd committed it to memory within minutes of her giving it to him.

The phone rang once. Twice. Three times.

She was probably gone for the day, he thought with a stab of disappointment.

He was just about to hang up when she said, "Natalie Ferrenzo." She sounded breathless.

"Happy New Year, Natalie."

"Thank you. Happy New Year to you, too."

"I thought maybe you'd gone for the day."

"I was across the hall using the copy machine. It took me a few minutes to get to the phone."

How was it that just the sound of her voice could make him feel so happy? "I'm sorry."

"No, that's okay."

For a moment, he couldn't think of anything else to say. "Did you have a good Christmas?"

"Yes, it was wonderful. And you?"

He almost gave her the usual everything-was-great answer that most people expected when they asked this kind of question. But somehow he couldn't. "I survived."

She didn't immediately answer. When she did, her voice had become quieter. "Are things that bad, then?"

"Natalie . . . I . . ." His voice was rough with unspoken emotion. "Can I see you tonight? I need to talk to someone. No, that's not true. I need to talk to *you.*"

"Oh, Adam, I don't think—"

"Please don't say no."

Silence.

"Natalie?"

An audible sigh floated clearly across the wire. "When I agreed to see you again, I wasn't thinking straight."

Adam closed his eyes.

"I'm sorry, Adam," she said softly. "But I think it's best for both of us if we don't see each other again."

"I understand," he said dully. The hell of it was, he did understand. From her point of view, she was doing the smart thing. From his point of view, he felt like jumping off a cliff. His life—barren and joyless—stretched ahead of him like an endless desert.

"Take care of yourself," she said.

"You, too."

"Good-bye, Adam."

"Good-bye."

After hanging up, Adam sat numbly. It had hurt him to give Natalie up twelve years ago, but that pain was nothing compared to the desolation that flooded him now. Twelve years ago, he hadn't fully understood what it was he was losing.

Now he did.

Tears ran down Natalie's face. Oh, God, he'd sounded so desperate. And so unhappy. And she'd wanted to say yes to him so badly.

Why did I have to see him again?

If she hadn't run into him that night at Rockefeller Center, she would have been okay. But seeing him again had ripped away the protective bandages she'd applied twelve years ago, and now she had an open, throbbing wound. One that was not going to heal easily.

She blew her nose into a tissue. Thank God no one else was around tonight. If anyone saw her crying like this, she would be mortified. Bad enough she felt so awful. She sure didn't want anyone knowing about it.

She took a deep, shaky breath. Okay, so it hurt to see Adam again—to have that tantalizing glimpse into what might have been—and then not be able to continue to see him. But that was life. You couldn't always have what you wanted.

She'd known that for a long time.

Seventeen

~~~~~~~~~~~~~~~~~~~~~

For the next few days, Adam functioned.

He worked. He ate. He slept. He made polite conversation with Julia.

What he didn't do was think.

Each time his mind veered toward the subject of his marriage or Natalie, he ruthlessly rerouted it.

On the fourth day, in the middle of a busy afternoon, when he should have been concentrating all of his attention on the upcoming Jamison Insurance Company hearing, his willpower gave out, and no matter how he tried not to, his marriage and Natalie were all he *could* think about.

At four o'clock, no longer able to stand being in the office, he put on his coat, scarf, and gloves and told Mary Beth that he would see her in the morning.

Her face showed her surprise—he never left this early—but, like the excellent employee she was, she quickly recovered and said, "Have a good evening, Mr. Forrester."

"You, too."

It was a bitterly cold day with gray skies that promised snow. Adam left his building and walked aimlessly for a while. Eventually, he found himself at Rockefeller Center.

He grimaced. Subconsciously, he must have been heading there the whole time.

A few hardy souls were skating on the rink below, and for a few moments, he watched them. He kept remembering the night he'd met Natalie here. Their dinner afterward. The way she'd looked. The way she'd sounded. He knew it was stupid to torture himself this way, but he couldn't seem to help himself.

He had to see her again. No matter what she'd said, he simply had to see her.

He eyed her office building, the top of which was visible from his vantage point. He knew exactly where her office was located, because he'd looked it up.

Glancing at his watch, he saw it was almost five. Most of the employees of her company would be leaving at five, especially on a day like this. Would she?

Suddenly, he knew what he was going to do. Walking rapidly, he covered the distance to the front of her building in less than three minutes. As he approached, people were just beginning to pour through the revolving doors.

He was reminded of all the times he'd waited for her all those years ago. How her face would light up when she saw him and how they could hardly wait to be alone. The memories were so vivid he could almost feel her in his arms.

Making another snap decision, he entered the building. There were leather benches in the lobby, and he walked over to the one that faced the bank of elevators he knew she would have to take to exit the building.

No matter how long it took, he would wait.

Natalie was bone tired. Ever since her conversation with Adam, she hadn't been sleeping well. Nothing seemed to help, not Tylenol-PM, which was her usual remedy for sleeplessness, not warm milk with cinnamon, not giving herself one stern lecture after another.

Trouble was, she thought tiredly, no matter how much

she knew she'd done the right thing, she was hurting.

Rubbing her forehead and hoping she wasn't going to end the day the same way she'd ended too many others in the recent past—with a blinding headache—she decided she wasn't staying late tonight. Whatever work she had to do could be done tomorrow. Tonight she was going home early, downing a couple of Advil, taking a hot shower, putting on her most comfy flannel nightgown, and watching TV in bed until her eyes finally closed.

"Leaving at a normal time tonight, huh?"

The question had come from Bobbi Chen, one of the assistant editors. Natalie smiled at her. She liked Bobbi, who reminded her of how enthusiastic and eager she used to be when she'd first started with the company. "Yes. I'm beat."

"Well, have a good one," Bobbi said.

"You, too."

Natalie headed for the elevators. Luckily, she only had to wait a couple of minutes for one to come, but it took forever to reach the lobby, because it stopped at nearly every floor. Finally, the doors opened at ground level. Natalie tightened her scarf around her neck and followed the crowd to the exit. Just as she reached the revolving doors, someone grabbed her arm.

"Natalie."

Her heart knocked against her rib cage. It was Adam. "Wh-what are you doing here?" She allowed herself to be guided away from the doors and over to a corner where they would be out of the way of the people rushing to exit the building.

"I'm sorry. I know what you said, but I had to see you." His eyes looked haunted.

She couldn't think what to say. She knew it was wrong, but her traitorous heart was filled with joy at the sight of him.

"Will you come and have a cup of coffee with me?"

"I—"

"Please?"

She wet her lips. "All right."

Together, they left the building. Once outside, he took her hand and tucked it under his arm. Then, heads down against the wind, they walked to the corner, where there was a small coffee shop.

The manager put them at a window table. It was very warm inside, and Natalie unbuttoned her coat and took off her scarf. She avoided Adam's eyes. When she finally looked at him, she saw that he'd removed his overcoat. Underneath he wore a lawyerly looking gray flannel suit—Brooks Brothers, she was sure—paired with a white shirt and a burgundy striped tie.

He started to say something but stopped when their waitress, a skinny blonde with black roots showing, approached. Once they'd placed their orders and the waitress had brought their coffee, Adam leaned toward her. "Ever since that night we met at Rockefeller Center, I haven't been able to stop thinking about you." His voice vibrated with emotion. "I know I have no right to say this, but I still love you. You're the only woman I've ever loved."

Natalie tried to ignore the explosion of joy she felt at his words. Because allowing him to talk like this was wrong. Admitting their feelings for each other wouldn't change anything. It would only make their present circumstances harder to bear. "Oh, Adam, please don't say anything more."

"I have to. You have to listen."

She knew she should get up, this very minute, and walk away. Before it was too late and she wouldn't be able to.

"My marriage is a sham," he said, his eyes boring into hers.

"Adam . . ."

"For a long time I thought I could live with it, but I can't anymore—"

"This isn't the place to talk about this," Natalie said desperately.

"Let's go somewhere else then."

Please, God, help me. But if there was a God, he wasn't listening, and Natalie no longer had the will to resist. "We could go to my place," she said faintly. Her heart was going like a tom-tom.

What was she doing? She almost said, *Wait, I didn't mean that,* but Adam had already thrust his arms back into his overcoat and thrown several bills on the table. He stood.

Natalie got up, too. Fingers fumbling, she rebuttoned her coat. Wordlessly, they left. The wind was blowing even harder now, and he put his arm around her as they walked quickly toward Fifth Avenue, where he said it would be easier to get a cab. Once they reached the corner, Adam went out to the street. It took a few minutes for him to flag down a cab, but he finally managed to snag one. Moments later, they were on the way to her apartment.

Once they arrived, Natalie was relieved to see the super wasn't in evidence. Although he wouldn't know Adam, and she certainly wouldn't have to explain who Adam was, she still felt funny about Jim seeing him.

It's your guilty conscience.

"The stairs are quicker," she said when Adam turned toward the elevator.

"Okay." He looked around with interest. "This is a nice building."

"Yes."

"Have you been here long?"

"Five years. Before that, I lived in Brooklyn."

For the first time that evening, he smiled. "Brooklyn?"

"There's nothing wrong with Brooklyn."

The smile got bigger. "I know. Some of my best—"

"Friends live in Brooklyn," she finished with a chuckle. But the chuckle was tinged with sadness, too, because it reminded her of all the times they'd teased each other about their respective schools.

Still, the lighthearted exchange relieved some of the tension, and by the time they'd climbed the stairs and reached her apartment, Natalie was almost back to her normal self. Yet the moment they walked inside and shut the door behind them, her heart started beating harder.

This is a mistake, she thought, suddenly filled with panic. Yet she managed to keep her voice from betraying her fear, saying, "Take your coat off and make yourself comfortable." She motioned to the sofa that took up most of her living room. "I'll be back in a minute."

Without looking at him, she escaped into her bedroom, shutting the door behind her.

Closing her eyes, she leaned against it. *Dear God, why did I bring him here?* Her cats, who spent their days sleeping on top of her bed, eyed her. Isabella meowed, but Gabriel didn't move, just gave her the evil eye. He didn't like it when she brought people home with her. He particularly didn't like men.

Natalie took off her coat, scarf, and boots. Slipping into her black pumps, she walked over to her dresser and peered at herself in the mirror. Her cheeks were red from the cold, her hair a mess from the wind. She brushed her hair and freshened her lipstick. Then, knowing she couldn't hide in her bedroom forever, she took a deep breath and walked to the door.

Natalie's apartment reflected her interests and personality, Adam thought as he looked around. It was cozy and without pretension.

Books were everywhere. Overflowing the bookcase on the opposite wall, stacked on the floor by the navy and green print couch, piled on the coffee table. A healthy-looking philodendron and a cup filled with pens and pencils took up most of the rest of the surface of the coffee table.

The only other piece of furniture in the room was a sturdy-looking oak rocking chair, over which was folded a knitted afghan in shades of green. A framed Renoir print—two young girls sitting in a rowboat in the middle of a lake—adorned one wall, and photographs of people Adam assumed to be Natalie's family were hung on the other free wall. He got up to look at them. He was studying a portrait of a nice-looking older couple he assumed were her parents when he heard the door to her bedroom open.

He turned, and his chest tightened painfully. Even dressed plainly in a black skirt and unadorned black sweater, she was beautiful. The love he felt for her filled him with a fierce longing.

As she walked toward him, she didn't quite meet his eyes. "Those are my parents," she said, looking toward the portrait.

"I thought so."

"And that's Rose and Chris and their children." She pointed to another portrait.

"Rose looks like you."

"Yes. Everyone says so."

She told him the names of all the other people whose pictures were on the wall, and he'd been right. All of them were members of her family. He was envious. It must be great to have so many close relatives. And it was obvious from the warmth in her voice that they *were* close. But he'd known that, hadn't he? He'd known it from the very first time he'd seen her.

She finished identifying the people in the pictures, but she still hadn't looked at him directly.

He touched her shoulder. "Natalie," he said softly. "Please look at me."

Slowly, she turned to face him and raised her eyes.

"I love you."

She shook her head. "Don't say that."

"You can deny it, but it'll still be true."

"I just . . ." She closed her eyes for a moment. When she spoke again, her voice was firmer. "It's just that your saying it only makes things harder, don't you see?"

"I'm sorry. I don't want to make things harder. But I can't pretend anymore."

"You're married."

"Believe me, I know that better than anyone." He wasn't able to keep the bitterness out of his voice.

"Then what's the point?"

"I . . ." He took a deep breath. "I'm thinking of leaving Julia."

Slowly, her eyes met his again. "Because of me?" she whispered.

"Because our marriage is a sham. Because I don't love her the way I should. Because I want to be with you."

Tears welled in her eyes.

"Do you love me, Natalie?"

The question hung in the air for what seemed an eternity to Adam.

"Please. I have to know."

For a moment, he didn't think she was going to answer. Finally she did.

"Yes." Now the tears overflowed. "Yes, God help me," she said with trembling lips, "I still love you."

"Oh, Natalie." As he'd been wanting to ever since seeing her in the lobby of her building, he pulled her into his arms. Crushing her to him, he lowered his mouth to hers.

Natalie lay in the circle of Adam's arms. She was trying not to think, for if she did, she might have to acknowledge the fact that she had done something she never would have believed she could do. She had slept with another woman's husband.

"You're awfully quiet." Adam kissed her temple. "You're not sorry, are you?"

"No." No, she wasn't sorry. She was just numb from everything that had happened today.

"Good. I don't want you to be sorry." His arms tightened around her. He nudged her chin up. Gave her a tender smile. "I love you so much."

"I love you, too."

"We'll work this out."

"Will we?" She desperately wanted to think they would.

"Yes." He kissed her softly, letting his lips linger against hers. "I won't lose you again."

She didn't want to lose him again, either, but she also couldn't close her eyes to reality. After all, this wasn't exactly the kind of situation a woman dreamed of. Nothing would change the fact that Adam was married to someone else.

"What if Julia won't agree to a divorce?" she finally asked.

"I'm not going to lie to you, Natalie. She won't be happy about it, but I think even she will finally realize that we'll both be better off if we split up."

Natalie thought about this for a while. "Adam, can I ask you something?"

"Anything."

"If you've been so unhappy, why haven't you left Julia before this?"

"I could never even have considered leaving her until I'd paid her father back."

"Oh. Does that mean you *have* paid him back?"

"Almost. I'll have the money to pay the rest at the end of this month."

"What about your job?"

"What about it?"

"Won't you have to find another firm if you and Julia divorce?"

"Not necessarily. I'm a full partner at Hammond, Crowley. They can't force me out. But you're right. I wouldn't want to stay there once Julia and I are no longer married. But that's not a problem. There are a lot of good firms that would be very glad to have me." He smiled. "Heck.

I might even look into the district attorney's office."

She bit her bottom lip. "You make it all sound so easy."

He tucked her head under his chin. "I don't mean to sound as if divorcing Julia will be simple or that I don't feel bad about it. I do. I never wanted to deceive her, and I sure don't want to hurt her now. But staying married to her is not fair to either one of us. So no matter how hard or how complicated, I think this is the right thing to do." He kissed her. "For all of us."

Natalie hoped so. She wanted Adam. There was no denying that. But she'd learned a long time ago that nothing came without a price.

"Now quit worrying," he said. "It'll take awhile, maybe a month or two, for me to get things at the firm in order and to discharge the rest of that debt to Julia's father, but when I do, I'll talk to Julia." He tipped her head up again. Smiled down into her eyes. "I love you, Natalie Ferrenzo. When I'm free, will you marry me?"

Natalie wanted desperately to believe this was possible. That Adam could be free. That they could build a life together. But she was afraid to count on anything, because she knew how easily things could go wrong. "Adam," she finally said, "ask me again when you really *are* free, okay?"

He searched her eyes for a long moment. Then he nodded. "Okay."

This time when he kissed her, there was no more talk.

Eighteen

"I'm going to tell Julia this weekend." Adam and Natalie had just had dinner together in her apartment. They were now finishing the cleanup.

Natalie switched on the coffeemaker. "Oh, Adam, are you sure?" She still felt guilty about being the cause of another woman's marriage breaking up, even though Adam kept reassuring her that eventually the marriage would have dissolved, anyway.

"Very sure." He put his arms around her, resting his chin on the top of her head. "I want more than this, Natalie. I'm tired of only getting to see you once or twice a week, of never being able to spend the night, of having to sneak around. I want us to be together all the time. To wake up in the morning and see your head on the pillow next to mine." He kissed her temple. "I want everyone to know we love each other. I want to take you places proudly and introduce you as my wife."

"I want all that, too, and yet . . ."

He tipped her face up and searched her eyes. "And yet what?"

"I just can't help feeling sorry for Julia."

"I know, but staying married to her isn't right. She deserves to be with someone who really loves her." He grimaced. "Last night she wanted me to make love to her. She didn't say so, but I know the signs. And I pretended I didn't understand what she was getting at. I stayed downstairs reading until nearly two in the morning so I could be sure she'd be asleep when I went upstairs."

"Oh, Adam." Natalie had tried hard not to think about this aspect of his relationship with Julia.

"Sooner or later, she's going to figure out why we no longer have a sex life."

Natalie nodded, but she was still filled with doubts. The question had nagged her for weeks now. Were they really doing the right thing taking their happiness at Julia's expense? "Isn't this the weekend of her mother's party?" she finally said.

"Yes. That's why I decided to tell her then."

"Doesn't that seem awfully cruel? To spoil the weekend for her like that? And what about her parents? Aren't they going to be terribly upset?"

He ran his hands through his hair, a gesture Natalie knew meant he was frustrated. "Look, I've thought and thought about this. If I tell Julia when we're here in Manhattan and then leave, she'll be all alone. At least this way, she'll have her parents with her." He sighed heavily. "She's not real strong, Natalie. I have no idea how she's going to react. If she goes all to pieces, she's going to need somebody afterward."

Nothing Adam had said made Natalie feel better. In fact, she now felt worse. But if Adam was going to leave Julia, Natalie was sure he was probably right; it *would* be better to tell her when she would be surrounded by people who loved her.

Adam kissed the tip of her nose. "Take that worried look off your face," he said gently. "It's going to be all right."

She wanted to believe that. She wanted to believe it more than she'd ever wanted to believe anything in her entire life.

Yet long after Adam had gone home, as Natalie lay in bed and tried to sleep, her doubts refused to be banished. Over the past weeks, Adam had told her a lot about Julia and their marriage, and Natalie was afraid that no matter how Adam rationalized what he was doing, no matter how many times he told himself Julia would be better off without him, Julia was going to be devastated when he told her he wanted out. It was clear to Natalie that Julia had built her entire life around Adam, and once he was gone, that life would have no meaning to her.

Yes, it was wrong of Julia to have done this; she needed to have a life and identity of her own, but that didn't change the fact that she *had* done it. That his leaving would be catastrophic to her.

And yet, what else were they to do? Because Adam was right about one thing: It wasn't fair to him to expect him to spend the rest of his life with a woman he didn't love just because that's what she wanted. As Adam had pointed out more than once, he'd given Julia more than twelve years. Wasn't that enough? Wasn't he entitled to some happiness, too?

"It would be different if we had children," he'd said. "I probably would never have called you again if that was the case, no matter how much I loved you."

Eventually Natalie fell into a troubled sleep, but the dilemma and its possible outcome continued to nag at her all day Friday. Adam sensed her continued concern when he called her on Friday afternoon.

"Please, darling, stop worrying," he said. "It'll all be over soon."

Natalie knew he had enough facing him. He certainly didn't need to be worrying about *her*, so she forced herself to sound upbeat. "I know. I'm okay."

"Are you sure?"

"Yes." She took a deep breath. "So when are you leaving?"

"About six. I'm going home in just a few minutes."

"And you're driving up to her parents' house tonight?"

"Yes."

"When . . ." Natalie swallowed. "When do you plan to tell her?"

"I'm not sure. I'll have to play it by ear. Either tomorrow night after the party or first thing Sunday morning. It all depends on how she acts and what happens."

"And then you'll come back to Manhattan?"

"Yes. Immediately."

"And . . . you'll call me?"

"The minute I get back."

"No matter what time it is? Even if it's the middle of the night."

"Even then," he promised. His voice deepened. "Just keep remembering how much I love you. That very soon we're going to be together the way we should have been all along."

Now it was Saturday, and she was waiting. The day seemed to crawl by, even though she kept herself busy cleaning her apartment, shopping for groceries, and taking care of other errands. Throughout, she kept looking at her watch and trying to picture where Adam was then and what he was doing.

Was he hanging around the house, watching the preparations for the party? Helping out, maybe? Or had he gone into town to escape all the hoopla? Natalie knew that when the weather was nice, Adam and his father-in-law played golf at Julius Hammond's club or sailed on the Sound. But February weather wasn't conducive to either activity.

At six o'clock, she knew Adam was now getting ready for the party. Showering and dressing. He'd said it was a black tie affair. She pictured him dressed in his tux. Slipping his feet into shiny black shoes. Julia asking him to zip up the back of her gown. His hands would touch her bare skin. Maybe she would ask him to fasten her pearls.

Natalie squeezed her eyes shut. She didn't want to think

about the intimacies of their marriage. She didn't want to think about them as a couple at all. Even though, as Adam had said, they weren't sexually intimate right now, they were still husband and wife. They undressed in front of each other. They slept in the same bed.

Stop it! she told herself. *You know he loves you. He's going to ask Julia for a divorce. What more do you want?*

But no matter what she said to herself, she couldn't seem to stop thinking about them. To reassure herself, she touched her talisman, the golden heart studded with tiny diamonds that hadn't been taken off since Christmas, not even when she honestly believed she would never see Adam again.

At seven o'clock, she knew the party for Margarethe Hammond was just beginning, and she thought about how Adam would be feeling as he and Julia stood in the receiving line with her parents and greeted all the guests.

Adam had said the party would be lavish, that more than one hundred fifty people had been invited. The buffet dinner was being catered by one of the top catering firms in Westchester County and there was going to be a five-piece band playing for dancing afterward. Natalie could imagine the beautifully dressed guests wearing dazzling jewels. The fragrance of expensive perfume and fresh flowers. The smiles and happy greetings.

By eight she knew all the guests would have arrived. Waiters would have spent the last hour circulating through the crowd with trays of hors d'oeuvres and flutes of champagne. But now people would start to move toward the dining room and the buffet. They would ooh and aah over the ice sculptures and the flowers and the food.

Would Adam be able to eat? Or would he be too nervous and worried? Earlier, Natalie had fixed herself a turkey sandwich, but she had only been able to manage a few bites.

At eight-thirty, she opened a new Maeve Binchy novel. At nine, she gave a weary sigh and closed it, even though normally she adored Binchy's work. She had read the same page at least five times without understanding a single word.

At nine-thirty she picked up the phone. She couldn't stand one more minute of solitude. She had to talk to someone. She would call Rose. Thirty seconds later, she put the receiver back into its cradle. It was too late to call Rose. She and Chris would probably be sitting with their feet up, finally relaxing after a busy week. The last thing Rose would want was to get up and talk to Natalie, especially since Natalie wouldn't be able to tell her sister the *real* reason she'd called.

At nine-forty, Natalie headed for the bathroom. Maybe a long, leisurely bath followed by a glass of wine would make her sleepy.

At eleven o'clock, she poured herself a second glass of wine and watched the late news on Channel 5. At midnight, she tuned into *The Tonight Show*. Although Johnny, Ed, and Doc were their charming, entertaining selves, and she did—for short periods of time—forget about her problem, inevitably her thoughts zoomed straight back to Adam and what was happening in Mamaroneck.

Was he telling her even now?

Adam closed the bedroom door softly. His in-laws and their other guests had already retired for the night; he didn't want to disturb them.

He dreaded the next few minutes, but there was no sense putting this off. He spoke gently. "Julia, there's something I want to talk to you about."

"Wasn't the party *wonderful,* Adam? And didn't Mother look beautiful? No one would have *ever* guessed she's seventy years old if we hadn't told them, don't you agree?" With a contented smile, his wife picked up the silver-backed, monogrammed brush that belonged to the vanity set her parents had given her on her sixteenth birthday. She began to brush her long blond hair, which—until just a few minutes ago—had been twisted up into her usual chignon.

Adam walked over to the dressing table and stood behind her, placing his hand on her thin shoulder. A wave of compassion hit him, but he forced himself to go on. "Stop that, would you?"

Her pale blue eyes met his in the mirror. Frowning in bewilderment, she carefully set the brush down and swiveled around to face him. "What is it, darling?"

He backed up and leaned against the post of the canopied bed in this largest of the Hammonds' guest bedrooms. For a moment, the only sounds were the faint ticking of the Seth Thomas clock on the marble fireplace mantel and the muted whistle of the February wind as it buffeted the house.

Julia leaned slightly forward, and the pale pink negligee she wore gaped open, revealing a sheer matching nightgown edged in lace. It saddened Adam that the sight of her in the elegant nightwear made him feel nothing but pity. "There's no easy way to say this. But I . . ." He took a deep breath. "I want a divorce."

For a long, frozen moment, she stared at him, saying nothing. When she finally spoke, her voice trembled. "Y-you're joking."

He shook his head. "No," he answered softly, "I'm not."

"I-I don't believe you." Despite her words, her eyes were filled with fear.

"Julia, please. I don't want to hurt you, but this can't be that much of a surprise to you. You must know things haven't been good between us for a long time."

"No! No!" she cried. "That's not true. Why would you say such a thing? Why, we've been *happy*! You know we've been happy." Tears sprang into her eyes, and she jumped up, coming over to him and flinging her arms around his neck. She pressed her mouth against his.

Adam closed his eyes. He didn't return her kiss.

Couldn't. Yet his heart smote him, for he could feel how her frail body was trembling, and he knew her reaction probably wasn't an act. She had convinced herself that they'd been happy. She would never have allowed herself to believe anything else, otherwise she might have had to face the truth; that he had married her because he'd been forced to. Gently, he put his hands on her shoulders and pushed her away so he could see her face again. "Please, Julia, we have to stop pretending. You know why I married you."

"*I'm* not pretending! I love you, Adam," she said in a broken voice. The trembling increased. "I've always loved you. Ever since I was a little girl."

"Julia . . ." Adam felt like crying himself. She *did* love him, in her way. But he couldn't stay with her out of guilt. He had given her twelve years. He couldn't give her any more.

"I'm so sorry," he said. "But you'll be better off without me. Now maybe you'll be able to find someone who will love you the way you deserve to be loved."

"No! Don't say that! I don't want anyone else. I don't care if you don't love me. I don't care! Please don't leave me. I-I can't live without you, Adam. I'll kill myself! I will!"

"Julia, please don't say things like that."

"I mean it. I can't live without you. You're everything to me! Everything! You always have been. You . . . you're my whole reason for being. Without you, I'm . . . I'm *nothing*." Her face contorted, and she tried to put her arms around him again.

Telling her had been even worse than he'd imagined it would be. And yet, as sorry for her as he felt, he wanted to shake her, too. Couldn't she see that their entire marriage was a farce? Couldn't she see that they would all be better off once they admitted it? Why did she want him? Why would anyone want someone who didn't want them?

Pulling away from her clinging arms, he walked to the closet and removed his suitcase. It was best to just go. Talking about this would only prolong the agony.

"Why?" she sobbed. "Why are you doing this?"

This was the part he had dreaded the most. And yet, now that she'd asked the question, he wouldn't lie to her. There had been enough lies. He wouldn't look away, either. Meeting her gaze squarely, he said, "I'm in love with someone else. We want to be together." Because he knew it would accomplish nothing but hurt Julia more, he didn't add that he had always loved Natalie, that Natalie was the one he'd wanted to marry in the first place.

"No," she moaned. "No. You can't mean that!" Rushing over to where he stood, she fell to her knees and wrapped her arms around his legs.

Pity flooded him, but it didn't sway him. He had given Julia too much of his life already. She would learn to live without him. In the end, she would be better off.

He leaned down and unwound her arms. Trying to ignore her hysterical weeping, he took his suitcase over to the bed and began to shove his clothes into it. When he was finished, he zipped it shut. "I'll be at our house in the city tonight," he said. "But tomorrow I'll find somewhere else to stay."

Abruptly, she stopped crying. Then, startling him, she whirled around, yanked open the door and, before he could even react, was running down the hall, the heels of her satin mules sounding like gunshots as they hit the oak floors. He dropped the suitcase and ran after her. Behind him, he could hear the door to her parents' bedroom opening.

"What the devil?" Julius Hammond said.

"Julia?" called her mother anxiously.

Adam ignored her parents and raced after Julia. Catching up with her at the head of the stairs, he grabbed her arm, but she wrenched it away. "Don't touch me!" she shrieked. "Don't you dare touch me!"

She shrank away from him. And then, in an instant

Adam knew he would relive in his nightmares for years to come, she stepped back too far. He lunged for her, but it was too late. She teetered, then lost her balance, and plummeted down the stairs.

"Julia!" screamed her mother.

The next few minutes would forever be a blur in Adam's mind. Racing down the stairs. The thundering footsteps of her father behind him. Margarethe screaming. Other voices shouting. And then, at the bottom of the stairs, Julia herself, lying so still, looking so fragile and so white.

"Adam?" she murmured when he reached her side.

"Oh, my God," Adam said, kneeling next to her.

"Get away from her," Julius Hammond said through gritted teeth.

"Daddy?"

"Julia, sweetheart . . ." Her father's eyes filled with tears. He shoved Adam out of the way and put his hand under her, as if he were going to lift her up.

"Julius, don't touch her. She may have injuries we can't see, and moving her could make them worse."

Adam looked up. It was Peter Bendel speaking. A house-guest for the weekend, he was not only an old family friend but also the family doctor. Moving both Julius and Adam aside, Dr. Bendel knelt beside Julia. While feeling her pulse, he said gently, "Can you move, my dear?"

"I . . ." Julia's voice seemed weaker to Adam. "I don't know." She made a visible effort, grimacing as she did. "I-I can't feel my legs."

The doctor looked up. And in his eyes, Adam saw something that caused his stomach to clench with fear. Suddenly he knew with a certainty that came from somewhere deep inside that there would be no divorce. No new life with Natalie. No anything that earlier he had anticipated with so much hope for the future.

His shoulders slumped in despair as guilt and sorrow and a desperate pity for Julia mingled with the bleakness filling his heart.

Nineteen

Natalie was jolted awake by the ringing of the bedside phone at three-thirty-five in the morning. Heart pounding, she snatched up the receiver. "Hello?"

"Natalie?"

"Adam?" For a moment, she hadn't recognized his voice. "I've been thinking about you ever since you left. Are you home now?"

"No, I—" His voice broke. "Something terrible has happened." He sounded distraught.

"What?" Alarm caused her heart to pound.

"I'm at the hospital here in Mamaroneck. Julia . . . Julia had a bad fall."

"Oh, no! Is she okay? What happened?"

"Listen, I'm at a pay phone, and I can't talk long. But I wanted you to know so you wouldn't wonder why I hadn't called you. I'll explain everything when I get back to New York."

"But what *happened*? Did you tell her about us?"

"Yes," he said wearily. "I told her. And she was so upset she ran out of the bedroom and out into the hall. When I tried to stop her from running down the steps, she lost her balance and fell. She . . . she's hurt pretty bad."

"Oh, Adam, I'm so sorry."

"Natalie . . ." His voice was ragged. "She can't move her legs."

Natalie gasped.

"Whether the paralysis is temporary or permanent, they don't know. They won't know until they can do some tests."

Dear Heaven. Julia . . . paralyzed. The implications were too terrible to contemplate.

"I've got to stay here," Adam continued.

"Yes, of course, you must," Natalie answered numbly. "Don't even think about coming back."

"Natalie . . ." His voice shook. "I love you."

"And I love you," she whispered. There was a lump in her throat so big she could hardly talk.

She managed to hold onto her composure until he'd hung up. But then she fell apart. She was shaking and crying so hard, the cats became alarmed. Isabella kept rubbing up against her and meowing, and Gabriel's ears stood at alert while he watched her warily.

Later, when her tears had finally dried up, Natalie sat dully. She couldn't stop thinking about poor Julia. And her parents. Natalie could only imagine how they must be feeling.

Oh, dear God, what have we done?

What if Julia never walked again? The thought was chilling.

This, then, was their punishment, hers and Adam's, for wanting something at the expense of someone else. If Julia was permanently paralyzed, for the rest of their lives, they would have to live with the knowledge that they were responsible for ruining Julia's life.

After calling Natalie, Adam walked slowly back to the waiting area where Julia's parents and Trudy Bendel were sitting. Julius glared at him as he approached. Adam wondered how much of the scene between him and Julia his father-in-law had heard earlier. Too much, he was afraid, if Julius's attitude now and right after the accident was any indication.

Adam sat down across from the group. Margarethe's eyes met his briefly. She didn't say anything, and Adam couldn't tell what she was thinking. Julius continued to glare at Adam. Adam wanted to say something to them, but what? *I'm sorry I caused your daughter to get hysterical and fall down the stairs and become paralyzed?* Jesus. How could this have happened? Adam had never felt more sick at heart.

What if Julia never walked again?

Just as the horrible thought formed, Dr. Bendel, accompanied by the neurosurgeon that had been called in for an emergency consultation, walked around the corner into the waiting area.

Julius immediately leapt to his feet. Adam and the two women rose more slowly. Adam's heart was filled with dread as he saw the serious expressions on the faces of both the doctors.

"Peter, how is she?" Julius demanded.

Peter Bendel sighed wearily. "I'll let Dr. Burke answer your questions, Julius. Jeff, this is Julius Hammond, Julia's father." He turned to Adam. "And this is her husband, Adam Forrester."

Adam shook hands with the doctor and tried to ignore the daggers Julius was sending his way.

Dr. Burke said, "Why don't we all sit down?"

"Is my daughter going to be okay?" Julius said sharply. He had never liked being told what to do.

"Please, Mr. Hammond, sit down."

"Julius . . ." Margarethe touched his arm.

He shook her off, but he finally sat. Dr. Burke's gaze moved to meet Adam's. "The answer is a qualified yes."

"Meaning?" Julius demanded.

"Meaning there are no life-threatening injuries."

"Oh, thank God," Margarethe said. Her eyes filled with tears.

"What about her legs?" Julius asked. "She said she couldn't feel anything."

"Yes, that's true. She has a spinal cord concussion, which is affecting her legs."

Margarethe cried out, and Julius swore. Trudy Bendel, who had moved over to sit beside Adam, touched his hand in a gesture of comfort. Adam was numb.

"But you can do something about this," Julius said, his blue eyes burning into Dr. Burke's.

"Yes, there are a number of things we can do, but first let me explain something. We believe your daughter was predisposed to this kind of traumatic spinal cord injury. There are signs that she has mild cervical canal stenosis, possibly congenital."

"Are you saying it's *our* fault this happened?" Julius exploded.

"Julius," Peter Bendel said, "no one is blaming you. Dr. Burke is just trying to give you a better understanding of Julia's condition."

Margarethe took Julius's hand. For a moment, Adam thought he was going to shove her away again, but this time he didn't.

"Is there anything you can do about this?" Adam asked.

Dr. Burke turned to Adam gratefully. "We want to keep her here for a few days so we can give her steroids to reduce swelling. Then, once she's stable, we'll send her to Rehab for physical therapy. While there, she'll either be fitted for a walker or a wheelchair, depending on her condition."

Margarethe bit her bottom lip.

"But you think she'll eventually be all right?" Adam pressed.

"We can't be certain of any—"

"Let's cut the bullshit," Julius interrupted furiously. "From now on, you will address your answers to *me*. And I expect you to give it to me straight. Is my daughter going to walk again or not?"

Dr. Burke looked at Adam.

"It's okay," Adam said. If the situation hadn't been so critical, and if he didn't feel so guilty about his part in it, he might have told Julius to take a flying leap. As it was, there was no sense in making more of a scene than Julius was already making. It would only make things harder for everyone, especially Julia's mother.

"I wish I could tell you what you want to hear, Mr. Hammond," Dr. Burke said quietly. "Unfortunately, there are no guarantees. The best I can say is the majority of patients with this type of injury do recover, most within hours or days. There are, however, a few who don't, although there's always a chance. I do have to caution you, though, that if a patient doesn't recover quickly, the chances that he or she will eventually recover are diminished."

Adam hadn't prayed in a long time, but right now he was pleading with God to let Julia be one of those people who make a full recovery. Otherwise, how would he live with himself?

"Where is she? I want to see her," Julius said.

"She wants to see her husband."

Julius jumped up. "I don't want that bastard anywhere *near* my daughter."

"Julius!" The shocked response came from Margarethe.

Both Peter Bendel and Dr. Burke had expressions of consternation on their faces as they looked first at Adam, then back to Julius.

"I don't care, Margarethe," Julius said grimly, pushing away her restraining hand. "You might not have heard what went on between him and Julia tonight, but I did! It's his fault she fell. His fault she's paralyzed!" As he talked, he shook his fist at Adam, his face getting redder and redder. "She never would have been so upset if it hadn't been for you!"

"Julius, please, can't we talk about this like two—" Adam began.

With a roar, Julius covered the distance between them in two long strides, and before Adam or any of the others could react, he had his strong hands around Adam's throat.

"I'll kill you!" he shouted. "I'll kill you!"

Adam tried to pull Julius's hands away, but his father-in-law was so enraged, he seemed to have almost super-human strength.

It took both Peter Bendel and Dr. Burke, as well as Trudy Bendel, to get him away from Adam. Margarethe was weeping.

Adam held his bruised throat and wished he was anywhere but there. He couldn't even be angry with Julius, who he knew was beside himself with worry. Who knew? If Adam were in his shoes, he might behave just as irrationally.

The two doctors were still trying to calm Julius. "Julius," Peter Bendel said, "I don't know what happened tonight, but anyone can see that Adam is just as upset as you are. He loves Julia, too, and—"

"He doesn't love Julia," Julius spat out. "That's what he was telling her tonight. Didn't you hear her crying? Begging him not to leave her?"

"Whatever passed between Julia and Adam doesn't matter right now," Dr. Bendel said, taking hold of Julius's shoulders and looking him straight in the eyes. "What matters is getting her well. Isn't that what we all want?"

Margarethe was still crying softly, and Trudy had moved over to sit beside her and had her arm around her shoulders as she tried to comfort her.

As suddenly as Julius had become inflamed, he quieted, sinking back into his chair like a deflated balloon. And then, stunning Adam, Julius put his head in his hands and began to cry.

"Are you okay?" Dr. Burke said as Peter Bendel tended to Julius.

"I'm all right." Adam's throat hurt, but he didn't think

Julius had done any real damage. "Don't worry about me."

"Come with me, then. Your wife has been asking for you ever since she got here."

A couple of minutes later, Adam stood in the open doorway of Julia's room. She lay motionless in the bed. Her right wrist was bandaged, and he could see that bruises were quickly forming on her arms and face. She didn't stir, even when he walked into the room. But once he reached her bedside, she turned her head and her eyes met his.

"Adam?" she whispered. She gave him a wan smile.

Adam would have given anything to turn the clock back. "Julia," he said softly, "how are you feeling?"

"I'm okay."

"I'm so sorry about this."

"I don't want you to feel bad. It's not your fault I fell." She tried to lift her bandaged hand and winced.

Adam reached out, placing his hand over hers. "Let's not worry about who's at fault. Let's just concentrate on getting you well. Because you *are* going to be okay. It might take awhile, but eventually you'll be just as good as new."

She smiled again. "I know that. I'm not worried. As long as I have you, Adam, as long as we're together, I'm not worried about anything."

When Adam returned to the waiting room to tell Julius and Margarethe that Julia wanted to see them now, Julius had regained his normal self-control.

"You go on in," he said to his wife. "I'll be there in a few minutes."

"You're not coming with me?" Margarethe said in disbelief.

"I want to talk to Adam first." Inclining his head toward the other end of the hall, Julius strode off. Adam followed reluctantly. He hoped there wouldn't be another scene.

Once they were out of earshot of Trudy and Peter Bendel, Julius, face hard, said, "Now listen, you little shit. My wife might be in denial and still think you're a great guy, but I know better. I heard most of what you said to Julia. I know you've got yourself some other fancy piece and that you told Julia you wanted a divorce."

"Look, Julius, please calm—"

"Here's the way it's going to be," Julius continued through gritted teeth as if Adam hadn't spoken at all. "If Julia tells me she never wants to see you again, you can go, and the faster the better. But if she still wants you, you're not going anywhere, do you hear me?"

Adam reminded himself of the enormous strain his father-in-law was under and fought to keep his tone as free of anger as possible. "You say you want straight talk, Julius. All right. I can appreciate how upset you are, and I can also understand that all you care about is protecting your daughter. That's why I'm going to ignore your insults and your threats. *Not* because I'm afraid of you. But let's get one thing straight. Whatever happens to our marriage in the future is between Julia and me and no one else. Understood?"

Julius didn't answer him, just gave him another scathing look, then whipped around and stalked off down the hall.

Adam watched him go with a heavy heart. Despite his tough talk to his father-in-law, he felt sick inside. What would happen to them all? he wondered. Would any of them ever be happy again?

Somehow Natalie managed to get through Sunday. But by ten o'clock that night, when she still hadn't heard back from Adam, she was a wreck.

At midnight, just when she'd given up hope of hearing from him, the outside buzzer rang. Racing to the intercom, she said, "Yes?"

"Natalie? It's me. Adam."

"Adam!" She pressed the release for the door lock. Five minutes later, he was at the door of her apartment. He looked awful. Unshaven and exhausted, with red-rimmed eyes and clothes that looked as if he'd slept in them. Tears brimming, she opened her arms.

Wordlessly, he held her.

They stood, arms wrapped around each other, for long minutes. Natalie could feel the tremors in his body, and she knew he was near the end of his rope. Through her tears, she murmured, "It's okay, Adam. I'm here, and I love you."

With a deep shudder, he said, "How can it be okay? Julia may never walk again, and even though I've been trying to tell myself it's not my fault, when it comes right down to it, it is."

"Come inside." They were still standing in the open doorway. She freed herself from his arms and, taking his hand, led him into the apartment and over to the sofa. Then she shut and locked the door.

Adam put his head back and closed his eyes. She went over to him and sat down. Taking his hand in hers, she said softly, "I've been thinking about you and Julia ever since you called last night. At first, I was like you, thinking what happened was our fault. But you know what, Adam? I've changed my mind. What happened wasn't your fault or my fault or anyone's fault. It was an accident."

"Everyone blames me," he said bleakly. "Julius hates me."

"Julius is Julia's father. He's upset."

Adam turned his head to look at her. "Natalie, you don't seem to understand. I can't leave Julia now."

"I know. I've known that ever since you told me what happened." She raised his hand to her lips and held it there for a long moment. When she spoke again, her voice was strong. "If you were the kind of man who could walk out on her now, you wouldn't be the kind of man I could love."

Adam grimaced. "Don't try to make me feel better."

"I didn't say that to make you feel better. I really mean it."

He shook his head, turning away from her. "I can't believe I'm doing this to you again."

Taking his face in her hands, Natalie made him look at her. "Adam, listen to me. What happened to Julia doesn't change the way I feel about you. I know you have to stay with her, but that's okay. It doesn't matter that we can't marry." She took a deep breath. She hadn't intended to say this, but now that she was, she knew it was the right thing to do. "I'll always be here for you, my love. Maybe we won't have the kind of life we'd hoped for, but we can still be together."

Gradually, as the import of her words penetrated, the bleakness in his eyes faded. Yet still he held back. "I can't ask you to do this."

"You're not asking me," she said fiercely. "Don't you know that I will only have half a life without you?"

"But I can never give you my name. Never give you a home. All the things you deserve."

"A name is just a name. And home is anywhere you are," she whispered.

He searched her eyes. "Are you sure?"

Remembering how she'd asked him this same question only days ago, she gave him the same answer. "I've never been more sure of anything in my life."

And then she pulled his head down and tried to show him with her kiss how much she loved him and always would.

Part Three

Twenty

New York City, New York
April 1995 to December 1997

For the past two weeks, New York City had been experiencing glorious weather: balmy breezes, blue skies, lots of sunshine, and temperatures in the midseventies.

Central Park was filled with people enjoying the interlude between the harshness of winter and the enervating heat of summer. Mothers and nannies pushing strollers. Kids on Rollerblades. Lovers strolling hand in hand. Old men sitting on benches and soaking up the sunshine. The twenty- and thirty-somethings jogging around the reservoir. Parents sitting on blankets while their kids tossed a Frisbee to the family dog. Young boys bopping to music from their Walkmans. Chic young professionals in suits taking a break from stuffy offices. It seemed as if all New Yorkers wanted to be outside as much as possible.

Natalie and Adam were no exception. They had fallen into the habit of meeting in the park whenever possible. Even if they were unable to be together any other time during the week, they had a standing date on Saturday afternoons. He would work in the office until about two, then he'd walk over to meet her. Their favorite spot was a bench near the lake and the boathouse.

Sometimes she would bring a lunch for them to share. Other times, they would just buy hot dogs and soft drinks from one of the vendors. Today, the last Saturday of the month, Natalie had brought hard-salami sandwiches on crusty rolls, sliced tomatoes, two fat nectarines, brownies that she'd made earlier in the week, and two bottles of water.

She sighed with pleasure as she watched the boaters. The water sparkled enticingly under the afternoon sun. Natalie wished she'd worn shorts instead of jeans. Maybe she could have gotten a little sun on her legs, which were still winter white.

A teenage couple had spread a blanket over the grass nearby and, oblivious to the people around them, were necking. Natalie couldn't suppress a twinge of envy as she watched them. How wonderful to be so young and so free, so unafraid to show your feelings. Although she was only thirty-six years old, hardly decrepit, sometimes Natalie felt ancient, weighted down by the life choices she'd made.

Mostly, she didn't regret those choices. But there were times—times that came more often lately—when she couldn't shake the feeling that life was passing her by. She hated feeling this way. She had always been an optimistic, upbeat person: someone whose cup was half full instead of half empty, someone who looked forward to each day and the possibilities that existed. Even after Adam had left her to marry Julia, she had managed to retain that positive outlook once she got over the hurt and pain of their parting.

But since Julia's accident, no matter how Natalie tried to stay upbeat, she had periodic attacks of depression. She tried never to reveal these episodes to Adam. His life with Julia was difficult enough without having to worry about or feel responsible for Natalie's state of mind.

The trouble was, she hadn't known how hard it was going to be to exist on the periphery of Adam's life. To get the leavings. To never be able to talk about him or go places with him. To never be able to introduce him to her family.

To never have his child.

And there was the crux of the problem. Lately, every time Natalie saw a baby, she felt this enormous yearning. It was hormonal, no doubt of it, but knowing that made no difference. The fact was, she was rapidly moving beyond the optimal baby-bearing age. In four years she would be forty. Every one of her sisters—even Carol, who had had such trouble conceiving—already had at least one child. And Grace, who had always declared she was never going to marry, let alone have "one of those icky-sticky rug rats," was a mother.

Natalie smiled, thinking how goofy Grace was over Sarah and Shawn, her year-old twin girls. And Rick, her husband. The last time Natalie had been home to visit, it had hurt her to see their little family, and even Grace's complaining about lack of money and never having a moment to breathe let alone sleep didn't disguise the obvious fact that she wouldn't have it any other way.

Natalie sighed again. Yes, she would trade her life for Grace's in a heartbeat, no debate necessary. She looked at the kids on the blanket again. She wished them well. Maybe they'd be some of the lucky ones, and their hopes and dreams would be realized.

Just then, she saw Adam approaching. As always, the sight of him lifted her spirits, and much of the sadness she'd felt moments earlier faded. She smiled as she watched him. Since Julia's accident three years ago, Adam no longer met with clients on Saturdays, so he had taken to wearing casual clothes to the office. Today, he was dressed in khaki pants, a dark brown knit shirt, and loafers. His step looked springier than usual, and as he got closer, Natalie saw he was smiling in that way he had when he had something good to tell her.

He plopped down on the bench beside her, put his arm around her shoulders, and gave her a quick kiss. Then he sat back and grinned.

"You look like the cat that ate the canary," she said.

"Do I?" He chuckled.

Natalie couldn't help smiling herself. "Yes."

"Why is that, do you think?"

She gave him a playful smack on the hand. "Come on. Don't tease me. What's going on?"

"Nothing much. I've just got a business trip to Montreal on Tuesday, and I'm really looking forward to it."

"Oh." For a moment, she felt disappointed that he was so happy about leaving her.

His eyes twinkled. "I want you to come with me."

"Come with you! How can I do that?"

"Easy. Monday morning, tell your boss you have a chance to go to Montreal with a friend, all expenses paid, and you want to take four days' vacation."

Her heart leapt in excitement. They had never gone anywhere together for longer than overnight, and the thought of four whole days alone with Adam was tantalizing. No snatching a few hours here and there. Being able to sleep together in the same bed the entire night. Eating meals together. Seeing a beautiful city together. And she did have the vacation time. In fact, she had more than three weeks accrued right now.

"Oh, Adam, I'd love to go." She knew she was grinning like a fool. "But—"

"But what?"

"What about Julia?"

Adam rolled his eyes. "Dammit, Natalie, you worry about Julia more than her mother does! Julia will be fine. I'll send her to Mamaroneck if she doesn't want to stay in the city while I'm gone, but hell, it's not like she's alone. She's got Olga *and* Alma with her."

Natalie felt bad that she'd upset him with her question, but even though three years had gone by since Julia's accident, Natalie still couldn't help feeling guilty about her role in the whole mess.

"I'm doing the best I can," he continued. "I give Julia everything I have to give her, but once in a while, I need something for myself."

"I know you do. I'm sorry. I shouldn't have brought up her name."

He sighed. "It's okay. I'm not mad at you." He took her hand and raised it to his lips. "I love you, Natalie. And being with you the little bit of time we manage to have together is what keeps me sane. It's what enables me to stay with Julia. So you're not taking anything away from her. If anything, you're helping her."

Natalie nodded mutely.

"Now come on," he said, "smile. Let's be happy today. Let's go rent a boat and talk about the trip to Montreal."

As they walked hand in hand to the boat rental booth, Natalie told herself Adam was right. Today she would not think about the past or the future. She would not think about the things she didn't have and never would have. She would simply seize the moment and enjoy this beautiful afternoon with the man she loved.

"But why can't you send Phil?" Julia said with that whine in her voice that had become de rigueur lately.

"Because I speak French, and Phil doesn't. Because I've built up a rapport with Pierre Broussard, and Phil hasn't." Adam spoke patiently. "It's not for long, Julia. I'm only going to be gone four days. And Alma and Olga are both here. Plus your parents are just a phone call away. In fact," he added, "I'll bet your mother would love to come and stay with you unless you'd rather go to Mamaroneck?"

"I don't want to go anywhere," she said stubbornly. "And *you're* the one I want, not my mother or Alma or

Olga." As happened so often, her eyes filled with tears.

Adam gritted his teeth. There was a time her tears had never failed to move him, because he had felt so guilty and so sorry for her, but she cried so often—any time she wanted to get her way, in fact—that her tears no longer generated sympathy. Sometimes he could hardly remember the sweet, understanding person she had been when they'd first married. And yet, how could he blame her for changing? Her life was so different now, so limited. If he'd been in her shoes, he'd have lost his mind by now. So when he answered, he answered gently.

"Julia, I can't be here twenty-four hours a day." He didn't add *I wish I could* because he lied to her enough as it was. He would not pretend to feelings he didn't have.

"All right," she said in an abrupt about-face, "if you have to go, fine. Take me with you."

"What?"

"I said, take me with you." Now she sounded mutinous. The tears had disappeared. In their place was a steely determination.

Telling himself she couldn't possibly know he wasn't going to Montreal alone, that this unprecedented request had nothing to do with any suspicion on her part but was only another manifestation of her possessiveness, he forced himself to answer calmly. "Taking you with me is impossible, and you know it."

"Why is it impossible for me to go with you? Other men take their wives on business trips."

"Julia, come on, be reasonable. First of all, what would you do with yourself during the day while I was at Broussard and Pinot? Secondly, you couldn't be left on your own. Olga would have to come with us. No. It's impossible, I can't take you with me."

Now she did start to cry, but Adam turned away. Even though he pitied her and tried to give her what she needed, he was so tired of her constant demands. So tired of the ways in which she manipulated him, whether it was unintentional or not. So tired of feeling guilty every time he looked at her. But guilt or not, there was no way he was giving up this trip with Natalie. He needed it. He needed it desperately. He had tried not to let on to Natalie, but lately he had become more and more disheartened. It had been over three years since Julia's accident, and she was no closer to walking than she'd ever been. And he knew that with each day that passed, the chances of her recovery became less and less.

Olga, the live-in physical therapist, worked with Julia every day. And even she had confessed to Adam just the other day that she was stymied by Julia's lack of progress.

"When I first began to work with her," she'd said in her heavily accented English, "I thought she would recover long ago, Mr. Forrester. I don't know why she hasn't. The doctor, he says there's not a physical reason that she still can't walk."

Ever since, Adam had been thinking about Olga's statement. Was it possible Julia didn't want to walk again? Maybe, on some level, she was afraid that if she got well, he would leave her the way he'd wanted to before her accident, so she was subconsciously resisting a recovery.

They never talked about the scene that had precipitated her fall. She had never alluded to his request for a divorce. It was as if that scene had never taken place, as if her fall had simply been an accident that could have happened at any time. She had chosen to believe he had never wanted to leave her and, because it would serve no purpose except to make her even more miserable, he went along with her fantasy rather than try to force her to acknowledge reality.

Turning, he studied Julia thoughtfully. She had stopped crying and had wheeled herself over to her dressing table where she was applying cold cream to her face. Their eyes met in the mirror.

"I'm sorry," she said. "I know I'm a burden to you. I know you're sick of me."

"Julia . . ."

"Oh, you don't have to pretend. What man *wouldn't* be sick of a wife who can't do anything?" To emphasize her point, she struggled to raise herself from her chair. In the process, she fell forward, and dozens of perfume bottles and jars and tubes of lipstick clattered onto the glass top. One of the bottles of perfume popped open.

Adam leaped toward his wife, grabbing her before she slid to the floor. The air reeked from the spilled scent, which had started trickling onto the carpet. "Jesus Christ," he swore softly. "What are you trying to do, Julia?"

Now she was openly weeping. She wrapped her arms around him and sobbed into his neck. "I'm so *sick* of being in this chair. So sick of it!"

All of Adam's earlier irritation disappeared, to be replaced by the horrible mantle of guilt that never left him for long. No matter what anyone said in their attempts to make him feel better, he knew he alone was responsible for Julia's condition.

"I know, I know," he said soothingly.

"Oh, Adam . . ." She held on tighter. "I love you so. Thank you for being so good to me. I know I can be unreasonable at times, but it's just because I'm so frustrated. I want so much to be a good wife to you."

"I know."

She kissed his neck. "Adam, oh, Adam. I love you. You love me, too, don't you?"

"Yes," he said wearily. "I love you, too." And he did. Just not the way she loved him.

His heart was heavy as she finally calmed down and he lowered her back into her chair.

Suddenly, with a certainty that settled into his gut like a truckload of stones, he knew he would never be free of her. For better or worse, they were bound together until one of them died.

• • •

Natalie told herself not to get too excited about the trip to Montreal until she knew for sure that Jack would let her go on such short notice. Monday morning, as soon as she was sure he was in, she walked down the hall to his office. The door was open, a good sign. When he didn't want to be disturbed, he closed the door.

She tapped on the doorframe. "Jack?"

He looked up and smiled. "Hey, Natalie, come on in."

She liked Jack. He was smart and knew the publishing business backward and forward. He was also a great boss: fair and not afraid to delegate.

"What's up?" he said, waving her to a chair.

"Jack, I know this is short notice, but I want to take the rest of the week as vacation."

He raised his eyebrows.

"I have this chance to go to Montreal, and I'd really like to go."

He nodded. "How's your workload?"

"Under control."

"No fires to put out?"

"Not that I'm aware of."

He shrugged. "Then go."

She managed to say, "Thank you, Jack," decorously, even though she felt like doing a happy dance.

"Don't mention it."

She could hardly wait to call Adam. Normally, she didn't call him at his office. He felt, and she agreed, that were she to call too often, Mary Beth would recognize her voice and become suspicious. Neither she nor Adam wanted that. It was bad enough that their relationship had to be clandestine; it would be intolerable if people began gossiping about them. Natalie knew she couldn't stand that. So Adam normally called her. Weekdays he called twice a day, once first thing in the morning, just to say hello, then again late in the afternoon. If anyone but Natalie answered her private line—which occasionally happened if she were in a meeting or away from her desk and her assistant happened to hear the phone—Adam simply said, "Sorry, wrong number."

On weekends, he called her at home, either from his office or from his private line, which was downstairs in his study. At first, Natalie had worried about him calling her from his home, but he had assured her there was no chance Julia would ever overhear them. "She spends most of her time upstairs with Olga. And when she *does* come downstairs, I hear the elevator." The elevator had been installed in their home shortly after Julia's accident.

But today was an exception, so Natalie dialed Adam's office. When his secretary asked who was calling, Natalie said, "Sandra, from Bloomingdale's," as she and Adam had prearranged.

"Well?" he said when they were connected.

"I can go."

"That's great." She could hear the smile in his voice. "I'll pick you up at seven. Our flight leaves Kennedy at nine."

The following morning, Natalie, butterflies of anticipation in her stomach, was ready by six-thirty, but she waited until ten minutes to seven before going down to the lobby.

"So you're off, eh?" said Jim, who was posting a notice on the bulletin board.

Natalie smiled. "Yes."

"And you're comin' back on Saturday?"

"Saturday morning."

Just then, Adam's car pulled up to the curb. Natalie waved and reached for her suitcase.

"I see your young man is here," Jim said. He walked to the door and opened it for her.

Five minutes later, her suitcase safely stowed in the trunk of Adam's BMW, Natalie and Adam, smiling at one another, were on their way.

Twenty-one

"I wish we could stay here forever." Natalie was standing at the window of the Ritz Carlton Hotel on Rue Sherbrooke, looking out at the wonderful view. Montreal was a charming and beautiful city, green and hilly, filled with parks and museums and lovely old buildings like Notre Dame Cathedral.

She loved being there. Loved the food, the quaintness of the old town, walking along the river, the sounds of French spoken everywhere, the hills and the flowers and the chic, cosmopolitan people. But mostly she loved how far it was from New York and real life.

The luxurious hotel that had been their home for the past three days was ideally situated. On the fringes of Westmont, the most exclusive and beautiful section of the city, it was only a few blocks from McGill University in one direction, the Museum of Fine Arts in the other, and was surrounded by a shopper's mecca including dozens of interesting restaurants within walking distance.

In fact, she and Adam had just returned to the hotel after a delicious dinner at a wonderful Thai restaurant, followed by a long walk.

But soon this idyllic interlude would be over, for to-morrow they had to go home.

"Come here," Adam said, patting the bed beside him.

"Why?" Natalie teased. "So you can have your way with me again?"

"That, too."

"Too? What else did you have in mind?" She walked over to the bed and sat beside him.

"This." Reaching into his pocket, he withdrew a small blue box that Natalie recognized as having come from Tiffany's.

"Adam!" She gave him a startled look. "What's this?"

He smiled at her. "Open it."

Her heart beat faster as she lifted a velvet ring box from the outer container. Slowly, she snapped open the lid. Then she gasped. Inside, tucked into the satin lining, lay the most beautiful ring she had ever seen: a magnificent round aquamarine surrounded by tiny diamonds.

"Since I can't give you a wedding ring," Adam said gruffly, "I had to settle for your birthstone." Lifting the ring out of the box, he slipped it onto her finger.

Natalie couldn't speak. Her hands were trembling. The ring was breathtaking. She stared at it, stunned by its magnificence. She couldn't imagine what it had cost. "Oh, Adam, it's so beautiful," she finally said.

"Not as beautiful as you are," he said softly. Taking her face in his hands, he kissed her. "I love you so much. I don't think I could have made it through these last few years without you."

"But Adam, I love you, too. And I've wanted to be with you."

"I know, but I also know it's been hard on you. You've sacrificed a lot, and I wanted to do something to try to make up for a little of that."

"I-I understand, but I don't want *things*. I especially don't want you to feel you have to buy me expensive jewelry."

"That's not why I did it. I needed to give you something lasting. Something that when you look at it, you'll think of me and you'll know how much I love you. How much I'll always love you."

Natalie's lips trembled, and her eyes filled with tears.

"Ah, Nat, don't cry."

"I'm sorry. It's just that sometimes I—" She stopped. What was the point of putting the sadness that hit her so often and so unexpectedly into words? There was nothing to be done about their situation. She knew that. Saying what she felt would only make Adam feel bad.

"I know." He pulled her close, tucking her head under his chin. "I know."

This time when he kissed her, she wound her arms tightly around him and kissed him back with all the passion and longing and love she had to keep hidden so much of the time. This was their last night here. She wanted to make the most of it.

"I've decided. I want you to fire Olga."

Adam put his book down and looked at his wife. "All right, let's talk about this. What brought this on, anyway? Why do you want to get rid of Olga?"

"I don't like her," Julia said. She set her own book aside.

Adam told himself to go carefully. Julia could be stubborn about some things, and this seemed to be one of them. For days now, ever since he'd returned from Montreal, she'd been relentlessly talking about firing Olga.

"I don't see why I have to have a live-in, anyway. I think it makes more sense to have a therapist come in for a few hours a day."

"Julia, you know that's impossible. How would you get dressed? How would you bathe? How would you get in and out of your chair?" Remembering the scene before he'd left for Montreal, he gentled his voice. "You see what happened when you tried to get up last week."

"I was upset then."

"Julia . . ."

"Well, I *was*."

Sighing, he rubbed his forehead. He could feel a headache coming on.

"Adam, please listen to me. Alma's here. She could do those things for me."

"Alma is getting up in years, and she's not a nurse. She's a housekeeper."

"Olga's not a nurse, either," Julia said.

"You know what I mean."

"Yes, darling, I do, but I just wish you could see this from my point of view. I'm tired of not having any privacy. And I don't need a twenty-four-hour warden."

"Aren't you exaggerating?"

"No, I'm not. You don't know what it's like . . . having someone constantly watching you, constantly making you do things you don't want to do. She's like a Nazi drill sergeant! I despise her."

"Maybe you need a drill sergeant if you're ever going to regain the use of your legs," he said as mildly as he could manage considering how obstinate she was being. "Don't you want to walk again?"

"Of course I want to walk again! How can you even ask such a question?" The tears that came so easily now filled her eyes. "But maybe . . ." She bit her bottom lip. "Maybe we should face facts, Adam. Maybe I'll never walk again." This last was said piteously.

"Don't say things like that, Julia."

"Why not? If they're true." She wheeled her chair closer to him and reached for his hand. "I know you don't want to talk about this, Adam. I know you feel guilty because I'm in this chair, but I don't blame you. I really don't." She gave him a soft smile. "I never have, and I never will."

Christ, she sure knew how to twist the knife. "Whether I'm at fault or not isn't the issue. I don't think getting rid of Olga is in your best interest."

The tears overflowed, rolling down her cheeks. "Please,

Adam. I can't stand her. You don't know what it's like to be trapped here all day with someone you can't stand."

Fingers of pain stabbed at his temples. "You're right, I don't know what it's like. But I do know what it'll be like if you don't have someone to help you do the things you can't do on your own. You have to have someone here full time. If you don't want it to be Olga, fine. We'll start looking for someone new, someone you *can* like, but until we find that person, Olga is staying. Unless, of course, you want to go and stay with your parents in the meantime." He knew she would not want that. Since the accident, she never wanted to leave him, not even for a weekend.

"I'm not going to my parents' house," she said mutinously. She swiped at her tears. "And I don't want someone full time. Why can't I just get someone to stay during the day while you're at work? *You* can help me do the things I can't do by myself in the evenings and on the weekends, can't you?"

Unspoken but implied by her tone was the suggestion that it was the least he could do for her. She could say she didn't blame him for what had happened to her a million times, but Adam knew down deep she *did* blame him, and at moments like these, her feelings were evident. "Sometimes I have to work in the evenings and on the weekends. You know that."

"You don't *have* to. You want to."

Adam sighed. They were getting nowhere. He was going to have to be firm. "Julia, I am not going to debate this. I can't always be here, and you need someone. If it's not going to be Olga, we'll have to hire someone else."

For a long moment, he thought she was going to continue arguing with him. Finally she capitulated, saying, "Oh, all *right*! I'll call Dr. Swann's office in the morning and see if they can recommend someone. But I do not want another therapist. I want a nurse or a nurse's aide, someone who will think about my comfort. And she doesn't have to live in. She can go home at night."

"What about when I have to travel?"

"Then she can stay the night. But when you're here, I don't want anyone else around except Alma."

Adam nodded. He was too tired to argue further. "All right. See if you can set up the interviews for Monday. I'll take the afternoon off and be here to talk with them, too."

Later, after Julia had gone up to bed, Adam remained in the library where they'd spent the evening and poured himself a snifter of brandy.

He wondered what had *really* brought on this sudden dislike of Olga. Was it the fact Olga was frustrated by Julia's lack of progress and had talked to Adam about it?

At times like these, he wished he was still on good terms with Julius. He'd have liked to discuss Julia's health and her attitude toward it with his father-in-law. But Julius hated him, and Adam knew it. Sometimes Adam was sure Julius knew he was still seeing Natalie. Whether he did or not, there was no question of confiding in Julia's father.

Adam didn't blame his father-in-law for the way he felt. In his shoes, he would feel the same, he was sure. Yet Julius didn't have all the facts. Adam was sure the older man had no idea Adam had never wanted to marry Julia in the first place.

Yet what difference would it make if he did know? Julia was Julius's beloved daughter. He would not look kindly on the information that Adam had never loved Julia the way he should have. It certainly wouldn't change his view that Adam had ruined Julia's life.

Adam sipped at his brandy, wondering as he had so often over the past three years, what he could have done differently.

He sighed deeply. What was the use of thinking about what-ifs? Better to put his energies toward helping his wife cope and praying the woman he loved would not get sick of him and his situation and decide she wanted something more out of her life.

Because if Natalie left him, he wasn't sure he could keep going.

"You are firing me?" Olga said in disbelief.

"I'm sorry, Olga. You've done a good job here, and I'll give you a good reference," Adam said.

"I don't understand. If I do such good job, why you are doing this?" When Olga was upset, her English deteriorated and her German accent became more pronounced.

Adam hesitated. "Because Mrs. Forrester wants a change."

Olga pressed her lips together. "Mrs. Forrester, she doesn't want to get well."

"You have to understand how frustrating her condition is. I think she thinks if she has someone different, maybe she'll get better faster."

"No, Mr. Forrester," Olga said, shaking her head. "You are wrong. I feel sorry for you. You are nice man. But your wife, she is not nice woman."

After she was gone, Adam hoped he'd done the right thing in acceding to Julia's obstinate stance where Olga was concerned.

Penny, the practical nurse they had hired to take Olga's place, was scheduled to arrive at two o'clock. Julia had seemed to like her immediately, and even Adam had to admit, Penny seemed very capable and had come to them with glowing references. She was also much milder-mannered and deferential to Julia than Olga had been, and Adam knew that, as far as Julia was concerned, that deference had been the major selling point in her favor.

He decided he would not worry about this. He would keep close watch on the situation, and if Penny didn't work out, if he thought she couldn't handle Julia, he would find yet another therapist.

Because no matter what Julia subconsciously felt, she was going to continue with her therapy. She might have given up hope of ever walking again, but Adam never would.

Twenty-two

"Do you think it's wise to have let her talk you into firing Olga?" Natalie leaned back in her chair and stretched. It was a few minutes before five o'clock, and she and Adam were talking on the phone as they did most afternoons.

"I don't know. Tell you the truth, I was just tired of fighting her on the subject."

He sounded tired, period, Natalie thought. Suddenly she really wanted to see him. "Adam."

"What?"

"Do you think we could have dinner together tonight?"

"I was just going to suggest the same thing."

Natalie smiled. "When and where do you want to meet?"

"Outside your building. I'll be there in, say, thirty minutes?"

The smile got bigger. "It's a date."

Mary Beth Mahoney looked at the pretty Wedgwood clock on her desk. It had been a gift from Adam, purchased several years ago on a trip to England. It was almost five o'clock. She eyed Adam's closed door. She knew he was on the phone. His private line was lighted. She also had a pretty good idea who he was talking to, even though she didn't know the woman's name.

Mary Beth wanted to think less of her boss. After all, he was committing a mortal sin. He was an adulterer, having an affair with another woman while his wife was stuck at home in a wheelchair. But no matter how many times she told herself what he was doing was horribly wrong, she just couldn't make herself believe it.

Julia Forrester was a fake, Mary Beth thought. Oh, she put on a sweety-sweety act, but Mary Beth didn't buy it for a minute. Maybe Julia wasn't snotty like Matt Crowley's wife, but she still thought she was better than Mary Beth and people like her who weren't born with silver spoons in their mouths.

And Adam was so nice! Mary Beth adored her boss. She would have done anything for him. In fact, if she wasn't married already and crazy about her Patrick, she might have been interested in warming his bed herself. She always felt guilty when she had these thoughts, as if Father Flynn knew exactly what she'd been thinking.

Mary Beth would never forget how wonderful Adam had been to her mother when she was so sick and her insurance company had refused to let her have a bone marrow transplant. Adam had taken on her mother's case, free of charge, and fought that company until they'd finally given in. Not only that, he'd paid her mother's deductible out of his own pocket.

And that wasn't all he'd done over the years that had won her respect and total devotion. He didn't talk about his donations to Covenant House or make a big deal about the money he gave to homeless shelters and the women's crisis center over on Twenty-ninth Street, but Mary Beth knew about them. He was a wonderful man. He cared about everyone, not just people with the right pedigree.

She just felt so bad for him. She had known he was unhappy for a long time, way before his wife had had her accident. In fact, Mary Beth had wondered why he didn't divorce Julia. After all, he wasn't a Catholic. And they didn't have any kids.

And then, right before Julia had her accident, he'd seemed like a different person. He whistled, he smiled, he even walked lighter. Mary Beth had immediately known he'd met someone, and she'd been so glad for him. And then the unthinkable had happened.

And now . . .

Mary Beth wondered if the woman in his life was the same one who had put that sparkle in his eyes in the months before Julia's fall. It didn't really matter, though. Whoever she was, Mary Beth was glad she existed. Adam deserved some happiness, and if this unknown woman could give it to him, good for her.

Mary Beth was also glad no one else here at the firm seemed to suspect what she suspected. She knew if they did, she would have heard about it, for nothing was sacred at Hammond, Crowley. The other employees weren't like she was. Her lip was zipped. She would never, not in a million years, spread gossip about Adam.

Just then, his door opened. He had put his suit jacket on and was carrying his briefcase. "You still here?" he said, giving her a smile. "It's after five."

Mary Beth smiled back. "I was waiting for you."

"Well, I'm leaving now. Taking a potential client to dinner."

A potential client wouldn't have put that look of anticipation on his face. "All right. See you in the morning."

"Now don't you stay late. There's nothing that can't wait until tomorrow."

"I won't. I just want to do this last letter, then I'll be off."

"Good night, then, Mary Beth."

"Good night, Mr. Forrester."

Once Adam was gone, Mary Beth opened a new document. She loved her computer and smiled every time she remembered how she'd fought against getting one. For years, she'd done all her typing on an IBM Selectric type-writer, and she had vowed she was never giving it up. But Adam had gently insisted, and it wasn't long before she had to admit the other secretaries had been right all along. God, her work was so much easier now.

She finished the letter, printed it, and was in the middle of reading it to see if she wanted to make any changes when Adam's private line rang.

"Mr. Forrester's office," she said briskly.

"Mary Beth, this is Mrs. Forrester. It's urgent that I speak with Mr. Forrester immediately."

Julia sounded panicked, and Mary Beth wondered if something was seriously wrong. "I'm sorry, Mrs. Forrester. He left a few minutes ago. He was taking a potential client to dinner. Can I help you?"

"Oh, dear. I don't suppose you have any idea where he might be? What restaurant he might be going to?" She sounded upset.

"No, I'm sorry, I don't. Is . . . is something the matter?"

"Yes. My . . . my parents have been in an accident." Now her voice trembled. "It was very serious. I-I don't know if they're going to make it."

"Oh, no. Oh, I'm so sorry." Even though Julia Forrester wasn't one of Mary Beth's favorite people, she couldn't help feeling bad for her in these circumstances. "Let me call around and see if I can find him for you."

"Thank you."

Mary Beth called every restaurant she could think of, with no luck. Finally, she had no choice but to call Julia back and tell her she hadn't been able to find Adam.

"Thank you, anyway." Julia seemed much calmer now. "If you should happen to hear from him, tell him I'm going to Mamaroneck, to the hospital. I've hired a limo to take me, and my nurse is going with me. He can come later. I'll leave a note for him."

Mary Beth sat thoughtfully after the connection was broken. Then she got up and went into Adam's office.

Picking up his phone, she hit the Redial button. It rang twice and then a soft voice said, "Natalie Ferrenzo."

Mary Beth's heart beat faster as she said nervously, "Um, Miss Ferrenzo, we've never met, but I'm Mary Beth Mahoney, Adam Forrester's secretary."

For a few moments, there was only silence on the line. Then, on a sudden intake of breath, Natalie Ferrenzo said, "Oh, God, nothing's happened to Adam, has it?"

"No, no, nothing like that," Mary Beth said. "It's just that his . . . his wife called a few minutes ago, and I really need to get a message to him. I was hoping you knew where he might be."

Again there was a brief moment of silence. "How did you know my number?" Natalie finally said.

"I didn't. I just hit the Redial button on Mr. Forrester's phone."

"Oh."

"Miss Ferrenzo, I promise you, no one here knows about you except me, and until a few minutes ago, I didn't know your name. And I would never have called you if it wasn't really important." Because, for some reason, Mary Beth felt it would be wrong to tell her Julia's private business, she didn't explain further.

"All right. I, um, I'm supposed to meet Adam in about ten minutes. I'll tell him to call you."

"Okay. Thanks."

Mary Beth sat at her desk until the call came, almost exactly ten minutes later. "I'm so sorry, Mr. Forrester," she said when he was on the line. She explained about Julia's call.

"Thank you, Mary Beth. I'll go right home. I'll call you from Mamaroneck in the morning. And would you mind calling Julia and telling her I'm on my way?"

After they'd hung up, Mary Beth made the phone call. She was very glad when Alma, their housekeeper, answered the phone, because if Julia had asked her how she'd managed to find Adam, Mary Beth wasn't sure what she would have said. It was one thing to feel sympathy for Adam; it was quite another to lie for him.

Suddenly Mary Beth couldn't wait to get home to Patrick and her uncomplicated, totally ordinary life.

Twenty-three

"Natalie?"

"Brooke! Hi! How *are* you? It's been ages." *It's Brooke*, Natalie mouthed at Adam, who was standing at the stove in her tiny kitchen dropping angel hair pasta into a pot of boiling water.

He smiled.

"We're all doing fine," Brooke answered. "But I didn't call to chat, because I can tell you everything when I see you. Sam and I are coming to New York."

"You *are*? When?" In all the years Natalie had lived there, neither Brooke nor Sam had ever visited.

"Next week."

"Next week! For how long?"

"We'll probably be there a week, maybe longer. It all depends on how long Sam's firm needs him." Sam was an entertainment lawyer whose firm was headquartered in Los Angeles. Six months ago, they had opened an office in New York.

"That's wonderful. I can't wait to see you. Are you bringing the kids?" Brooke and Sam had two children— a boy, ten, and a girl, eight.

"Not a chance. Sam's mother is coming out to stay with them while we're gone. We need some time alone."

"I hear you," Natalie said. She'd heard this refrain from her sisters often enough.

"Is there any chance you can take a day or two off while I'm there?" Brooke asked eagerly.

"I'm sure I can." Her pleasure over the upcoming visit was tempered by the fact that no matter how much she would enjoy seeing Brooke, the visit probably meant she would not be able to spend time with Adam while they were in town. Even though Adam and Sam had remained in touch through the years and Adam still considered Sam a good friend, and Natalie still thought of Brooke as her best friend, neither Sam nor Brooke knew about Natalie and Adam's involvement. And that was the way Natalie intended to keep it.

The only person who did know was Adam's secretary, and that was bad enough, Natalie thought, even though Adam had assured her Mary Beth would never tell anyone.

"As soon as I know which hotel we'll be in, I'll let you know," Brooke was saying. "Oh, Nat, I can hardly wait. It'll be just like old times."

"I wish I could put you up in my apartment, but it's so small," Natalie apologized. "Unless you wouldn't mind sleeping on the sofa. It does pull out to make a bed. And it's pretty comfortable."

"No, don't worry about it. The firm is paying for the hotel. Anyway, I'm just glad I'm getting the chance to see you. We're gonna have a great time!"

"I'm glad, too." And Natalie was. But she couldn't help wishing she and Adam could do things with Brooke and Sam like any normal couple.

"I haven't been to New York since the summer before my senior year in high school."

"Is there anything special you want to do? Should I try to get some show tickets? I haven't seen *Chicago* yet, and I'm dying to." When she said this, she didn't look at Adam, because she knew if she did, he would think her remark was a criticism of him and all the things they never were able to do together.

"Ooh, I'd *love* to see *Chicago*. Is Bebe Neuwirth still in it?"

"I don't know. I'll check. I know Marilu Henner was supposed to join the cast, but I'm not sure if she's there now or not."

"Oh, it doesn't matter. Get tickets for whatever you can, day or night."

"For Sam, too?"

"Sam may be tied up at night, so we won't worry about him."

"Okay. Great."

"I can't wait, Nat."

"Me, either."

As she hung up the phone, Natalie wondered if Brooke and Sam would be invited to Adam's home. It hurt to think they would be entertained by him and Julia. Natalie didn't like herself when she had thoughts like these, because after all, Julia was an invalid, and more importantly, Adam didn't love her. But at times like this, Natalie couldn't help realizing that she had no official role in Adam's life. She was now and always would be the other woman, the one who had to remain hidden behind the curtain while Julia occupied center stage.

"What's wrong?" Adam said, frowning.

Natalie gave herself a mental shake. "Nothing." She smiled. "Brooke and Sam are coming to New York."

"I gathered that from your end of the conversation." The frown was gone, but a puzzled look remained in his eyes. "Aren't you glad they're coming?"

"Of course I am. I haven't seen Brooke in years. It'll be great to have them here."

He nodded. "The pasta's almost done. Want me to drain it?"

"Yes." Natalie stooped to open a bottom cupboard and pulled out her colander. She handed it to him. When she did, their eyes met. For some ridiculous reason, Natalie felt close to tears.

"Nat . . ."

She stood. "What?"

"You know how much I wish things were different, don't you? How I'd like to be able to tell everybody in the world how I feel about you. How I'd like to be able to go to the theater with you. How I wish we could see Sam and Brooke together—"

Natalie put her hand over his mouth. It no longer surprised her that he almost always knew what she was feeling, whether she articulated it or not. "Don't say any more. I'm being stupid. Don't pay any attention to me."

"You're not being stupid," he said softly. He put his arms around her, cradling her head against his chest. "I don't deserve you. I don't know why you put up with me."

Natalie's eyes filled. "Don't say things like that," she whispered. "I love you."

"But you deserve so much more than this. I—" He broke off, pulling away slightly so he could look at her. "I want you to know something, Nat," he said fiercely. "If you ever want out, I would never blame you."

"Adam, don't . . ."

"I mean it. It would hurt like hell to lose you, but I'd understand if you wanted more."

"I'm not leaving you. I love you. I just get sad sometimes, that's all, but it doesn't mean anything, not really." She smiled shakily. "Now let's finish getting dinner ready, okay? Before the pasta gets mushy."

"Slave driver."

She laughed in spite of herself. "And if you think I'm making you work hard now, just wait'll I get you in bed."

"But I thought you were going to Mamaroneck this weekend," Adam said. Ever since the car accident two years ago that had claimed her mother's life and put her father

in a nursing home, Julia usually spent every other weekend in Mamaroneck.

This weekend, in addition to the time she spent with
her father, she was supposed to be deciding about the
disposition of all the furnishings in her parents' home. It
had taken this long to get Julius to agree to sell the place.

Adam still wasn't sure selling the family home was a
good idea; maybe someday Julia would regret it, but she
seemed adamant, and after she'd said, "My place is with
you," for the dozenth time, he'd finally stopped trying to
talk her out of it.

"That was before I knew Sam and his wife were coming
to New York," Julia said now. "I've heard so much about
him, and I want to meet him." She smiled. "Let's invite
them to dinner on Saturday."

Adam wanted to object, but how could he? It was perfectly reasonable that she would want to entertain his oldest friend and that friend's wife. She could have no idea
how uncomfortable such an evening would be for Adam.

What if Sam or Brooke inadvertently made reference
to Natalie? Adam didn't think they ever would, but they
could forget themselves and slip up. He would have to
warn them to be careful, and then he'd have to explain
himself, because they were sure to wonder why a long-
ago romance would make any difference now.

He had never intended for Julia to know Sam and
Brooke were coming to New York. Unfortunately, Sam
had called the house and left a message, and then Adam
had had no choice. "Won't having a dinner for them be
too tiring for you?" he finally said.

"Oh, Adam, I'm not that helpless!"

Couldn't prove it by me. Adam was immediately
ashamed of the flippant thought. Julia didn't have an easy
life. At least he could get away by himself when he felt
the need. But she was rarely ever alone and never would
be. And, of course, most importantly, he had Natalie. His
saving grace, he thought gratefully.

"I'll ask Alma to get salmon fillets and bake them in that wonderful orange/honey sauce she does. And we'll have new potatoes and fresh asparagus, and I'll have her make popovers the way Mother always made them. Let's see, for dessert we could have raspberry tarts or peach cobbler. Which do you think they'd like best?" Julia looked more animated than he'd seen her look in months.

"They might already have plans," Adam warned.

"Then we'll do it another night."

"All right. When Sam calls tomorrow, I'll ask him."

The next morning, before placing his habitual good-morning call to Natalie, Adam debated whether he should mention the dinner invitation he planned to extend. He knew it would hurt her, but if he didn't tell her, and Brooke did, it would hurt her even more. Besides, he had never lied to Natalie, and he didn't want to start now.

"Oh," was all she said.

"I wish it could be you and me, you know that, don't you?"

"Yes, I know."

Adam hesitated, then decided to say what he was thinking. "If you don't mind Brooke and Sam knowing about us, we *could* do something together."

"No!" she said quickly. "No, I don't want that."

"Nat, I'm sorry."

"I know you are. Please don't worry about it."

All morning, he kept remembering that resigned tone in Natalie's voice. The way she'd seemed suddenly distant from him.

Five years.

It had been five long years since Julia's accident, and now . . . now it was even worse than when she'd first lost the use of her legs, because then, at least, she'd had her parents.

Now her mother was gone, and her father might as well be. The stroke he'd had, the one that caused him to lose control of his car and had resulted in the auto accident that had taken Margarethe's life, had been a bad one. His left side was completely paralyzed, and he could barely speak. And lately, according to Julia, his mind seemed to be going, as well. His doctor had hinted that Julius might be in the beginning stages of Alzheimer's disease.

The future looked bleak. Once there was at least hope. Hope that Julia would recover. Hope that Adam could leave her. Now there was nothing ahead but endless years of pretending.

Sometimes Adam thought about chucking everything: packing a bag, grabbing Natalie, getting on a plane, and never looking back. The rest of the time, he knew he would never run away. Escape from responsibility was not in his genes.

I'm trapped forever, for only a monster would leave Julia now.

In a burst of misery and frustration, Adam hit his desk. Papers scattered all over the place, and a moment later, Mary Beth knocked on his door, saying, "Is everything all right, Mr. Forrester?"

"Yes, Mary Beth. Everything's fine." Adam put his head in his hands. "Everything's just wonderful."

"So tell me everything," Brooke insisted. "Are you dating anyone?"

Natalie shrugged. "Haven't you heard about New York? How it's virtually impossible to meet guys? How single women outnumber single men by several hundred percent?" The two of them were having lunch at Alaina's, a popular tea room in SoHo. They had spent the morning in and out of the shops and galleries that characterized the area.

"Shoot, Nat, maybe you should move to L.A. Sam and I know lots of single guys. One in particular is a really cute screenwriter and—"

"I'm not moving to L.A., so you might as well save your breath."

"Why not? I mean, New York is fun to visit, but I never did understand why you wanted to live here. Our weather is ten times nicer."

"There's a little matter of a job I love."

"Somebody as smart as you could find a great job in L.A. We'd help you. Heck, that screenwriter I was trying to tell you about could probably give you all *kinds* of leads. You'd probably even make more money."

Natalie chuckled. "That wouldn't be hard. But anyway, Brooke, I'm not moving to L.A. Even if it wasn't for my job, you know how I feel about being close to my family."

"You'd only be four hours away by plane."

"I know. But it wouldn't be the same."

Brooke sighed. "Oh, well, it was worth a try. Speaking of your family, catch me up on what everyone's doing."

So for the next half hour, Natalie did.

"You're so lucky," Brooke said when she'd finished. "I'd give anything to have the kind of family you do."

"You're lucky, too, you know. You have Sam and the kids."

Brooke grinned. "Oh, I know I am. I adore the kids, and Sam is great. Funny, isn't it? I never thought I'd end up with him. Remember when I told you guys like him and Adam never married girls like us?"

Natalie's heart gave a little hop at the mention of Adam's name, but she managed to keep her voice light. "Well, in my case, you were right."

Brooke's forehead creased. "Oh, Nat, I'm such an idiot. I'm sorry."

"For what?"

"I shouldn't have said that about Adam."

"Oh, for heaven's sake, Brooke. That was a long time ago. In fact, I was going to ask you if you and Sam planned to see him while you're here."

Brooke grinned. "I've been *dying* to tell you, but I didn't know if you'd want to talk about him. We've been invited to dinner at his house tomorrow night."

"Really?"

"Yes," Brooke said eagerly. "And I can't wait to go. I'm dying to meet his wife."

"Well, if you hadn't eloped with Sam and had a normal wedding, you'd probably have met her then," Natalie said.

"You never *will* let me forget that, will you?"

"Nope. You cheated *me* out a wedding, too. I was counting on being your maid of honor." After a few more minutes of teasing, Natalie sobered. " You'll have to tell me all about the dinner."

"Really? You won't mind hearing?"

"Oh, come on, Brooke. Why would I mind?"

"I don't know. I just thought . . . but like you said, it was a long time ago."

After that, the conversation turned to Brooke's job as a mortgage loan officer, and no more was said about Adam.

Twenty-four

Alma had worked for the Forresters for nearly seventeen years, and she had never seen Mrs. Forrester so flustered or nervous about anything. What was so special about these people coming to dinner tonight?

As far as Alma knew, it was just some old college friend of Mr. Forrester's and the friend's wife. Nobody really important, at least not the kind of importance Mrs. Forrester usually recognized.

But for some reason, she really wanted to impress these two, because she'd had Alma running around like a chicken with her head cut off all day.

Get this, do that, have you done that, why not . . . ? At one point Alma almost said she was not a scullery maid, she was a sixty-year-old housekeeper, and she had a bad knee.

But of course, she hadn't. Normally, Mrs. Forrester wasn't unreasonable, although she was demanding and didn't believe in giving you lots of praise.

Now Mr. Forrester, he was different. He was always telling Alma how much he appreciated her, especially since Mrs. Forrester had had her accident. On the first of every month, he gave her a couple of hundred dollar bills in an envelope, saying he knew she was having to work much harder than she should.

He never said not to mention the extra money to Mrs. Forrester, but he didn't have to. Alma knew his wife knew nothing about the money, and that if she did, she would be angry.

Alma liked her job well enough and planned to stay with the Forresters until she was sixty-five and could collect the maximum Social Security, but much of her satisfaction was due to Mr. Forrester and the way he treated her. Alma wasn't sure she would still be willing to stay there if he wasn't part of the picture, because Mrs. Forrester could be hard to take sometimes.

"Alma! Alma! Where are you?"

Alma sighed and walked to the bottom of the stairs. "I'm down here in the laundry room, Mrs. Forrester."

"Well, would you please come upstairs? I want you to set the table now."

Alma sighed again. It was only two o'clock, but it would do no good to remind Mrs. Forrester that there were still five hours to go before the dinner guests arrived. When she wanted something done, she wanted it done immediately.

Alma abandoned the basket of laundry she had intended to fold. She could do it later. Slowly, favoring her arthritic right knee, she climbed the stairs.

An hour later, the dining room looked as perfect as Alma, directed by Mrs. Forrester, could make it. The dark walnut table, covered with a Belgian lace tablecloth, was set with Mrs. Forrester's favorite Royal Doulton china and Baccarat crystal. The centerpiece, ordered from Mrs. Forrester's favorite florist, was a beautiful arrangement of baby orchids in a shade of peach that Alma knew must have cost a fortune.

"I think you should get started on the raspberry tarts now," Mrs. Forrester said after she pronounced the table acceptable.

Alma knew better than to argue, so she put the unfolded laundry out of her mind and headed for the kitchen. Again, she wondered what was so special about these people coming tonight. Suddenly, she was glad Mrs. Forrester hadn't hired any extra help to do the serving as she had hinted she might, because Alma didn't want to miss a single word.

"Wow," Brooke said. "Nice." She looked up and down the street where Adam lived. "And only a block from the park."

"Yep," Sam said, "definitely a high-rent district."

"Adam must be doing really well."

"He told me his father-in-law bought the house and that it's in Julia's name."

"Oh, really?" Brooke wasn't sure how she'd feel about that if she were in Adam's shoes. From what Sam had told her about the situation, Adam had practically been forced to marry Julia. Brooke couldn't wait to meet her.

"Now, remember," Sam said as they walked up the steps to the front door, "not a word about Natalie."

"I know, I know, his wife doesn't know about her." Brooke wondered why it would matter if Julia did know about Natalie. After all, college was a long time ago, and he'd married Julia. Then again, some women were extremely jealous, so Brooke guessed it paid to be cautious. Especially since Adam's wife was in a wheelchair and she was sure he didn't want to do anything to make her feel bad.

Sam rang the bell, which was answered almost immediately by Adam himself. He looked great, Brooke thought. This was the first time she'd seen him since they'd been in New York, although Sam had had lunch with him yesterday. She liked the wings of gray at his temples and the fine lines around his eyes. Both gave him a maturity that sat well on his shoulders.

"Come in," he said, smiling. He pumped Sam's hand,

then turned to Brooke. Kissing her cheek, he said, "Brooke, you're even prettier than I remembered."

Brooke grinned. "Flattery will get you anywhere." But she knew she did look good. Living in L.A., she wouldn't have dared to let herself go. Too many gorgeous California girls around to tempt Sam.

Inside, the house was even more impressive than outside. Brooke and Sam owned a contemporary stucco in Manhattan Beach, and Brooke had always thought she preferred a modern home, but there was something to be said for a lovely old house like this one.

"Julia will be down in a few minutes," Adam said, leading them into the living room, which was beautifully furnished in shades of blue, peach, and cream. Gesturing to a pair of blue-and-cream satin striped love seats that flanked the fireplace, he added, "What would you like to drink?"

"You know me," Sam said. "I'm a beer man."

"English, German, or Mexican?"

"Have you got Beck's?"

"Of course."

Sam smiled happily. "Beck's it is."

"What about you, Brooke?" Adam asked. "Do you still like beer?"

"I'd prefer wine. Something sweet." She made a face. "I'm not a connoisseur."

"I've got a really fine port that a client gave me." He smiled. "You'd like it."

"That sounds good."

While Adam busied himself at the bar, Brooke and Sam sat next to each other on one of the love seats. Brooke looked around, thinking how perfect everything appeared: the shining surfaces of the wood furniture, the immaculate Oriental carpet, the crystal vase filled with roses on the coffee table, the gleaming black grand piano in the corner, the objets d'art placed here and there. She couldn't help but compare this graceful, orderly room with her own living room, which was usually littered with the detritus of daily life with one too-busy wife, one who-cares husband, two children, two dogs, and one long-haired cat. She smothered a smile as she tried to imagine the two black Labs here in this room. It boggled the mind.

As Adam approached with their drinks, Brooke heard a sound she couldn't place.

"Elevator," Adam explained. "We had one installed after Julia's accident."

A few minutes later, a thin, fragile-looking blonde wheeled into the room. She was dressed very simply, but Brooke knew at a glance the dark brown crepe dress was a designer model and had probably cost more than Brooke spent on her entire winter wardrobe. She was smiling.

Sam stood, and Brooke followed his lead.

If Brooke hadn't known Adam for such a long time and seen him with Natalie, she would never have known there was anything questionable in his manner or his tone of voice. *How interesting,* she thought as Adam made the introductions. He was gentle and solicitous of his wife. You could tell he cared about her, but something vital was missing.

He doesn't love her, Brooke decided. Not the way he'd loved Natalie. Brooke wondered if he ever thought about Natalie. God, those two had been so in love, it had almost hurt to look at them.

"I'm so pleased to meet you both," Julia was saying. She gave them a charming smile. "And please, do sit down again." She turned her smile to Adam. "Darling, would you get me some white wine?"

Adam went to do his wife's bidding, and Sam and Brooke sat down. Julia wheeled herself closer. Adam came back with her wine and a bottle of beer for himself. He sat on the other love seat, and Brooke noticed that although he could have sat close to Julia, he chose the other end of the sofa. *No. He doesn't love her.*

For a moment, there was an awkward silence, then

Adam, Julia, and Sam all began to talk at once. Everyone laughed, and the men deferred to Julia.

She looked at Brooke. "I know about Sam, of course, since he and Adam have been friends since their under-graduate days. But what about you? Did you go to Yale, too?" Her voice was very precise, her tone just the tiniest bit arrogant. Even if Brooke hadn't known Julia came from a privileged background, that Eastern finishing school voice would have been a clear giveaway.

"No, I went to Southern Connecticut." She laughed. "It's the poor man's school in New Haven."

"Yes, I know the school."

Brooke sensed rather than saw Adam's sharp look.

"Why are you so surprised, darling?" Julia said with an amused smile. "I'm not *entirely* uninformed." Not waiting for him to answer, she turned her pale blue eyes on Brooke again. "So how did you and Sam meet?"

"Well, actually—" Sam said.

"We met at a party," Brooke hurriedly interjected. Surely he wasn't going to say *Adam* introduced them!

"It was love at first sight," Sam said, giving Brooke a look that said *I'm not stupid.*

"No, it wasn't," Brooke retorted. "It took him years to get around to asking me to marry him."

"You asked *me!*" Sam protested. He winked at Adam. "She won't admit it, but she did."

Brooke rolled her eyes.

"Adam and I knew we were going to be married when we were just children," Julia said. "Didn't we, darling?"

"Really?" Brooke murmured. She looked at Adam, but he didn't meet her eyes. "I thought that only happened in books."

For a moment, no one said anything. Then, in an abrupt change of subject, Julia asked, "Are you a lawyer, too?" She was looking at Brooke.

"Me?" Brooke said. "No. I'm a mortgage loan officer."

"How fascinating."

But Brooke knew Julia Forrester didn't think it was fascinating at all. *She's a snob,* Brooke thought. *She's gracious and charming and polite, and she'd never say anything overt, but she's still a snob.*

"I wouldn't be married to a lawyer," Sam said. "Lawyers are the scum of the earth."

Adam laughed. Julia smiled, but Brooke knew she wasn't amused. Suddenly, perversely, Brooke wanted to say something that would shock Adam's wife out of her perfect manners. She was immediately ashamed of herself. Damn. What was wrong with her? Julia Forrester was paralyzed. So what if she had a faintly superior attitude? Brooke had two good legs, a husband who loved her, and two wonderful kids.

The conversation turned to Sam's firm, and Sam told a couple of funny stories about famous clients of theirs, which Adam seemed to really enjoy. Julia smiled politely, but Brooke could tell she wasn't really interested. Hollywood celebrities would not be important in her world. Now, if Sam represented some New York dignitary, that would be different.

While they were still discussing Sam's firm, a small, dark-haired woman of about sixty appeared in the open doorway. "Dinner is ready, Mrs. Forrester," she said in a soft, faintly accented voice.

"Thank you, Alma."

Brooke and Sam followed Adam, who pushed Julia in her chair, to the dining room across the hall. As in the living room, everything was perfection, down to the smallest detail.

But Brooke had already decided she didn't envy Julia Forrester her pedigree or her perfect house or her money. It might be a cliché to say that money didn't buy happiness, but in this case, it was certainly true.

The dinner itself was delicious. But Brooke hadn't expected any less. It was served quietly and unobtrusively by Alma, and Brooke wondered if the woman had done the cooking, too, or if Julia had a cook as well as a maid.

"The salmon is wonderful," she said.

Julia smiled. "Thank you."

"So are these popovers."

"They're made from a recipe of my mother's."

"Really? Did you make them?"

"No, Alma did, under my instruction."

"Did Alma fix the entire dinner?"

"Yes."

"Well, she did a great job."

"Yes, she's a marvelous cook. When I hired her as our housekeeper, I didn't realize I was getting two in one. I'd fully expected to have to hire a cook, as well."

"You're lucky."

"Do *you* have help?"

"Yes, I have a marvelous cleaning woman who comes in once a week."

During this exchange, the men had been conducting their own conversation, which had taken a political turn and had become a bit heated.

"That's crazy, Adam," Sam was saying.

"No, your idea is the crazy one," Adam countered.

"Darling," Julia admonished, "in polite society one does not talk politics or religion at the dinner table. Especially when one's guests don't agree with your opinions."

"Hey, I don't mind." Sam grinned. "I like arguing with Adam. We used to debate this kind of thing all the time when we were in law school."

"Well, *I* don't like it," Julia said. She didn't smile.

"I apologize," Adam said. "Julia's right. Besides, if we keep it up, I'll prove you wrong, and then you'll be embarrassed."

Sam laughed. "In your dreams."

"Enough," Brooke said, giving her husband a warning look. Actually, she didn't care what the men talked about or how heated the discussion became, but it was clear

Julia did. "Let's talk about something else."

"Tell me what you've been doing since you came to New York," Julia said.

"I've been working," Sam replied. "She's been goofing off."

"By goofing off, he means I've been shopping and sight-seeing," Brooke said. "And going to the theater."

"Oh? What have you seen?"

"Well, the other night Nat—" She stopped. "My friend Nancy and I went to see *Chicago*." Holy shit. She'd nearly done it. She'd nearly said Natalie's name. "Nancy and I went to high school together," she added in a rush. She was afraid to look anywhere. She could just imagine what Adam was thinking, because he probably realized what she had *really* started to say.

"How nice for you . . . to have a friend in New York," Julia said.

Was it Brooke's imagination, or were Julia's eyes about ten degrees colder?

"Did you enjoy the show?" Julia continued.

"Oh, yes, it was wonderful. The dancing was fabulous. Bob Fosse is brilliant, don't you think?" Oh, God. Now she was blathering like an idiot.

"I haven't seen one of his shows, so I really wouldn't know."

"You haven't seen one of his shows? And you live in New York?"

"I prefer plays to musicals," Julia said. "Especially the classics."

Oh, please, Brooke thought. Could Julia be more tight-assed? Suddenly she didn't even care that she'd almost slipped up awhile ago. She hated people who put on airs, the kind who said they never watched TV and wouldn't be caught dead reading Danielle Steel. She'd just bet if the subject turned to music, Julia would say she never listened to pop and that she didn't like rock music, either.

But as quickly as her irritation flared, it burned out,

because the bottom line was, Julia Forrester was trapped in that wheelchair of hers. And as a result, no matter how snooty she might be, no matter how many airs she effected, she was not a woman you could hate.

Suddenly, Brooke couldn't wait for the evening to be over. Sam might not be as handsome as Adam or as smart, and their house might not be as beautiful and they might not have as much money, but there wasn't anything in the world that anyone could have offered Brooke to make her want to trade places with Julia Forrester.

"Sam?"

"Hmm?" He was sitting on one of the chairs by the window, working on his laptop, and he didn't look up.

Brooke was already in bed, propped up against the pillows. She'd been reading but hadn't been able to stop thinking about the evening at Adam's. "What did you think of Julia?"

"She seems nice," he said distractedly. He kept tapping at the keys.

"Sam! Would you stop that for a minute and pay attention to me?"

He finally looked at her. "Brooke, I've got to finish this report before the meeting tomorrow." But he set the laptop aside. "What? I answered your question."

"I asked the wrong question."

"And what question did you mean to ask instead?"

"Do you think Adam loves her?"

Sam rolled his eyes. "Ah, Brooke, come on, gimme a break. How the hell should I know?"

"Well, you talk to him. I don't."

"Guys don't talk about that kind of thing."

"What do you talk about, then?"

Sam laughed. "We talk about all the gorgeous babes we'd like to fuck."

Brooke threw her pillow at him. The next thing she

knew, he had jumped on the bed and was pulling her on top of him.

"Come to think of it," he said with a wicked gleam in his eyes, "I wouldn't mind fucking *you*."

"Be still my heart," Brooke said dryly.

He buried his face between her breasts, which were shown to advantage in her low-cut satin nightie. "Be nice, okay? I'm feeling horny tonight."

"A minute ago you said you had to do a report."

"The report can wait."

Brooke wanted to sigh with pleasure as he gently squeezed her nipples. Instead, she pulled away and swatted at his hands. "Not until you answer my question."

"What question?"

"Do you think Adam loves Julia?"

Suddenly Sam became serious. He shook his head. "No, I don't think so."

Now Brooke did give a satisfied sigh. "I didn't, either. And you know what else?"

"What?"

"I have this feeling . . ."

"Uh-oh."

Brooke grinned. It was a standing joke between them that when she had "this feeling," she was going to say something really out there. "I can't help it, Sam. I do."

"And what are you *feeling*?"

"I can't say why . . ."

"Dammit, Brooke, will you just spit it out?"

"I think Adam and Natalie might be seeing each other."

"*What?* Did she say something?"

"No. It's what she didn't say."

"What do you mean?"

"Well, when I asked her if she was dating anyone, she never answered directly. In fact, anytime the conversation got around to her personal life, she'd answer my questions with a question. It was like she was *evading* being specific."

"But—"

"And another thing," Brooke continued. "She didn't seem at all surprised that Adam lived here."

"Hell, Brooke, that doesn't prove a thing. I mean, we all knew he was headed for Manhattan after law school."

"I know, but that was eighteen years ago. He could have moved anywhere by now. The thing is, when I mentioned him, she could have said something like, 'Oh, is he still in New York?' But she didn't."

For a few moments, Sam didn't say anything. Then, giving her a rueful smile, he said, "Well, you know what? I really don't care if they are seeing each other or not. And you know what else? This is really none of our business."

"I know. I'm just curious, that's all."

"You know what they say about curiosity."

Brooke grinned. And then, feeling kind of horny herself, she got back on top of her husband and lowered her mouth to his.

"That's more like it," he muttered.

Natalie couldn't sleep. She couldn't stop thinking about Brooke and Sam and their dinner at Adam's. All night, no matter what she was doing, she kept picturing them sitting at Adam and Julia's dining room table. Laughing and talking. Two old friends and their wives. All night, Natalie had fought against tears.

Disgusted with herself, she'd gone to bed. But shutting out the lights couldn't shut out her thoughts.

You chose this life, she reminded herself over and over again. *You knew what it would be like.*

But no matter how many times she told herself this, it didn't help. She could no longer stop the tears. Eventually, she cried herself to sleep.

Twenty-five

Natalie wondered if she was coming down with something. For the past couple of weeks, she hadn't felt like herself. Maybe she was anemic. She certainly looked pale enough. Of course, everyone in New York looked pale at this time of year. It was the week after Thanksgiving, and the sun hadn't shone in days.

Sighing, she decided maybe she should call her doctor and make an appointment to go in. Come to think of it, it was about time for her yearly exam, anyway. She always had her yearly checkup in January because the start of a new year made it easy to remember, but maybe she'd go early this time.

She headed for the phone and actually had her hand on it when it rang. She jumped, then laughed at herself. "Hello?"

"Natalie, hi! It's Grace."

"Hi, sweetie. What's the occasion?" Her youngest sister didn't call often. Firefighters didn't make much money, and Grace was a stay-at-home mom, so she watched her pennies carefully.

"I'm coming to visit you," Grace said.

Natalie grinned in delight. "You *are*? When?"

"This weekend."

"How'd you finagle that?"

"Rose and Carol thought I needed to get away, so they bought me a train ticket as a birthday present. Carol's even taking the kids for the weekend, since Rick is on duty." Grace and Rick now had three children: their twin girls, who were four, and a little boy, eighteen months and a holy terror.

"That's terrific. What time does your train get in?"

Grace gave Natalie all the information, and Natalie said she'd meet the train.

"You don't have to do that."

"I want to."

After they hung up, Natalie thought, as she had when Brooke and Sam came to visit, how much more excited she'd be about Grace's visit if she could introduce her to Adam. If they could take Grace out and really show her the town. But, of course, that was impossible.

She also would not be able to wear her ring, just as she hadn't worn it when Brooke visited. The ring was just too big and too beautiful. A person didn't have to know jewels to know it had cost a small fortune, and if Natalie had worn it when Brooke was there, Brooke's eyes would have popped out. She'd have started asking Natalie questions, and she wouldn't have rested until she'd pried the truth out of her.

Grace was a little more naive than Brooke, but still, Grace wasn't stupid. She would put two and two together and realize there had to be a man in Natalie's life. And if Natalie didn't talk about him or let Grace meet him, Grace would know there was a reason. It wouldn't take long for her to figure out what that reason was.

Natalie sighed again, then smiled ruefully. Lately, all she seemed to do was sigh. The ring would have to be hidden. Thank goodness Natalie had never allowed Adam to leave anything in her apartment, so at least she didn't have to worry about going around and hiding a robe or a toothbrush.

Oh, she hated this! Hated the sneaking. Hated the lying. Hated the loneliness. *I'm tired,* she thought. *I'm really, really tired. . . .*

Which reminded her, she had been going to call her doctor when Grace's call had come in. Picking up the phone, Natalie punched the buttons for Dr. Sandstrom's office and made an appointment for the following Tuesday.

The next morning, when Adam called, Natalie told him about Grace's upcoming visit and how that meant she wouldn't be able to see him over the weekend. Although he didn't say so, Natalie knew he was disappointed. Julia was going to Mamaroneck, and he and Natalie had talked about getting away themselves.

"I'm sorry," Natalie murmured. "I'm disappointed, too."

He didn't answer for a minute. When he did, saying, "I've never met any of your family," he sounded sad.

"I know."

All morning, the forlorn note in Adam's voice haunted Natalie. *He's unhappy, too.* Well, she'd known that, hadn't she?

And then, in one of those bursts of insight—the kind that when you have it, you wonder why you didn't realize it before—she understood something. Maybe by clinging to each other, to a dream that wasn't to be, they were making their lives much harder than they had to be.

Maybe, if Natalie could muster the courage to break off with Adam, she would be doing all of them a great favor.

Maybe, once she was gone from Adam's life, he could begin to build something with Julia.

Natalie pushed away the line edit she'd been working on and stared into space.

He can't leave Julia. He will never be able to leave her. So we have no future together. We will just go on like this, year after year.

Getting up, she walked to her window. The sky looked gray and overcast.

Our love won't survive.

She wanted to deny the truth of that thought, but she couldn't.

What we're doing, and what we're missing, will eat away at us until we feel more and more resentful. Until there's nothing left.

For the first time in the nearly six years since she and Adam had begun their love affair, Natalie knew it couldn't last. The knowledge brought tears to her eyes. A life without Adam, she thought in despair. How could she bear it?

For the rest of the week and throughout the weekend, the same thoughts kept going round and round in her head. Could she do it? Could she make the break?

She was so preoccupied, Grace noticed and commented.

"Is something wrong, Natalie? You don't seem like your normal lively self," she said on Sunday morning. The two of them were sitting in one of the little cafés near Union Square having bagels and hot chocolate.

"Not really," Natalie said, rousing herself.

"You sure?"

"It's just work. I'm trying to make a decision that'll affect my future, that's all."

"Want to talk about it?"

Natalie shook her head and forced herself to empty her mind of her problem. This was Grace's last day in New York. Natalie didn't want to waste it. "What do you want to do this afternoon? Anything special?"

"Promise you won't laugh."

Natalie grinned. "I promise."

"I want to do touristy things, like go to the top of the Empire State Building and ride the Staten Island Ferry."

"Actually, I think that sounds like fun."

The sisters smiled at each other.

• • •

"This is really a great city," Grace said later as they stood looking out from the viewing level of the Empire State Building.

"Yes." From here Natalie could see her building. She could also see Adam's, but she didn't want to think about Adam today.

"You sure there's nothing wrong?" Grace said softly. "You seem sad."

Snap out of it, Natalie. Forcing a smile to her face, Natalie said, "Sad? Really? I'm anything but."

Grace nodded, but she didn't seem convinced.

They ended their tour in Little Italy, where they had pizza and red wine at Natalie's favorite trattoria, then they took the subway back to Natalie's, where they picked up Grace's luggage. Once Grace was ready, Natalie splurged on a cab and rode to the station with her sister. They didn't have long to wait before Grace's train arrived.

"I had a wonderful time," Grace told her.

"Me, too."

They embraced, then Grace turned to board the train. A second later, she came rushing back. "Nat, I know you haven't been worried about work this weekend. This is about a guy. No, don't bother to shake your head. I know it is, I can tell. I just wanted you to know, if you need to talk, I'm always ready to listen." Then she gave Natalie another hard hug, waved, and was gone.

Adam thought about Natalie and her sister all weekend. He hoped they were having fun. That the sadness he'd seen in Natalie's eyes more and more often lately was gone and that she was laughing and happy.

He'd known Natalie was unhappy for a long time now. He just hadn't wanted to deal with it, because he also knew there wasn't much he could do to make her feel better. Unfortunately, his situation was unchanged and looked as if it would always remain that way.

Sometimes he wished Julia would die. Then he hated

himself for wishing it. None of what had happened was Julia's fault. Just as none of what had happened since was Natalie's fault. Yet both women were paying the price for his mistakes. But were they really mistakes? What else could he have done, either in 1979 or in 1992? Both times, he had been trapped by his own sense of duty and honor. He would always be trapped.

The question was, What should he do now?

If you really loved Natalie as much as you say you do, you would set her free.

Just the thought made him feel sick.

Natalie told her boss she probably would not be back after lunch. "Depends on how long I have to wait at the doctor's office."

Jack nodded. "I won't look for you, then."

Her appointment was for two o'clock. She arrived ten minutes early and, to her great surprise, she didn't have to wait. Ginny, the receptionist, called her name promptly at two. Natalie was shown into one of the examining rooms, told to undress, and given a paper robe to put on.

Dr. Sandstrom, a tall, no-nonsense woman with a dry sense of humor and a gentle bedside manner, had been Natalie's primary physician for the past seven years. Natalie really liked the doctor. Moreover, she trusted her and always enjoyed seeing her. The two women had struck up a rapport at Natalie's first visit, and that hadn't changed over the years.

A few minutes later, Jodie, Dr. Sandstrom's nurse, came in. She asked Natalie questions, made notes in her chart, then took her pulse and her blood pressure. "Dr. Sandstrom will be in in a few minutes," she said before leaving Natalie alone again.

Five minutes later, the doctor knocked, then entered the exam room. "Hello there. How're you doing?" she said, smiling at Natalie who was perched at the end of the exam table. She picked up Natalie's chart and quickly read the nurse's notes. "Feeling a bit tired, are you?"

Natalie nodded. "Yes."

"And how long's this been going on?" Dr. Sandstrom placed her stethoscope against Natalie's chest and listened.

Natalie shrugged. "I don't know. A month? More?"

"And you're also feeling queasy at times?"

"Yes."

"Has that ever happened to you before?" Now she put the scope on Natalie's back. "Take a deep breath."

"Not that I can remember," Natalie said, breathing in, then out.

The doctor moved the scope. "Again." When she was finished listening, she peered into Natalie's ears. "Maybe you're pregnant."

Natalie's heart lurched. "No, that's impossible. I always use a diaphragm."

Dr. Sandstrom grimaced. "Nothing's one hundred percent foolproof, Natalie." She picked up the chart again. "I see where you weren't sure when you had your last period."

"Well, no, I . . ." Natalie frowned. "I think it was sometime in early October. But I'm not certain. You know I've always been erratic."

"Well, let's just check you out." The doctor pulled on a pair of disposable gloves and reached for a tube of lubricant.

Natalie always dreaded having a pelvic. She could never relax, and today was no exception. The whole time the doctor was probing and feeling her abdomen, Natalie's mind was racing. She wasn't pregnant, she knew that. But maybe something else was wrong. Maybe she had cancer. That could explain the tiredness and the queasiness.

"Okay," the doctor said when she was finished. She patted Natalie's leg. "You can sit up now."

Once Natalie was up, the doctor met her gaze. I was right. You *are* pregnant."

Natalie stared at her. Her heart galloped in disbelief. "Are . . . are you sure?"

"Yes, there's no doubt of it." The doctor's green eyes were compassionate. "I'm guessing this isn't good news."

Natalie still couldn't take it in. Pregnant. She was pregnant. With Adam's baby. *Oh, my God.* With trembling hands, she touched her abdomen. A baby. She was going to have a baby. She didn't even realize she was crying until she felt the tears running down her cheeks.

Dr. Sandstrom touched her shoulder gently. "Natalie. It's okay. There are options, you know."

Natalie brushed at the tears, tried to regain control of herself, but she couldn't seem to stop crying. "I-I'm sorry."

"No, it's okay," the doctor said. She handed her a box of tissues. "It's a big thing, finding out you're pregnant. Take your time. When you feel calmer, I'll leave you to get dressed, then we can talk in my office."

Natalie nodded. She took a long, shaky breath, then blew her nose. "I'm all right now."

"Are you sure?"

"Yes."

"Okay. Go on into my office when you're dressed."

Ten minutes later, Natalie sat waiting for Dr. Sandstrom. Her mind was spinning. She still found it hard to believe. She was thirty-eight years old, almost thirty-nine. She had thought she would never be a mother. And now . . . now she was pregnant!

Just then, Dr. Sandstrom came in and sat behind her desk. "Feeling better?"

Natalie nodded.

"How do you feel about this pregnancy now that you've had a few minutes to get over the initial shock?"

"I don't know. I'm still stunned."

"Is having a baby impossible for you?"

Natalie swallowed. "No. I-I just . . . My mind is whirling. It's hard to think. This . . . this is just so unexpected."

Dr. Sandstrom nodded thoughtfully. After a moment, she said, "What about the father? Would he be support-ive?"

Adam. Dear God. Adam would be thrilled, she knew he would. He didn't talk about his feelings regarding chil-dren much, just as she didn't. But she knew how he felt. He had told her long ago what a disappointment it was to him that he and Julia had not had children. And now, every time they saw families with children, she saw how he smiled, how his eyes followed them. Yes, Adam would be thrilled.

Natalie's eyes met the doctor's. "I think he would be, but I'm not sure I want to tell him." She hesitated, but only for a few seconds. "You see, he's married."

Dr. Sandstrom nodded. "All right. You obviously have some thinking to do. Why don't you go home, think about everything for a few days, then give me a call. If you decide you want to have the baby, either to keep or to give up for adoption, we'll talk about prenatal care. If you decide you don't want to have the baby, we'll talk about options there, too. In the meantime, I'll have Jodie give you a supply of vitamins to take and some reading ma-terial." She smiled at Natalie. "Do you have any ques-tions?"

"Just one. I'm almost thirty-nine. Will that present any problems for me?"

"None that I can see. You're healthy. You should have a healthy baby."

Still in a daze, Natalie left the doctor's office and began to walk. It had turned colder, and a few snowflakes drifted down, but Natalie hardly noticed. She walked east on Fifty-sixth until she reached Fifth Avenue, then turned south. It wasn't until she came abreast of St. Patrick's Cathedral that she realized she had never intended to go back to her office. She'd been heading for the beautiful old church the whole time.

Except for the times she went home to Emerson, Natalie hadn't set foot in a Catholic church the entire time she'd been in New York. But as she entered the venerable cathedral, all of the worry, all of the doubt, all of the sadness of the past months lifted from her shoulders, and she felt an overwhelming sense of calm and peace.

Sinking into one of the pews, she sat for a long time. She didn't try to think. She closed her eyes and let all her doubts and fears, all her confusion and turmoil drift away.

When she finally rose, she headed for the niche that held the Virgin. Kneeling before the statue, she lighted a candle and bowed her head. She prayed for the wisdom to know the right thing to do and the strength to do it. And she gave thanks for the gift she had been given today: a gift she knew she didn't deserve and had never expected to receive.

Dearest Mother, I thank you from the bottom of my heart, and I promise I will be the best mother I know how to be.

And then, tears blurring her eyes, she walked out into the gathering dusk.

Part Four

Twenty-six

$\backsim$ ⁂ $\diagup$

December 1997 to April 1998

Natalie had never seriously considered moving to California. She'd only told Adam she might go there because she didn't want him contacting her. It was going to be very hard for both of them, but Natalie knew a clean break was best. She simply couldn't take a chance on Adam finding out about the baby.

She felt terrible about keeping the information from him when knowledge of the baby would have brought him so much joy, but it was absolutely necessary. Above all else, Natalie wanted a secure, normal, happy childhood for her baby—one that was not rooted in secrecy and lies. That meant removing herself from Adam's sphere and starting over again with a clean slate.

She tried not to think about how hurt he would be if he knew what she was keeping from him. Occasionally, she wavered. Maybe she *could* tell him. Adam was an honorable man. Surely, if she explained how she felt, he would respect her wish that he stay away.

But each time she started to weaken, she told herself she simply could not take the chance. No. She must keep her priorities straight. Her feelings and Adam's feelings weren't the most important factors in this situation. What was best for their unborn child mattered most. And that meant keeping the fact of the baby's existence a secret from Adam.

Natalie had been truthful about going home to Emerson for the holidays, though. Before going, she'd worried about the trip home and the questions she'd have to face from her family. Even after she got there, she still hadn't determined whether to tell her parents about the baby then or wait until after she was settled somewhere. She kept asking herself if she really wanted to spoil their Christmas, for her announcement would surely bring them pain, especially when they realized why the father of her baby would not be involved in their lives.

After agonizing over the problem, she finally decided she would just play it by ear. If an opportune moment arose while she was home, she would take advantage of it. If not, she would wait. There was no hurry. She wasn't showing yet.

They did know she was leaving New York, though, because she'd had to tell them something about why she was bringing her cats home with her. But when they'd pressed for details, she had explained that she would tell them all about it when she saw them.

"But, Natalie," Grace said when the two had their first chance to talk after Natalie's arrival in Emerson, "I don't understand. I thought you loved your job."

"I *do* love my job, but I'm tired of living in a tiny apartment and battling the crowds every day. You know me, Grace. At heart I'm really a small-town girl. So when I found out there was a possibility I could still work for Bramwell, but be based somewhere else, I decided to explore that option."

Grace's eyes widened. "You mean your boss *agreed* to that kind of arrangement?"

"Yes, he did."

"Wow. He must think a lot of you."

"Well, after that author of mine won the Newbery Medal, my stock did go up quite a bit."

"So are you planning to stay in Emerson?"

This was it. The time to tell Grace the truth. Taking a deep breath, Natalie said quietly, "Let's go for a walk. I need to stretch my legs."

Grace obviously realized Natalie wanted privacy, for she readily agreed to the suggestion. A few minutes later, bundled up against the blustery day, the two sisters walked arm in arm down the familiar street where they'd grown up.

"Okay," Grace said once they were away from the house. "What's going on?"

"Do you remember what you said to me when you left New York? About me being involved with a man?"

"Yes."

"Well, you were right. There was a man. In fact, he was a part of my life for a long time."

"Was?"

"Yes. Was. I—" She stopped. This part was going to be hard. Natalie cared what her family thought, and she was afraid her coming revelation would bring her down a notch in Grace's eyes. "I've been involved with him for a long time, but I-I just couldn't keep on going, so I broke it off." Not looking at Grace, she took a deep breath, then said, "You see, he's . . . he's married."

"Oh, Nat," Grace said softly.

Without warning, Natalie's eyes filled with tears. "I know what you're thinking."

"No, you don't."

But Natalie nodded her head fiercely. "I do, and I don't blame you." Trying to gain control of herself, she groped in her pocket for a tissue. Finally finding one, she swiped at her eyes. "I'm sorry. I thought I could talk about this without crying, but . . ." Her lip trembled. "It hurts."

"Look at me," Grace said, stopping and forcing Natalie to stop. Her eyes, the same color as Natalie's, blazed with emotion. "I do not think any less of you because of what you've told me. You're my sister. I love you. Besides, I know you and the kind of person you are. You would never get involved in this type of relationship lightly. Now, I want you to tell me about him. I think if you do, you'll feel better."

In a shaky voice, Natalie began. She started with New Haven and how she and Adam met and fell in love. Talking about those carefree days and how happy she'd been brought it all back in vivid detail. Oh, God, she'd loved him so much! If only they could have . . . But all the if onlys in the world would not change things.

Grace remained silent throughout, but her soft smile said she remembered those feelings, too. Occasionally, she'd squeeze Natalie's arm, and Natalie knew she understood.

When Natalie told her why and how the romance ended all those years ago, she murmured in sympathy, "Oh, God, Nat, that must have devastated you."

"Yes, I was pretty broken up."

"So how did you two hook up again?"

Again Grace listened quietly, but when Natalie told her about Julia's fall and her subsequent paralysis, she gasped.

"*Now* you think I'm terrible," Natalie said miserably.

"No. I-I just . . . Oh, God. What an awful situation. For all of you."

"Yes. It was awful. It still *is* awful. Julia will probably never walk again. And Adam . . ." Her voice cracked. "Adam's life is hell. He feels so responsible. So guilty."

For a long moment, Grace said nothing. Then she sighed. "It's very sad. He's trapped, and she's trapped, only in different ways."

"Yes."

"You still love him, don't you?"

Natalie nodded. "I think I'll always love him."

"So why did you break it off, then? Did something happen?"

Here it was. The moment of truth. "Yes, something happened. I found out I'm pregnant."

"Oh, my God!" Grace stopped in her tracks and stared at Natalie openmouthed.

If the situation hadn't been so serious, Natalie would have laughed at the expression on her sister's face.

"I . . . gee, I-I hardly know what to say. I'm . . . just *speechless*!"

Natalie smiled crookedly. "Shocked you, huh?"

"Yeah, I guess you could say that."

"I was pretty shocked myself."

Grace still seemed stunned. "Wh-when did you find out?"

"Three weeks ago."

"How far along are you?"

"Nine weeks."

"So you're due in . . ." Grace did a mental calculation. "July?"

"Yes." Natalie smiled. "July fourteenth."

"Gosh. How . . ." Grace bit her lip. "How do you feel about this?"

Natalie's smile softened. "Well, I wish the circumstances were different. But even though having a baby as a single mother isn't ideal, I'm thrilled."

"So you're planning to keep the baby."

"Yes. Oh, I thought about adoption, but in the end, I knew I wanted this child. Maybe it's selfish. Maybe if I were a bigger person, I'd give him or her the chance to grow up with two parents, but I just can't do it, Grace. I already love this baby. It . . . it's the only part of Adam I'll ever have." Overcome with emotion, she blinked back a fresh bout of tears.

Grace put her arm around Natalie's waist and hugged her. "I don't blame you, sweetie. In your shoes, I think I'd do the same thing."

By now they had reached the park that lay along the bank of the narrow river that bordered the town. This time of year, the park was deserted. The swings and sandboxes and picnic tables that were always packed with youngsters and their mothers in the summertime now sat empty and forlorn. A few yellowish leaves, the last of autumn's glory, dotted the winter-bare landscape. A lone cardinal, the only spot of color, sat on the back of one of the benches and called for his mate.

Natalie shivered.

"You're cold," Grace said. "Let's head back."

Natalie nodded.

They walked a little ways in silence. Then Grace said, "What *about* Adam? Does he know?"

"No, and I don't want him to."

"But Nat, why not? I mean, this is his baby, too. And you said he was really disappointed about not having any children."

"I know, and if we could be married, that would be one thing, but he can't leave Julia. And I can no longer be the other woman in his life."

Grace sighed. "You're right. I know you are, but it seems so sad for him."

Natalie nodded. She didn't trust herself to speak again. Maybe it was hormonal, but she seemed to cry at the drop of a hat these days.

"When are you going to tell Mom and Dad?" Grace asked after awhile.

"I don't know. It's going to be hard. They'll be disappointed in me."

"Maybe for a minute they will be, but they'll get over it. They love you, and they'll love the baby. You know how Mom is about her grandkids. Geez, she spoils Ricky to death."

"Yes, but all her other grandchildren have mothers and fathers who are married."

"I know, but I'm telling you, the fact that you aren't isn't going to make a difference. Not in the long run."

"I hope you're right."

"Listen, Nat, I don't know much, but I do know that. You don't have to worry about Mom and Dad. They'll always be there for you. And so will the rest of your family. Now give me a hug."

As they embraced, Natalie thought about how lucky she was to have the family she had.

"You never answered my question," Grace said. "Are you going to stay in Emerson?"

"No, that won't work. Once people know about me and my situation, they'll talk. It would be uncomfortable for Mom and Dad if I remained here. No, what I thought was—if Rose is agreeable—I'd go to Ohio."

"Agreeable! I think she'll be *thrilled*!"

"Thing is, I'd like to live with her and Chris until the baby's born."

"She'll be even *more* thrilled."

Natalie was pretty sure Grace was right, but she'd learned long ago not to take anything for granted.

"Oh, Nat, I'm excited! When are you going to talk to Rose?"

"Tomorrow. Mom said she and Chris and the kids would be in sometime in the afternoon."

"Good. Then by tomorrow night, everything should be settled."

"Nat! Of *course* you can come and stay with us! I can't believe you ever thought I might not want you."

Natalie and Rose were upstairs in the bedroom Natalie was using while at their parents' home. They'd come up on the pretext that Natalie wanted to show Rose a couple of new dresses she'd bought before leaving New York. Chris, his and Rose's two kids, and the elder Ferrenzos were downstairs watching television. Natalie had just finished telling her older sister the whole story of Adam and the coming baby. As Grace had predicted, Rose seemed thrilled about the prospect of having Natalie in Crandall.

"It'll be great having you. And a new baby . . ." Rose's dark eyes grew misty at the thought.

"Hadn't you better talk to Chris about this first?" Natalie said.

"He won't care. He *likes* you."

"Liking me and having me living with him for months on end are two different things."

"He'll enjoy it. To tell the truth, it's been a bit lonely with both kids away at college." Jenny was a junior at Ohio State, and Reagan was a sophomore. Rose grinned. "So it's settled. You're coming to Crandall. Oh, Nat, I'm so excited! It's going to be such fun having you there and helping you get ready for the baby." Then her grin faded. "I'm just sorry your Adam isn't going to be a part of this."

"I know."

"I wish I'd gotten to meet him."

"I wish you had, too."

"Do—" Rose stopped.

"What?"

"Do you have any pictures of him?"

Natalie nodded. "Not with me, though. They're packed away with my things."

"Someday will you show them to me?"

"Someday."

Rose put her arm around Natalie's shoulders and gave her a squeeze. "Nat, I know this isn't going to be easy for you, but Chris and I, heck, the entire *family*, we'll be behind you all the way."

Natalie nodded, but even though both Rose and Grace seemed to think their parents would accept her news and support her wholeheartedly, Natalie still dreaded telling them. Funny how no matter how old you were, you always wanted your parents to approve of you. Did a person ever outgrow that wish? Natalie wondered.

"When did you think you'd come to Crandall?" Rose asked. "Right after the holidays?"

"It depends. If Mom and Dad want me to stay awhile,

I will. But I'd like to come to you no later than the middle of January."

Rose smiled. "Great. Now maybe we'd better get downstairs before Mom comes looking for us. Or before they eat all the banana cream pie and we don't get any!"

Laughing, Natalie's dilemma momentarily pushed to the back of her mind, she followed her sister down the stairs to rejoin their family.

Somehow Adam made it through the Christmas holidays. Only once did he succumb to temptation and call Natalie's private office number. When it was answered by the switchboard operator, Adam hung up without identifying himself. The fact that she hadn't answered her phone didn't necessarily mean anything, he told himself. She might just be out to lunch. Or in a meeting. Hurriedly, before he could change his mind, he punched in her home number. After two rings, a recording told him the number he had dialed had been disconnected.

Numbly, he replaced the receiver.

Gone.

She was really gone.

For three weeks he had survived the ever-present pain of her absence by telling himself she might change her mind. She might call. It might not really be over.

But now he could no longer fool himself. Natalie was gone. Their relationship was over. He would never see her again.

Burying his face in his hands, he tried to blot out the memories that constantly assailed him: her eyes, her voice, the way she smelled and felt, the way she could lift his spirits with that irresistible smile. Yet no matter how he tried to put those painful images somewhere they couldn't hurt him, he knew it was impossible. Natalie was as much a part of him as his hands or his feet or his eyes.

Where was she now? Had she gone to California? He had a sudden vision of her sitting out on Sam and

Brooke's back patio. Instead of her New York black, she'd be wearing something bright and tropical looking, and she'd be smiling. Behind her, growing wild over the patio wall, would be a profusion of scarlet bougainvillea. There'd be lemon trees and flower beds filled with jasmine and oleander and hibiscus and the sparkling ocean in the distance.

And across the umbrella table would be a man—someone Sam and Brooke had invited to meet Natalie. Someone—

Breaking off the torturous thought, Adam jumped up. He had to stop this. He had to get a grip on himself. Slowly, he walked to the corner window.

From this height he could see most of the southwest end of Manhattan with the twin towers of the World Trade Center and the Hudson River beyond.

Normally, the impressive view thrilled him. Today he felt nothing but a great weariness. He wasn't sure he would ever be excited about anything again.

Yet no matter how weary he was, he knew he had to face facts. Natalie was gone. She wasn't coming back.

And somehow, some way, he had to learn how to live without her.

Twenty-seven

Natalie didn't tell her parents about the baby until New Year's Eve. She had finally decided it would be best to wait until it was just the three of them. That way, no matter what they were feeling or what they wanted to say, they'd be free to say it.

All evening she kept trying to get up her courage to broach the subject, but somehow she could never seem to find the right words to begin.

But when, a little after eleven, her father opened a bottle of Asti Spumante and offered her a glass, Natalie knew—courage or not—the time had come.

"Just some ginger ale for me, Dad. I'm not drinking alcohol."

"Natalie, it's New Year's. Besides, a glass of Spumante has very little alcohol."

Natalie shook her head. "No. Just ginger ale. I'm not allowed to have alcohol."

Natalie's mother frowned. "Is something wrong, honey? Are you sick?"

"No, Mom. I—" Natalie took a deep breath. She met her mother's eyes, then turned to look at her father. "I've been trying to get up my courage to tell you for days now. The truth is, I'm pregnant."

If Natalie had dropped a bomb in the middle of the living room, she didn't think her parents could have looked more stunned. Her mother was the first to recover and immediately began to fire questions at Natalie. Her father finished pouring himself a glass of Spumante and gulped down half before sitting down and staring at her. As calmly as she could, Natalie answered their questions. It hurt her to see the expressions on their faces when she told them about Adam, because no matter what Grace had said, the disappointment they felt was going to last a lot longer than a minute.

"I'm sorry," she said once the whole story was told. "I know I've disappointed you."

"Well, sweetheart," her dad said, "it's true we never expected anything like this, and it's probably going to take us a while to get used to it. I can't pretend I'm happy about you being pregnant by a married man, but that doesn't mean I won't support you in the decision you've made to keep your baby."

"I feel the same way, honey," her mother said. "Yes, I'm disappointed that something that should be a completely happy occasion is a bit less than that, but I'm proud of you for facing up to the problem and breaking it off with Adam."

"We'll help you in every way we can," her dad added.

"We love you, honey," her mother said. "And we're going to love your baby."

Her dad, emotional now, nodded and reached for her mother's hand.

Natalie's eyes misted over.

A moment later, the three of them were hugging. Once their emotions were again under control, both of her parents had a lot more questions, but this time the questions concerned her future.

"If you want to stay here in Emerson, we'll stand behind you," her mother said.

"I thought about it," Natalie admitted, "but I know how

hard it would be on you if I did. There'd be a lot of gossip."

"I don't care about that."

"Yes, you do, Mom. Besides, I care. I don't want people talking about me behind your back."

"But where will you go? How will you support yourself?"

So Natalie told them about her conversation with Rose and the plans they'd made.

Her mother smiled. "Oh, that's wonderful. I've hated Rose living so far away with none of her family around, and now she'll have you, and you'll have her."

Her father, more practical, said, "What about the baby? You'll need help if you're working. Are you going to look for a day care center or try to hire someone to come in?"

"Rose said the daughter of one of her friends does home day care and is just wonderful. I'm hoping she'll agree to take the baby in the fall."

"What about between now and then?" her father asked. "Do you have enough money to last you?"

"I think so. I've saved a little, and my boss at Bramwell has promised me as much work as I can handle." Besides, Natalie thought, if worse came to worst, she could always sell her ring. Before she'd left New York, she'd had the ring appraised. For what the jeweler had offered her, if she were frugal, she could live without working for a year.

Of course, she didn't want to sell the ring. The ring and her diamond heart meant a lot to her. But the coming baby meant more. If she had to sell the ring, she would.

"Sounds like you've got it all worked out," her father said.

"Yes, I've given it a lot of thought."

"Still, the best laid plans . . ." he warned.

"I know."

"Well, if anything unforeseen should happen, your mother and I will help you out financially, won't we, Connie?"

"Of course we will!"

Natalie would scrub floors or clean toilets for a living before she'd ask her parents for a penny. This was her problem. She'd created it. She would solve it. But she didn't say this. She just smiled and thanked them—they were so wonderful, she was so lucky!—and the three of them hugged again.

"Do you plan to have an amniocentesis?" her mother asked awhile later.

Natalie shook her head. "Dr. Sandstrom said it was up to me. The test is usually done between the fifteenth and eighteenth week of pregnancy, and I'm only about ten, maybe eleven weeks pregnant. There's a slight risk to the baby, so I'm still thinking about it."

"Oh, I didn't know there was any risk," her mother said.

"Rose said she knows of a wonderful ob/gyn that a couple of her friends have used. I thought I'd see if he'll take me on as a patient, then discuss the possibility of the test with him."

Her mother nodded. Then, brightening, she said, "What about ultrasound? Do you want to know the sex of the baby ahead of time?"

"Yes. I definitely do." But Natalie was certain she was going to have a girl. She didn't know how she knew. She just did. She'd even picked out a name already. Francesca. Francesca Constance Ferrenzo. Sadness pricked her momentarily because it couldn't be Francesca Constance Forrester, but Natalie had made her peace with that, so she smiled the grief away.

Just then, cheering sounded from the TV set, and her mother turned to look. "Oh, it's almost midnight."

For a moment, all three watched the ball in Times Square drop, then, to the strains of "Auld Lang Syne," they lifted their glasses in a toast.

"To 1998 and our coming grandchild," Natalie's father said, smiling at her.

"To new beginnings," Connie said, her eyes soft with love as they met Natalie's.

Natalie took a deep breath and told herself not to cry. There'd been enough sadness. It was time to move on. "To the most wonderful parents any woman could ever have," she said huskily. "Thank you from the bottom of my heart."

Mary Beth was worried about Adam. In all the years she'd worked for him, she had never seen him so despondent. He'd been like this for weeks now. And she was sure she knew the reason. Something must have happened with Natalie. He no longer made that late-afternoon phone call on his private line, and as far as she knew, he went home from the office every night.

Oh, dear, she thought, her heart going out to him. He was so nice, and she was sure his life at home was no picnic. He deserved to have some happiness.

She sighed again. She wished there was something she could do to help him, but she couldn't think of a thing except to make sure she kept the office running smoothly and as free of stress as possible.

Why did life have to be so tough for some people while it was so easy for others? She thought about her own life, wondered how strong she'd be in the face of the adversity Adam had faced. She had no idea, because she'd never really been tested. Her parents were still alive and healthy. She had a great marriage and great kids. She and Patrick had no money problems. She loved her job and her boss. Come to think of it, she was one lucky woman.

Superstitious, she crossed herself, and just as she did, Adam's door opened and she jumped.

"Something wrong?" he said.

"No, no, you just startled me. I guess I was daydreaming." Then she smiled. "Actually, I was counting my blessings."

He smiled, but it was a pitiful effort, nothing like the smiles of old.

"I do that," she continued in a rush, before she lost her nerve, "whenever I start to feel sorry for myself. Because you know, Mr. Forrester, no matter how bad things seem sometimes, there's usually *always* something else you can feel grateful about."

He stared at her. For what seemed like hours, but was in actuality only seconds, silence thrummed between them. "Are you trying to tell me something, Mary Beth?" he finally said.

Appalled by her audacity and scared she'd offended him, she could only shake her head. "No, I just—"

"Why don't you get yourself a cup of coffee," he interrupted, "and while you're at it, get me one, too. Then come into my office and we'll talk."

A few minutes later, seated across the desk from him, Mary Beth sipped at her coffee and waited for him to take her to task. Why had she opened her mouth? she berated herself. His personal life was none of her damned business. *Oh, Mary Beth, you have such a big mouth!* Patrick would kill her if she got fired. But surely Adam wouldn't fire her, not after all these years together, would he? Her heart beat faster as their eyes met.

Adam knew exactly what Mary Beth was thinking. Her face was an open book. Taking pity on her, he said gently, "Don't look so frightened. I'm not angry with you."

"You're not?" She gave him a hesitant smile. "I'm sorry, though. Patrick is always telling me I speak before I think."

"Sometimes that's not a bad trait. I think too much." Looking into his secretary's soft, sympathetic eyes, Adam wanted nothing more than to spill his guts. He'd kept his pain inside for so long now, he could no longer contain it. Confession was good for the soul, isn't that what they said? And who better to be his confessor than Mary Beth, keeper of his office, keeper of his secrets.

"I'm the one who should apologize," he said. "I know I've been hard to take lately."

"Oh, no!" she protested. "I just . . . I know you're unhappy, and I feel bad for you."

He swallowed. Maybe talking to her was a mistake. He wasn't sure he could keep a lid on his emotions, and the last thing he wanted to do was fall apart in front of his secretary. *Keep your own counsel.* The advice, something his father had said dozens of times while Adam was growing up, popped unbidden into his mind. Yes, Adam thought bitterly, his father had kept his own counsel, all right, and look what had happened as a result. *I'm the one who paid the price.*

Jesus. Hadn't he come to terms with his father's weaknesses long ago?

"If you want to talk about it," Mary Beth said softly, "I'll listen."

Adam took a deep breath. "Thanks. I appreciate that. But you know what? I don't think it'll do a bit of good to talk about my problems. What I need to do is quit thinking about the past and, like you said, count my blessings."

She frowned.

"I'm okay, Mary Beth. Quit worrying about me."

She nodded.

He glanced at the clock on his desk. "Tell you what," he said, "I'm taking the afternoon off." He made himself smile. "And you can do the same."

Vanessa Forrester, who had refused to take her husband's surname of Zimmerman, was in the middle of making gnocchi. In the process, she'd done a lot of cursing. Several times, she'd almost picked up the entire batch of the damn stuff and thrown it into the garbage. But if she was anything, she was not a quitter. And ever since she and John had spent a month in Italy last year, she'd been determined to master making gnocchi.

"How hard can it *be* to make it look right?" she said furiously as her latest effort took on a decided resemblance to a toothpick instead of the oblong barrel shape it was supposed to be. "Goddammit! What am I doing wrong? No wonder there are so few women chefs. No woman in her right mind would spend this much time on something so unimportant! I must need my head examined."

In the middle of this tirade, the doorbell rang.

"Oh, fuck," she cursed. "Just what I need now. Some sales type or some religious zealot wanting to bend my ear or empty my bank account."

Without even bothering to wipe the clotted flour and potato dough off her hands, she banged down the rolling pin and marched off in the direction of the front door. All set to say "Get lost," she yanked it open.

But it wasn't a sales type, and it wasn't a zealot, unless you'd call an overworked, driven attorney a zealot, which she usually did. She grinned. "Adam! Come on in. What a surprise. What brings you out here to the boonies in the middle of a weekday?"

Her brother returned her grin. "Hey, Van, how's it going?"

Vanessa made a face. "It wasn't going well at all. Come on out to the kitchen. I'll give you a beer, and you can watch your sister make a fool of herself while she plays Barbie the Housewife."

He laughed. "That's the best offer I've had all day."

But when they got to the kitchen, she decided to abandon the gnocchi. Maybe she wasn't a quitter, but a wise person knew when something was a losing battle. Scooping up all the dough on her cutting board, she walked over to the garbage pail, toed it open, and dumped the dough in.

"Why'd you do that?" Adam said. "What was it you were making?"

"Trust me. You don't want to know." Opening the refrigerator, she hunkered down so she could see the bottom shelf where John always stashed their beer. "Let's see. We've got Elbeero, Carta Blanca, and Tecate."

Adam laughed. "What? You made a run down to Mexico?"

"What can I say? John's got a thing about Mexican beer right now. He swears the Tecate is awesome."

"Okay, I'm game."

"I think I'll have some, too," she said, reaching for two bottles.

Once she was seated across the table from him, and they were both sampling their beer—"Yum, it *is* good, isn't it?" she said—she studied her brother. He looked tired. Really tired. There were circles under his eyes and, for the first time ever, he looked every bit of his forty-four years. Well, God knows, the poor guy had a lot on his plate. Vanessa was sure she would have shot herself by now if she'd been married to Julia all these years.

Funny, she mused. Adam had always been the good guy and she'd been the bad girl. And in the end, what had being good ever gotten him? A wife that, even before she was paralyzed, was a noose around his neck, no kids, and from the looks of him, not much to make him smile. Whereas she, who didn't deserve any of it, had a saint for a husband (Hey, anyone who'd put up with her shit all these years had to be a saint!), two pretty decent kids, a nice house and, because her husband earned enough to support them without a second income, the freedom to spend her time on the causes she believed in. Not to mention a terrific sex life. Just proved what she'd always thought. There was no justice in this world.

Adam stared down at his beer. Cleared his throat. The clock on the wall ticked loudly in the background.

"Want to tell me about it?" Vanessa asked quietly.

He traced circles in the condensation on his bottle. "That's why I came here, I think." He finally looked up. "I almost spilled my guts to my secretary earlier."

"I'm safer."

He nodded. "Yes."

And then he began to talk. He talked and talked and talked. And the longer he talked, the sadder Vanessa felt. When he'd finished, he slumped back in his chair. He looked completely drained.

Vanessa wished she knew what to say. She wished she could wave a magic wand and make all the bad stuff go away so that the light that used to be in her brother's eyes would come back. Unfortunately, she was only a woman, not a miracle worker.

"Pretty sordid, huh?" he said.

"Not sordid. Just human."

"You don't think I'm a bastard because of what I did to Julia?"

"Adam, you didn't do anything to Julia. What happened to Julia is her fault, not yours. She's the one who's clung to you like a leech, the one who's never had a life of her own. She's the one who got hysterical instead of acting like a grown-up and facing the truth. You didn't push her down those stairs, no matter what her father or anyone else said. Now stop blaming yourself!"

He nodded slowly, but she knew he wasn't convinced. He'd never be convinced. Because every day he had to look at Julia in that wheelchair.

"I'm sorry about Natalie," Vanessa said.

"Yeah. Me, too."

"I wish I could do something to help."

He gave her a crooked smile. "You have helped. You listened. And you didn't judge."

"I don't believe in judging people."

"I know. How did you ever put up with me when we were young?"

"What do you mean?"

"I was always judging *you*."

Vanessa laughed. "Oh, Adam, you couldn't help it. You

got all the respectable genes in our family while I got all the wild ones."

"Self-righteous genes would be more like it," he said dryly.

Vanessa grinned. "Those, too." She stood. "Want another beer?"

"Better not. I drove."

"Tell you what, why don't you call home and tell that Patty or Penny or whatever the heck her name is to stay the night, that you're out here and you and your sister are gonna go out and have some Mexican food tonight and a whole ton of margaritas, and you'll be too smashed to drive. Then *you* stay the night here. We'll stay up late and play pinochle the way we did when we were kids."

"Who's going to drive us back from the Mexican restaurant?"

"John."

"Poor John."

"Oh, he doesn't even like margaritas. He won't mind. I'll tell him he can drink beer when he gets home. Now, come on, do it. You need a break from that life of yours." She wanted to say *from that wife of yours*, but she knew he knew what she'd meant, anyway.

She tried not to listen while he talked to Julia, but it was hard not to, seeing as how he whipped out his cell phone and didn't try to keep the conversation private. She could tell from what Adam said that Julia did not give him any grief. He confirmed as much when he broke the connection.

"I'm surprised," Vanessa admitted. "I'd've thought she would have complained about you being gone all night."

"No, it's a funny thing. I sure haven't been easy to live with lately, but she seems to be bending over backwards to be accommodating. She hasn't complained about anything in weeks."

"Well, that's good."

"Yeah, but it's odd, too." Then he shrugged. "Hell, I'm

not going to worry about it. Guess I ought to be grateful that she's being so nice."

A few minutes later, Vanessa heard the screech of brakes that meant her daughter's school bus had stopped out front. Sure enough, the dark head of her twelve-year-old soon passed by the window that faced the driveway. "Carly's home," she said, getting up and unlocking the back door.

"Uncle Adam!" Carly cried. She dropped her backpack on the kitchen floor and flung her arms around Adam's neck.

"Hey, short stuff," he said, returning her hug.

"Where's my hug?" Vanessa demanded. Carly was still loving toward her parents, so Vanessa took advantage of it. Soon enough the kid would turn into a moody teenager and then hugs and all other demonstrations of filial affection would disappear.

From then on, there was no more time for personal talk, but that was good, Vanessa thought. They'd said everything that needed saying. Now Adam just needed to be around people who loved him without expecting anything from him.

Getting up, she fished another Tecate out of the fridge and gave it to him.

"Thanks." He smiled. "For everything."

"Anytime," she said. "Anytime."

Twenty-eight

❧

Natalie laid down her knitting needles and lifted the baby blanket she'd just completed. It was beautiful, she thought, all pink and white and mint green. It would be perfect in the room she had planned for her daughter.

She sighed. If it wasn't for missing Adam so terribly, she would be completely happy. Her amniocentesis had shown all was well with her pregnancy, and her ultrasound had only confirmed what she had already known in her heart: her baby was a girl.

She touched the growing mound of her stomach. It was late April now and getting warmer and more springlike every day. All around her the world was bursting with new life, just as she was. She only had two more months to wait and then little Francesca would be there.

Tears misted Natalie's eyes as she imagined what it would feel like to hold her already-cherished baby in her arms—the baby she and Adam had created out of their love for each other.

Adam, oh, Adam. If only you could be here with me. If only we could share this miraculous experience. I would give almost anything to see the wonder in your eyes when you felt our baby kick. You'd make such a wonderful father. Our daughter would grow up idolizing you, just as

I do. Sometimes it hurts so much to know you'll never look at your child's face, never hear her voice, never see her first attempts to walk and talk. Please forgive me for denying you the chance to know your child.

"Aha, caught you daydreaming again."

Natalie shook off her sad thoughts and managed to give her sister a smile. "Guilty."

"You finished the blanket, I see."

"Yes. Like it?"

Rose took it from her and examined it. "It's lovely. You do nice work."

"Thanks to you."

Over the winter months, Rose had taught Natalie to knit, and it constantly surprised her that the skill should give her so much pleasure. There was something very satisfying about making something with your hands. The blanket was only one of a dozen baby things she'd knitted over the winter. Little Francesca would probably have more booties and sweaters and blankets than she'd ever need.

As if she knew her mother was thinking about her, the baby kicked a couple of times. "Oops," Natalie said at a particularly strong kick.

"Baby's active today, huh?" Rose plopped down on the other end of the sectional sofa that took up the lion's share of the family room.

"Very."

For a few moments, the sisters sat quietly, each lost in her own thoughts. Natalie gazed out the big picture window that overlooked Rose's backyard. She smiled at the antics of several robins who were splashing around in the birdbath Chris had installed only last week.

"I'm tired," Rose said, sighing. "Funny how doing nothing makes you almost more tired than working all day." Following in her mother's footsteps, Rose now worked as a school secretary at the elementary school her children had attended.

"It's the perfect job for me," she'd told Natalie a few years back. "I don't make a lot of money, but I have the bulk of the summer and all the Christmas holidays off. Plus I'm home by four-fifteen every day."

"You hardly did nothing today," Natalie reminded her now. "I seem to remember you went to the supermarket this morning, and when you got home, you cleaned out the refrigerator, and I also saw you doing laundry. *I'm* the one who's done nothing! Sometimes I feel completely useless here, you let me do so little."

"Pregnant women are supposed to rest."

"You spoil me."

"With the kids gone, I needed someone to spoil." Rose gave Natalie an affectionate smile. "Have I told you lately how much I'm enjoying having you here?"

"Only about a dozen times."

"Well, I mean it. Chris feels the same way. Only last night we were talking about how much we'll miss you when you leave to get a place of your own."

"You're so good to me, Rose. I'll never forget it. I just hope I'll have the opportunity to do something for you someday."

"Cut it out now. You're making me blush," Rose declared. She jumped up. "You know what? I'm in the mood for popcorn. What say I pop some and pour us some lemonade and we go out back and soak up some sun?"

"Sounds like a plan to me."

The smell of buttery popcorn made Natalie think of other Saturdays. Saturdays when she and Adam met in Central Park. Many's the time they had shared a bag of freshly popped corn that he'd picked up from one of the street vendors on his way to meet her. In a return of the melancholy that could attack her without warning, she wondered if he ever went to the park now. If he ever sat on their bench and thought about her. Did he miss her? Did he have any idea how much she missed him? How hard it had been to make the break? Or had he put her out of his mind?

"Nat."

Natalie blinked. "Hmm?"

Rose stood before her, holding a tray with their popcorn and drinks. "You're thinking about Adam again, aren't you?"

Natalie grimaced. "Am I that transparent?"

"Yes, when you have that sad, faraway look on your face."

"I'm sorry."

"Don't apologize. Come on. Let's go outside, and we can talk about it."

Natalie levered herself to her feet. It was getting harder for her to get up out of any low seat now. She, who had never been overweight in her life, had already gained twenty-something pounds, every bit of it in her stomach. Rose said from behind you couldn't even tell Natalie was pregnant, but from the side . . . oh, my! And Natalie still had two and a half months to go.

Once outside, Rose put the tray down on the black wrought-iron umbrella table where they ate their meals in fine weather. "Why don't you take the chaise?" she suggested.

"No, that's okay. I'll sit at the table with you." Natalie pulled one of the chairs out and lowered herself into it.

Rose sat, too, and reached for a handful of popcorn. Her dark eyes were thoughtful. "Listen, hon, if you miss Adam that much, you can always call him. I'll bet he'd be here on the next flight."

Natalie shook her head. "No. I'm not calling him."

"But maybe you—"

"Look, Rose. It's perfectly normal for me to feel sad once in awhile. I don't want you to worry. I'm fine."

Rose sighed. "All right. I'm sorry."

"It's okay, you don't have to apologize."

"Yes, I do. It's none of my business. I guess I just want

to be sure that *you're* sure. That you're not sticking to this decision just because you think we'd think less of you or something if you *did* contact him."

"I'm very sure. I've made my decision. It hurts sometimes . . . okay, it hurts a *lot*, but this is best for both me and the baby. It's the way things have to be. The way they are *going* to be. I won't change my mind."

"I hate asking you to go, Adam, but you're the only one in your firm who speaks good enough French."

Adam shrugged. He was talking with Yvon Roget, the CEO of Gaspard Ltd., a French banking and investment company that was one of Hammond, Crowley's most important clients. Adam and Yvon had gotten to be friends over the years, and Yvon knew Adam's situation. "It's okay," he assured the older man. "Julia's nurse can stay with her while I'm gone and, as you know, we have a live-in housekeeper."

Yvon nodded, but his dark eyes were full of sympathy. "You will apologize to your wife and tell her that I am sorry to be taking you away?"

"Yes, I'll tell her."

Later, as Adam walked from Yvon's office to his own, he wondered what Yvon would think if he knew Adam was glad to be going away—glad he had a reason to escape Julia for a few days. Would he think Adam was terrible?

Probably not. Yvon, like most Frenchmen, was pragmatic when it came to marriage. He had, in fact, once told Adam that he believed wholeheartedly in the principle of marrying sensibly for an alliance of families or fortunes.

"Is that what you'd want for your daughters?" Adam had asked.

With a typical Gallic shrug, Yvon said, "But of course. I would much rather see them with someone who is secure financially, someone capable of giving them a good life than with some penniless musician or artist they might fancy themselves in love with." Then he'd smiled. "You Americans, you think too much about love. What you call love usually disappears before the first wedding anniversary! And then what do you have?"

Adam wished he could feel as Yvon did, especially now when he no longer had Natalie in his life. How much better it would be, he thought, if he could be realistic and accept his situation instead of yearning after something he would never have.

Four months. It was more than four months since he'd seen Natalie, since she'd left New York, and the pain of their parting hadn't lessened.

Where was she? What was she doing? Had she gone to California? Several times over the past months, he'd been tempted to call Sam and casually ask, but at the last moment, he hadn't succumbed to the temptation. What was the point? Natalie had made her position clear. It was over.

Accept it, he told himself.

Accept it and move on.

That night, when he told Julia he had to go to Paris for a few days, he braced himself for what he was sure would be her objections. But she surprised him.

"Don't worry about me," she said. "Alma's been wanting to do the spring cleaning, so maybe we'll tackle that while you're gone." Then she gave him a wry smile. "Not that *I'll* be much help."

He smiled at her attempt at humor. Julia didn't normally crack jokes, especially at her expense, but she'd been in a good mood for months now. Sometimes he wondered if she could possibly know that he was no longer seeing Natalie, if that's why she was so agreeable lately. But that was ridiculous, wasn't it? She hadn't known he *was* seeing Natalie since the accident, so how could she know he'd stopped?

He was scheduled to leave for Paris the following evening, and he planned to go straight from the office, so he began to pack. Julia watched him, even making a few suggestions about what he should or shouldn't take.

"It can be cool in Paris, even in late April," she said. "And it rains a lot. Better take your raincoat." She smiled at him. "Now, make sure you do something for enjoyment while you're there. Don't just work the whole time."

Anyone listening to them or watching them would have thought they were a happily married couple, he thought, even as he wondered how long this good humor of Julia's would continue. He couldn't remember the last time she'd complained to him about anything. *Count your blessings,* he thought, remembering Mary Beth's advice.

Julia was in an even better mood the next morning. She kissed him good-bye with a smile, saying, "Don't worry about me now. I'll be fine."

"Do you want me to pick up anything for you while I'm there? Maybe a bottle of perfume?"

"That would be lovely, darling. What a sweet thought. Perhaps some Joy?" Like Adam's mother, Julia had always favored the expensive scent.

"Okay. I'll call you when I get there," Adam promised.

The morning seemed to fly by. Adam was busy, but that wasn't the reason the time went so quickly. The reason was, for the first time in a long time, he had something to look forward to. He was actually excited about the trip to Paris. He hadn't been there in years—not since before Julia's accident—but it was one of his favorite cities. And the people at Gaspard would treat him royally, he knew. Armand Gaspard in particular would show him a good time and had mentioned an evening at the Moulin Rouge, saying, "All American men want to see the can-can girls, so we'll be sure to go there."

At three o'clock, Adam gave Mary Beth last-minute instructions, told her he'd call her the following morning, then left the office for Kennedy Airport and his six o'clock Air France flight.

It was a good thing he'd left so early, he thought an

hour later, when the logjam of traffic due to a four-car accident on the Van Wyck Expressway turned the normally forty-five-minute trip into an hour and a half. In spite of the delay, he arrived at the airport in plenty of time for his flight. Because he wanted to make sure of his first-class seat—he'd been told he might have to settle for business class due to high demand for first class on this flight—he headed for the main check-in counter.

"I'm sorry to tell you, sir, but your flight has been delayed."

Adam sighed. "By how long?"

The clerk said she wasn't sure. "But we'll keep you posted. Why don't you go to the first-class lounge and relax? It shouldn't be too long."

Knowing there wasn't a thing he could do except be patient, Adam said, *"Merci,"* and followed the clerk's suggestion. Once in the lounge, he ordered a beer, found the *Times*, which he hadn't had a chance to read that morning, and settled in to wait.

At six o'clock, the intercom buzzed in the guest room.

Penny sighed. She looked longingly at the TV set. The movie *Witness*, which was one of her favorites, was on HBO tonight, and she'd been hoping to watch it while she ate the dinner that was waiting for her in the kitchen.

Hurrying down the hallway, she knocked on Mrs. Forrester's office door.

"Come on in, Penny."

Penny opened the door and walked in. Mrs. Forrester was sitting behind her desk, and at Penny's entrance, she looked up and smiled.

"Good news," she said brightly. "It won't be necessary, after all, for you to stay over tonight."

"But Mr. Forrester said—"

"My friend Liz is coming to spend the evening," Mrs. Forrester continued, interrupting Penny, "and between her and Alma, they'll help me get into bed. Trust me. I'll be fine. You can just come in the morning, the way you usually do, although I may want you to stay over tomorrow."

"But I thought this was Alma's night out."

"It is, but she'll be back by ten." Mrs. Forrester smiled. "You know she'd never miss *Law & Order*."

Penny grinned. "Well, if you're sure . . ."

"I'm positive," Mrs. Forrester said firmly.

Penny was elated. She hadn't wanted to stay over tonight because Joe, her boyfriend, had wanted to take her to a party at his uncle Rocky's, in the Bronx, but there was no way she could have refused Mr. Forrester when he'd asked her to be there while he was gone on his trip to France. Not if she hoped to keep her job, and even though Mrs. Forrester could be a pain in the butt sometimes, this was one of the best-paying jobs Penny had ever had.

But now she could go to the party with Joe. She couldn't wait to tell him and rushed back to the guest room to phone him, both the movie and the waiting dinner forgotten.

At seven o'clock, Adam's flight was still delayed. An announcement had been made that the delay was due to a mechanical problem "which should be fixed very soon." Maybe he should call Julia. But what could she do? And what difference would it make to her? He had said he'd call her tomorrow, so he'd call her tomorrow. Settling back down in his seat, he opened his briefcase and began to make notes on the Gaspard case.

At seven-thirty, Air France announced that Adam's flight was canceled. He rolled his eyes, knowing before he'd even checked, that he would not be going to Paris tonight. Whipping out his cell phone, he dialed home.

"Damn. Where the hell is Penny?" Adam said when voice mail kicked in after four rings with no answer. Then he shrugged. Maybe she'd taken Julia out for a walk. Occasionally, on fine afternoons or evenings, they did that. No big deal. He would just go home. He clicked the phone off without leaving a message, grabbed his suitcase, and headed for the cab stand.

Adam's cab pulled up in front of the house at eight-fifteen. Looking up, he saw there was still a light on in Julia's office. She had either forgotten to turn it off, or she was working on something.

Alma's lights were out, though. But this was her evening off. She probably hadn't returned yet.

Julia would be glad to see him, he knew. He wished he felt glad to be there.

Poor Julia, he thought. *You deserve so much better than me.*

Twenty-nine

As soon as Adam let himself in the door, he heard the music. Something by Bach or Beethoven, he thought, or maybe Brahms, but he didn't know what. Julia was the classical music buff, not him. Ask him anything about Clapton, the Eagles, or the Stones, and he could tell you not only what song but what album. When it came to the three Bs, he was clueless.

Leaving his suitcase in the foyer—no sense lugging it upstairs when he'd only have to lug it down again tomorrow morning—he climbed the stairs. First he'd let Julia know he was home and why, then he'd go back to his study and E-mail Armand to tell him about the change in plans.

Boy, she was playing that music loud. Wonder how Penny felt about it? He had a feeling Penny was probably just as clueless as he was when it came to the highbrow stuff.

When he reached the top of the stairs, he could see Julia must be in the master bedroom. The door was open, and that's where the music was blasting from.

He walked down the hall. The guest room door was open, but the room was empty. Penny must be in the bedroom with Julia. When he reached the open doorway to the master suite, he stopped, his attention caught by movement to his right. At first, what he saw didn't register. And then, in a rush of complete disbelief, it did.

Not six feet away, standing unassisted in front of the full-length antique cheval mirror she had purchased at auction years ago, was Julia. Julia. Standing. Julia wearing the shimmery blue Vera Wang evening dress she'd bought at Christmas. Julia pivoting from side to side to admire how it looked.

And then, in the seconds before she saw him, Julia walking—walking!—back to the bed where several other articles of clothing lay. Julia could walk! And from the looks of her, she'd been walking for a long time.

Adam's heart banged in his chest. The disbelief gave way to confusion, which quickly turned into understanding followed by rage so powerful, he could hardly breathe around it.

And in that instant, she looked up. Their eyes locked, and hers widened in fear and shock as her hand flew to her mouth. For a long moment, time stood still.

Then, shaking and furious, Adam stalked to the stereo and snapped it off. The abrupt silence pulsed around them as Adam fought to control his rage and the murder in his heart.

"Adam," she finally whispered. "Wh-what are you doing home?"

"Didn't expect me, did you?" he said bitterly. All this time when he'd felt so low and so guilty and so sorry for her, she'd been pretending! Because it was obvious to him that her recovery and ability to move and walk wasn't anything sudden. He knew enough about the type of injury she'd sustained to know it would have taken months of work to bring her mobility back. Maybe years of work.

"Adam, don't look at me like that. I know what you're thinking, but you're wrong. I just wanted to surprise you!"

Oh, she was a great actress. A great actress. "Congratulations. You've succeeded."

Turning his back on her, he walked to his closet, opened the doors, and took out his largest suitcase. Pulling clothes off hangers and out of drawers, he threw them into the suitcase.

Suddenly, his murderous thoughts disappeared. Suddenly, it didn't matter whether she'd been recovered weeks, months, or years. All that mattered was that he was finally free. Free!

"Adam, what are you doing?" Julia cried.

"What does it look like I'm doing?" He didn't look at her. "I'm leaving you the way I should have a long time ago."

"No! No!" She stumbled to where he stood. Falling on her knees, she clutched his legs. "You can't leave me! I love you! The only reason I didn't tell you about being able to walk was I wanted to give you a wonderful birthday present!"

But Adam ignored her and continued his packing. *Never again,* he thought. Never again would he allow himself to be manipulated by this woman.

She continued to cry and beg, and he continued not to pay any attention. When he had finally jammed as many of his belongings as he could into the suitcase, he zipped it shut. "I'll send for the rest of my stuff in a few days," he said, lifting the suitcase off the bed. He looked at her, at the streaked face, the tear-spotted gown, the terrified eyes, and felt nothing but dislike and an overpowering relief.

His gaze must have communicated what he was feeling, because as quickly as her tears had started, they stopped. The terrified look disappeared, and her eyes hardened. "Don't bother," she said, struggling to her feet. "Whatever you've left here will be thrown out tomorrow."

He shrugged. Who cared? "Good-bye, Julia."

"You're going to be sorry you did this, Adam. I'll take you for every penny you have. You'll be left with *nothing*!" Her eyes blazed, and there were two angry spots of color on her cheeks. "Then we'll see whether that woman still wants you! You didn't think I knew about her, did you? Well, I've known about your whore for a long time! I had you followed! So you're screwed, Adam. You'll lose everything!"

He almost felt sorry for her. "You don't get it, do you, Julia? I never wanted any of this. The money, the house, all the costly things you've filled it with, even the firm and the partnership, none of it means anything to me. You're welcome to it. All I care about is my freedom."

Without another word, he turned and walked out of the bedroom. Her screams and threats followed him until the front door finally shut them out.

Adam headed straight for his office. Once there, the first thing he did was find a hotel room for the night. The second thing he did was E-mail Armand Gaspard and tell him he'd had a family crisis and wouldn't be able to get to Paris this week after all. He added that he would call him in a day or two.

Then he called Sam and Brooke's house.

"I'm sorry, Adam, but she's not here," Brooke said when he asked about Natalie. "Whatever made you think she would be?"

It didn't even register with Adam until later that Brooke didn't seem surprised by his call or that he was looking for Natalie. "When she moved last December," he said, "she told me she would probably relocate out there. You mean she never talked to you about it?"

"I didn't even know she'd left New York," Brooke said.

By the time Adam did some explaining and they'd hung up, it was almost ten, but he decided it wasn't too late to call Natalie's parents. Even if it was, he couldn't wait until morning. He had to at least *know* where she was tonight or else he would not be able to sleep.

He had no trouble getting their number. There was only

one Ralph Ferrenzo listed in the Emerson directory. His hand shook as he punched in the number.

It rang three times before a soft female voice said, "Hello?"

"Hello, Mrs. Ferrenzo?"

"Yes?"

Suddenly nervous, Adam cleared his throat. "You don't know me, Mrs. Ferrenzo, but I'm an old friend of Natalie's and I'm trying to get in touch with her. Do you know where she's living now?"

"Which one are you? I thought I knew all Natalie's old friends."

"I'm Adam Forrester. Natalie and I were in New Haven together and then recently, we renewed our acquaintance in New York, but when she left, she forgot to give me a forwarding address."

"Maybe she didn't forget. Maybe she prefers not to hear from you again." Her voice had turned decidedly colder.

"Please, Mrs. Ferrenzo. It's urgent that I speak with her. Something's happened, something I know . . ." He took a deep breath. "Something I hope she would want to know about."

There was a long silence. Then, in a softer voice, she said, "Look, Adam, I know all about you and Natalie. She told her father and me about your relationship. It's been hard on her to leave New York and try for a new life, and I think you should respect that."

"I do respect that, but things have changed. I've left my wife, Mrs. Ferrenzo. I'm getting a divorce. Does that make any difference to you?" Adam hadn't prayed in a long time, but he prayed now as he waited for her answer.

"I just don't know."

Adam poured his heart and soul into his next words. "I love Natalie more than anything in the world, and if she'll have me, I want to marry her."

She made a sound that was a cross between a sigh and a laugh. "Oh, all right, I'm a sucker for a happy ending, and you've persuaded me. She's staying with her sister in Crandall, Ohio." Then she gave him the address and the phone number.

Heart soaring, Adam started to punch in the number. Halfway through, he changed his mind and put the phone down. He didn't want to call Natalie. He wanted to see her. He couldn't take a chance that she would refuse to see him. Besides, he wanted to see her face when he told her about Julia and how she'd been deceiving him for so long.

Excited now, he rushed down the hall to the library where he knew there'd be the latest Rand McNally atlas. Opening it, he quickly found the page he wanted. From what he could see, it was only about 400 miles between New York and Columbus, Ohio. If he started out now, he could be there in the morning.

Back in his office, he left a note for Mary Beth. Then once more, he gathered up his suitcases and headed out the door.

The smell of coffee and frying bacon awakened Natalie. She looked at the bedside clock. Seven o'clock. She might as well get up. As she swung her feet out of bed, her cats, who had been sleeping at the foot, stirred. But they didn't open their eyes.

"Too early for you, huh?" she said. She slid her feet into her slippers and reached for her satin robe. She could barely belt it around her tummy now and knew she'd have to get a bigger one if she intended to wear a robe during the next two and a half months. "Wonder if that ultrasound could be wrong," she murmured, patting herself. "Maybe it's twins in there."

After brushing her hair and teeth and splashing her face with water, she walked downstairs.

"Hey," Rose greeted. "You're up early." She was turning the bacon. "Before you sit down, would you mind going out and getting the paper?"

"No, of course not. Where's Chris?"

"He had to be at work at seven this morning, so he's already gone. And I'm leaving as soon as I eat."

Yawning, Natalie headed for the front door. It was a beautiful morning, she thought as she walked outside. The sun was up far enough to have bathed everything in a soft, pink gold light, and the grass shone with dew.

Natalie took deep breaths of the cool air as nearby a bluebird trilled. Almost as if she were answering, the baby kicked. Natalie laughed out loud. For some reason, she felt absurdly happy today.

The paper lay on the strip of grass between the curb and the sidewalk. Natalie held up her robe so the dew wouldn't stain it as she leaned over to pick it up. As she straightened, she saw a dark green BMW coming slowly down the street. Her heart gave a funny little hop. Adam had a dark green BMW. Honestly, she thought. When would she ever stop associating everything she saw and did with Adam?

She turned to go back up the front walk. The BMW had slowed, and she could see the outline of the driver's head as he peered at the houses. It was obvious he was looking for an address. She thought about waiting to see if she could help him, but really, how much help could *she* be? She only knew a couple of the families on the block.

She had covered half the distance between the sidewalk and the front door when the BMW pulled into the driveway of Rose and Chris's house. Slowly, she turned around.

Adam saw the woman when he was three houses away. As he drove closer, he realized she was standing in front of the address he wanted.

Closer still, he knew that he was looking at one of Natalie's sisters. A pregnant sister. He figured it couldn't be Rose. Rose had grown kids, if he remembered correctly, and was too old to be pregnant again.

Whoever she was, she looked almost exactly like Natalie. It gave him a start to realize there were two women in the world with the face he loved.

He wasn't sure exactly when he knew he wasn't looking at one of Natalie's sisters. Whether it was when she stopped and turned his way, or when he opened the door and climbed out of the car, or when their eyes met and recognition dawned in hers.

All he knew was his heart turned cartwheels as his gaze went from Natalie's eyes to Natalie's stomach and back again. As the realization dawned that Natalie, *his Natalie*, was pregnant, and from the looks of her, at least six or seven months along. It didn't take long for it to sink in that it was his baby growing in her belly. His baby she was now cradling so protectively with her hands.

My baby! Happiness, like a giant tidal wave, crashed over him. "Natalie!" he shouted, covering the distance between them in four giant strides.

"Adam!"

And then she was in his arms, and he was covering her face with kisses.

For Natalie, the whys and wherefores of Adam's unexpected appearance didn't matter. Nor did the fact that she hadn't wanted him to know about the baby. Nothing mattered except that he was there and she loved him. So she clung to him, her heart singing with joy, and her happy tears mingling with the taste of his kisses.

How long they stood there, she didn't know. Her first awareness of anything other than Adam was the sound of someone clearing their throat.

"I take it this is the father-to-be?" Rose said dryly. She was standing in the open doorway watching them.

Breaking apart, Natalie blushed, and Adam looked sheepish.

Rose walked out and extended her hand to Adam. "I'm Rose."

"Hi, Rose. I'm Adam." He grinned at her, keeping his free arm possessively around Natalie.

"Why don't you two lovebirds come into the house?" Rose suggested, "instead of giving the neighbors more fuel for gossip?"

It was only then that Natalie realized the cranky old man who lived next door had walked outside and stood watching them. She gave him an embarrassed little wave.

"Thank you," Adam said. "I'd like to." He looked at Natalie, a question in his eyes.

"Yes," she said. "Let's go in. We have lots to talk about." When he smiled, she knew that no matter what his reason was for coming, she was glad he had.

An hour later, Rose was gone, and Adam and Natalie were sitting together in the kitchen. He had just finished telling her how he had discovered Julia's deceit.

"You mean she could walk all this time?" Natalie said in disbelief.

"I don't know. I didn't stick around long enough to find out how long she's been recovered, because I don't really care. She hid it from me. The length of time doesn't matter."

"Oh, Adam, I can't help it. I feel sorry for her. She must love you an awful lot to go to such lengths to keep you."

"Don't feel sorry for her. Both of us have wasted too many years feeling sorry for her, and she doesn't deserve it. Anyway, what she feels for me isn't love. It's obsession. And it's sick. I don't want to talk about her anymore. I've left her and I'm divorcing her, and believe me, from the way she acted at the end, she'll be just fine." He grinned. "Nat, I'm *free!*"

Natalie wanted to be happy, but she'd suddenly wondered when he was going to realize that she had lied to him, too, when she'd kept the fact of her pregnancy a secret.

"What's wrong?" he finally said. "Aren't you happy about all this?"

"Yes," she whispered.

"Then what is it?"

"I—" She stopped. "You do understand why I had to leave New York, don't you? Why I couldn't tell you about the baby?"

"Of course I do. Has that been worrying you?"

Natalie nodded. "A little. Oh, Adam, I wanted to tell you. I just—"

"Shhh," he said, putting his finger over her lips. Then, grinning, he got off his chair and knelt in front of her. Taking her hand in his, he said, "Miss Ferrenzo, I adore you. Will you make me the happiest man in the world and agree to marry me?"

Natalie's eyes filled with tears. Too overcome to speak, she could only shake her head yes.

Adam stroked her belly. His own eyes looked suspiciously shiny. "I'll work hard to make a good life for us, Natalie."

"I know you will," she whispered.

"Because I want the best for you and our baby."

"Oh, Adam. If you're talking about money and possessions, none of that matters. Don't you know that right now, this very moment, I already have everything I could ever want?"

Epilogue

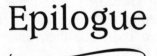

Crandall, Ohio
June 2000

"Careful, sweetheart!" Natalie called out just before
Francesca stumbled over a forgotten toy lying in their
backyard.

Adam jumped up to comfort their nearly two-year-old
toddler, whose little round face was already screwed up
to cry her outrage, although Adam knew his daughter
could not have been hurt. The grass was soft, and she had
not fallen hard. Still, he picked her up and held her and
kissed her silky dark hair until the urge to cry vanished.

While he stroked her head, Puppee, the newest addition
to their family, licked Francesca's leg. The dog, a three-
month-old black Lab, had come by his name through the
stubbornness of their daughter, who insisted on calling
him puppy even as Adam and Natalie tried to get her to
agree to a real name.

"No! Puppy!" she'd say, her lower lip sticking out in
a gesture that said she'd never change her mind. So Puppee it was, even though the name was bound to raise
eyebrows when the dog reached his full growth.

Francesca, stubbornness (inherited, Natalie insisted,

from her bullheaded father) included, was the light of their lives. Had been, from the moment she'd come yelling into the world. Adam knew he would never forget that momentous day. Along with the day he and Natalie had pledged their love and made their union official, it was the happiest day of his life.

Putting Francesca back on her sturdy feet, he returned to his lawn chair. It was early on a Saturday evening, and he and Natalie had just finished eating hamburgers Adam had grilled and were enjoying their coffee while watching their toddler's prebed playtime with the new puppy.

Looking at his wife's lovely profile as she gazed with amusement at their daughter's antics, Adam thought about the amazing ways his life had changed in the past two-plus years. He not only had a wife he adored and a daughter he would give his life for, he had also found meaningful work that gave him great pride and satisfaction.

Soon after settling in Crandall, he had made the acquaintance of a general practice attorney named Thaddeus Turner who was in his late sixties and really wanted to retire but who hated to abandon his long-time clients. The two men had struck up an instant rapport, and within two weeks of meeting him, Thaddeus had offered Adam a partnership. Julia's threats aside, Adam had been awarded half the worth of his existing partnership in Hammond, Crowley which, after learning about the impending birth of his daughter, he had prudently decided he could not afford to give away in a gesture whose meaning would be lost on Julia, anyway.

So a deal was made, and two weeks before Francesca made her appearance in the world, the new firm of Turner and Forrester was born.

Thaddeus, now seventy, spent very little time in the office, but he was always available to counsel and listen.

Adam discovered he loved practicing law in a small town and taking on all types of cases. The only ones he refused were divorce cases. He wanted no part of marriages gone sour. Thinking about divorce reminded him of how stunned he'd been to learn last month that Julia had married again. He was too happy to hold grudges against her, and he sincerely hoped she had finally found happiness with someone who loved her.

He thought about how Mary Beth, his old secretary from his Hammond, Crowley days, had once told him to count his blessings. Now he had so many he counted them daily without having to be reminded.

He would soon have another. Again his gaze rested on his beautiful wife, traveling from her face to her rounded belly. To their great delight, Natalie was pregnant again, and this time, she was expecting a boy.

Adam's cup runneth over.